Anna Spargo-Ryan has worked in digital marketing for fifteen years, including time on Ramsay Street, in the Formula 1 pits and on bus magazines. Her work has been published in *Kill Your Darlings*, *The Lifted Brow*, *The Big Issue* and *The Guardian*, among other places. She won the 2016 Horne Prize for her essay, 'The Suicide Gene'. She lives in Melbourne with her people, animals, and a cat called Norman. *The Gulf* is her second novel.

annaspargoryan.com

Also by Anna Spargo-Ryan

The Paper House

The GULF

ANNA SPARGO-RYAN

PICADOR
Pan Macmillan Australia

First published in 2017 in Picador by Pan Macmillan Australia Pty Ltd
1 Market Street, Sydney, New South Wales, Australia, 2000

Cataloguing-in-Publication entry is available
from the National Library of Australia
http://catalogue.nla.gov.au
Typeset in 12/16.5 Adobe Caslon Pro by Midland Typesetters, Australia
Printed by McPherson's Printing Group

I would like to show my respect for and acknowledge the traditional owners of the land on which I write and love and breathe, and recognise Elders past and present.

For my mum, in gratitude for her wisdom and courage

Galápagos tortoises are the largest of all living tortoises. They live on islands created by volcanos. The oldest Galápagos tortoise lived to be 170 years old. They eat leaves, lichen and even cactuses. When the sun goes down it gets cold, and they burrow into the mud to stay warm. Their only natural predator is the Galápagos hawk, an endemic bird that eats the hatchlings.

Galápagos tortoises are very peaceful creatures.

Australian Zoological Magazine

1

My mother had morphed into all kinds of versions of herself. She'd been a cowboy boot wearer and a biker chick and a Liberal voter. She'd been a person who went to raves in the bush and a person who watched horror movies and a person who had to sleep with the fan on. They'd come and go, and she'd snap back to the woman who watched cooking shows and took spiders outside.

And then there was Jason.

A week after they met in the Big W checkout line, Mum asked him home for dinner. She had her hair swept to the side and she made tuna mornay in little white pots. When the buzzer rang, she pulled us by our wrists into the corridor.

'You kids be good. Promise?'

'We're always good,' Ben said. Her lips curled up. She opened the door.

'Jason.' They kissed on the mouth. 'Jase.'

He looked around her and into the hall. 'Who are they?'

Mum gathered us together. 'This little guy is Ben.' Ben put out his hand and Jason stared at it. 'And the big one is Skye.' He was good-looking, in a balding, tattooed way, which had always been Mum's type.

'Didn't know you had kids.'

'You'll like them,' she said.

He gave her a bunch of flowers with a barcode on the side, just shoved them right into her hand. 'Right then. What's for dinner?'

Mum had the table laid out with placemats I'd never seen before. Cutlery from the picnic set she got with her Flybuys points that had handles made to look like ivory. She led him down the corridor by the hand with her feet floating above the ground. We sat around the table, all of us looking at each other at once.

'Hope you like tuna,' she said.

'Yeah,' he said. 'Got a mate with a boat, go out fishing for those bastards sometimes.' He clinked his fork against the white bowl. 'Never had it this fancy though.' He ate quietly, contemplating each mouthful. The mornay was lumpy. I pushed the balls of flour against the roof of my mouth and let them sit there in a film.

'Where do you live?' Ben said. Jason eyed him up and down, at the dinner table in his *Iron Man* pyjamas.

'North.'

'Where's that?'

'North of here.'

'Everywhere's north of here,' I said. He looked at me.

'Port Flinders, mostly.'

'Never heard of it.'

'Yeah, well. Why would you? No posh folk like you there.'

Mum put her hand on his arm. 'Port Flinders,' she said. 'How exotic.'

'Wouldn't call it that,' he said, and chewed his tuna with his eyes closed.

After dinner Mum brought out a Viennetta and told Ben to cut off a slice as big as he wanted. We ate it from plastic bowls in front of the TV. A blonde woman shouted about landscaping and pies with berries in them.

'Such good reception,' Jason said. Mum had pushed him into the three-seater and he ate around her head, which moved up and down on his belly as he breathed. Next door's TV was right on the other side of the wall. They were watching a movie. We could hear it every time *Better Homes* went to an ad break.

'Might get a blanket,' Mum said. We sat in the room with Jason and he didn't look away from the TV once. Mum came back with the blanket, tossed it over both of them and her whole body disappeared under it. Jason stared ahead.

'Are you going home soon, Jason?' Ben said. Mum looked up at him and the blanket moved.

'Dunno,' he said.

'I'm going to my room.' I took the bowls to the kitchen and watched the people from the window. From there you could see right across to the Westfield, all the families late-night shopping in their Corollas or their Astras, buying burgers in the food court and sitting together and probably laughing. They came through the doors with their arms swinging, heavy with bags. Gifts, maybe. I left the bowls to dry on the counter.

My room was stale and I opened the window to let the air in. Season-end crickets were doing their tango in the car park downstairs. Mr and Mrs Adelmann from number six shouting because he'd cheated again, or she had. The screeching of the train coming to a stop in the tunnel.

A man had died in there last week. On the news they said 'no suspicious circumstances', but Kirrily from school had seen it with her own eyes, the man laid out on the tracks with his legs sliced off and blood shooting out everywhere. 'It was pretty bad,' she'd said. 'I bet,' I'd said, which didn't seem like the right thing to say but I couldn't think of anything else.

On my bed, I had a copy of *Macbeth*, second-hand, bruised and beat up at the edges, someone else's notes inside. A cheat version. I read the lines again and again, trying to make myself understand all that mulched-up language. We were supposed to read from it in English on Monday, me as Lady Macbeth and some other kids reading the other parts. Not like a play, just to get the words right. And so our teacher didn't have to do any actual teaching. Too busy having his fling with our homeroom teacher, everyone said.

Mum appeared at the door with her hands together. She had a faraway look. Glassy. I read about the bloody dagger, tried to decipher someone else's handwriting in the margin. Mum coughed.

'Yes?' I said.

'What do you think of him?'

'I guess Lady Macbeth is the real brains of the operation.'

'What? I mean Jason.'

'Oh. I haven't thought of him.'

'Can't believe I met him in Big W. I mean, of all places. Just so romantic to bump into each other in the line. He let me go ahead of him, you know. Real gentleman.' I heard his voice from the kitchen, a mess of low growls. Mum sat on my bed. 'He runs his own business. How good is that? In Port Flinders.'

'Oh yeah? What does he do?'

'Something in trading. Import–export stuff. Too complicated for us to understand, I bet.' She touched her fingers to her face. 'I'm glad you like him.'

'I've got homework.'

'Oh sure, of course.' She lingered in the doorway, watching me. His voice came from down the hallway: 'Linda, oi. How d'you get the lid off this thing?'

Mum winked. 'Better get to bed,' she said.

The walls between my bedroom and hers were paper thin. I listened to them into the night, the rhythmic thud against the floor.

'At least wait until I'm asleep,' I shouted, and the noise stopped.

*

Three days later, Mum gave Jason keys to the apartment.

'He needs them, you know. Gotta come and go when you run your own business.'

I moved my homework to the kitchen table, watched him make phone calls from the couch. Ben sat next to me and drove his cars along the bench.

'This one's an HQ Monaro,' he said. 'And this one's a Ford Escort. Look.' They went drag-racing along the kitchen sink. 'The Escort wins at short distances but the HQ can go for longer. Peter Brock had one just like it.'

'Oh, right,' I said.

Jason whispered into his phone. Mum buzzed around him, sweeping and straightening. She bought a vacuum cleaner from Kmart and pushed that around him too, picking up dust that hadn't had time to accumulate yet.

'Linda,' he said, 'can you fucking not?' and pointed at his ear.

'I'll put it on eBay,' she said, and sat next to him on the couch with her hand on his knee. We stayed like that into the afternoon. Mum watching Jason do his business deals. Ben driving his cars around the kitchen. Me wondering if Lady Macbeth would get the blood off her hands.

Later, I walked Ben to the fish and chip shop. Jin wiped his hands on his apron: 'What can I get you two?' Minimum chips was three dollars and Mum had given us a bit extra to get some calamari rings. We took the paper packet to the bridge over the river and sat with our legs between the bars.

'What's on at school tomorrow?' I said.

'Spelling.' He pulled the thin tendons of calamari from the batter. 'Yiannis is gonna show me how to make a bomb out of a sparkler.'

'Sounds dangerous.'

'Sounds cool, you mean.'

'Give me some of that calamari.'

He ate two pieces, barely chewing. People walked around us on their way home from work, from university. We put our heads close together and tried to guess where they were going. A tall woman in leopard-print heels: to meet her boyfriend at the bar. A grandmother with three Myer bags to take to her grandson's birthday. A young guy on a skateboard on his way to jump the balustrade at Westfield.

I crumpled the oily paper and we took it home with us. 'Keep Australia beautiful,' I said. The apartment block car park was lit in a couple of corners by the two light posts still standing, and the apartments on the lower storey were cloaked in the night. Upstairs, some of the windows glowed yellow. All the twilight sounds came up from the road and lodged in the u-shaped building, as though it were a baseball glove.

The door at number six flew open and a shoe came hurtling out. 'Why is Mrs Adelmann always so angry?' Ben said. 'She wakes me up.'

'Let's put the rubbish in the downstairs bin.'

Mum had her legs around Jason on the couch. She looked at us as we came in, but didn't move.

'Where's my change?' she said.

'You told us we could get calamari rings,' said Ben.

'Like hell I did.'

Jason laughed. 'Don't suppose you got any for us?'

Ben looked to me. 'No?' he said.

I tipped two dollars from my pencil case and shoved it into Mum's hand. 'Get yourself something nice,' I said. Jason laughed again and she slapped his arm.

'Don't encourage her,' she said. 'Got enough kids in this house without you acting like one too.' She climbed off his lap. His phone rang.

I went out on the concrete balcony and watched the traffic go by. Over the road the new factories were going in, but on Sunday mornings they downed tools and if you strained, you could hear the river beating against the rocks.

I took Ben lizard hunting with Amir from the apartment next door. We went down to the river, where it went under the main road and into the park. Newts, they said. Sometimes. When the rain had been really heavy.

Amir's parents had come to Australia when he was a baby, from Pakistan. 'Don't think they've got many lizards in Pakistan,' Ben said.

'Can't remember,' said Amir. 'Pretty good food though I think.'

Ben nodded solemnly. 'They're teaching us about asylum seekers at school, now. Mrs Morris says they're locked up on some island.' He turned to Amir. 'Did you get locked up on an island?'

'Nah,' he said, and picked up a bit of broken cement. 'My dad's a bricklayer.'

'Oh yeah.'

They ran up along the edges of the canal, stopped to look at bits of graffiti with swear words in them, started shouting them at each other. 'Hey Ben! Fucking knobjockey! Fucking douche!' And Ben: 'Amir, you're a bloody shitrag!' People stopped on the bridge to look at them. My brother in his *Guardians of the Galaxy* t-shirt and Amir with his sandals slapping against the concrete.

'Slow down!' My voice bounced around the aqueduct. We reached the tunnel that would take us underground and through to the park. Amir stopped.

'What if the rain starts again?'

Ben farted, laughed. 'What do you mean?'

'Kids drown in these tunnels when it rains, you know. It rushes through and they get swept away.'

'No they don't.'

'It's true.'

The day was dry and warm. 'There's no rain coming,' I said.

Ben ran into the tunnel. 'The good lizards are this way, Amir!'

The younger boy stood at the entrance a good while longer, peering into the blackness of the tunnel. 'It's so dark,' he said.

'That's only because it goes around the corner,' I said. 'It's like fifteen metres and then you get to the bend and when you go round it, you're practically out.' He shifted from foot to foot. 'I can hold your hand, if you like?'

The movement stopped. 'Ben?' he called. Silence. Amir's hand slipped into mine and we walked together, his tiny legs going twice as fast as mine and his palm sweaty.

At the park a few people gathered around a barbecue, which hissed and spat into the midday air. A kid on a bike. The same kid falling off the bike, trailed by a mother with a bandaid. A girl on a swing. A boy on a swing. An adult on a swing. I sat at the edge of the canal and watched the way they were with each other, touching and laughing.

Mum didn't come with us to the park very often. Not at all, really. She said families depressed her, which was probably true. Lots of things upset her, especially people being happy in public, where she could see them. She never looked into the Westfield car park from the kitchen window.

A man watched the boys as they made their way along the creek bed. Ben's skin had flushed red in the sun and excitement. He laughed loudly, and it ricocheted. Another boy joined them, and another. The four of them picked over the rocks together, shouting at each sign of a webbed foot or a scaly tail.

Still the man watched. The littlest boy slipped where moss had grown against the concrete. He cried. Ben bent down to him, pulled him up by his hands. 'Are you okay?' he said.

The man was standing then. 'Oliver, get back over here.' The boy limped towards him. Ben came to sit next to me, pulled his cap down over his eyes. I wrapped my arm around his shoulders, the way I always did; he rarely pushed it off.

'Do you like Jason?' he said. His legs were so close to mine. I wondered if his sweat would fuse our skin together.

'Dunno,' I said. 'Do you?'

'I guess? I think Mum likes him.'

'Yeah. She busted me at the fridge in the middle of the night and didn't even yell.'

'Wow.' He looked at me. 'Was he still there when you got up this morning?'

'Don't think so.'

He turned over a heavy rock. 'Got one! Amir, look!' A gecko, skin so soft it was transparent. He held it in his open palm and we laughed at the dropped tail as it danced on its own. Watched its organs throbbing inside its bones.

2

My nonno lived on the side of a hill, and once, before Ben was born, Dad took me there for ice-cream in the backyard. There was a storm, a big one. The rain came down in sheets and we pointed at the lightning and tried to guess whose house it was striking.

'The Lothians, I reckon,' he said. The sky lit up. 'That butcher with the dodgy leg.'

Nonno tapped his pipe on the edge of the table. 'No, he died,' he said. 'Wife got him with a cleaver.'

'Oh,' Dad said, as the paddock over the hill erupted into flame.

Ben liked to go the long way to school, down the canal and through the park. Amir came with us a couple of mornings a week, when his mum was working down at the nursery. They skipped ahead of me with their *Avengers* backpacks, pockets jingling with bits of garbage they'd found wherever it was boys looked for trinkets. I walked in silence, going over the lines I'd rehearsed for English.

Their school was at the edge of the park. A dozen mobile pods on dead lawn, and a man at the gate with a fluorescent yellow vest. The lady who managed the crossing had pink hair and she scowled at every single child who interrupted her daydreaming. Blew her whistle with the enthusiasm of a half-drowned cat.

Blrrt. 'Get a move on.' *Blrrt.* 'Get a move on.'

I tried to kiss Ben's head but he ducked away.

'I'll meet you here after school, okay? Mum's at work.'

'Whatever. I can walk home on my own. Yiannis taught me how to make tear gas by keeping a pumpkin in an ice-cream container.'

I read the Lady Macbeth parts from memory, imploring my husband to seek his rightful kingship, breaking down at the blood on my hands.

'There's no need to show off, Skye.' Mr Pollock didn't look up from his desk.

Jessyka leaned across me. Her breath reeked of hot chips and something else I didn't recognise, something earthy.

'Hear your mum's got a new fella,' she said. Her eyes were bloodshot, black rings underneath.

'So what?' I said. Felt a little bile in my throat.

'So Jeremy says he's a pretty bad guy, you know. Saw him outside that house on Dyson Road with all the cars in the garden.'

'You don't know what you're talking about.'

'Just saying what I'm hearing. Get the sand out of your vagina.' She smiled. Mr Pollock shushed us.

It'd been a while since Mum had even had a boyfriend. Months, at least. For a while I thought she might have had more to do with the Adelmanns' arguments than she let on, although his wife always said hello to me when I went to the mailbox. There had been a bloke with one leg, for a bit, and Mum had let him stay in her bedroom while she collected his pension. Harold? Gerald? There was Noakes, skin black as embers and who always spoke in a whisper, even at the dinner table: 'How was your day, Noakes?' and then tiny unutterances, even though his mouth always moved plenty. At Christmas, Paolo, who was at least twenty years older than Mum, bought us all gifts wrapped in silver paper, and took us to his mother's house in the hills where we ate handmade ravioli with figs and chocolate. He was okay, Paolo. Rich, anyway. But Mum said she could hardly look at him, with the hair sprouting from a mole on his forehead.

At lunchtime I swapped my Le Snak for a ham sandwich and took it behind the tuckshop to eat while I read. Some of the boys had a soccer ball and it bounced off the bricks again and again, a hollow and metallic sound. I watched their feet move. Picking the ball up with their ankles, tossing it into the air. *Thud. Thud.* It reverberated in the back of my skull.

When Ben and I had been at the same school, I'd found him in the quadrangle and we'd eaten our sandwiches together. He showed me creatures he'd found: moths that shied away from the daylight; a fly with its wings cut off for fun. He and Yiannis would spread out their food like it was a picnic. Didn't seem to notice when the other kids stared at them. Plucked ants straight from the ground and kept them in a little jar in Ben's pocket.

'It's a colony,' Ben had said. 'We're going to breed them to make an army.'

I found an empty corner where the main buildings met, waited until Kirrily came to sit with me after her piano lesson.

'What's this they're saying about your mum's new boyfriend?'

I picked the greasy bits out of my sandwich. 'He's not a new boyfriend. Just a guy.'

'Jessyka says he's living at your place.'

'She's lying.'

'Fair enough.' She tapped her fingers along the ground, an imaginary piano. 'How was your *Macbeth* thing?'

'Shithouse. Everyone else just read from the book. Pollock said I was showing off.'

'Overachiever.'

'Yeah. Maybe I was showing off.'

We sat with our backs pressed against the bricks for a while. I listening to her breathing in and out, the pinched asthmatic squeak at the end.

'Hey, Casey is having a party this weekend. You in?'

'A party? Like, a party party?'

'Yeah, Skye. A party party. With boys and everything.'

'Am I invited?'

'Everyone is invited.'

'That doesn't necessarily mean I'm invited. Are you invited?'

'Everyone is invited.'

'I'll think about it.'

'Dad can get us some beers. He said he would. I guess so I don't drink someone else's or get my drink spiked. Haylee got her drink spiked.'

'Did she?'

'They found her in the back of Lachie's car. You know Lachie? That Year 11 guy?'

All the Year 11 guys looked the same to me. 'Black hair? Floppy fringe?'

'Nah, Lachie has brown hair.'

'Oh, I dunno then.'

'She had to get her stomach pumped.'

Kirrily's dad was American, ex-Army. She told us he'd been on two tours to the Middle East in the eighties as part of Desert Storm, and he'd lost part of his foot when another soldier's rifle went off in the tent. They sent him home but he was never the same. I didn't really understand what 'never the same' meant.

He'd met her Irish mother while they were both on respite in Vanuatu, and they'd moved to Adelaide in search of a new life, whatever that meant. A fresh start. So she said.

'Dad gets pretty good beers, too. Coopers. Do you like Coopers?'

'Don't think I've ever had it.'

'Well, I like it. You've got to roll it first to get the sediment mixed in.'

'How do you know?'

'Everyone knows.'

'Oh.'

We'd been to a couple of parties together. Mostly to laugh at the idiots getting drunk on cheap booze, we told ourselves, but we brought our own anyway. Kirrily had once got a hand in her t-shirt, and I'd hooked up with someone's gross cousin. And there was the time I'd reached behind me for my drink and grabbed a random's crotch instead. Some of my finest moments.

The bell went.

'Want to walk home with me?' I said.

'Can't,' she said. 'Hockey practice. Dad's picking me up.' She put her arm around me. 'We've got History last though. See you there.'

My shoulder warmed under her hand.

Jason sat on the couch, counting five-dollar notes into plastic bags in front of the afternoon news. The top of his head gleamed, sweaty and dirty.

'You're here. Again.'

He looked at me. 'School dresses always been that short?' Corner of his mouth curled up.

'Piss off.'

'Careful when you bend over. Not everyone's trustworthy like me.'

'I'm sixteen.'

He shrugged, pulled a bent cigarette from his top pocket and smoothed it between his fingers. ''Course you are. Sixteen-year-olds never shut up.'

Mum walked in, bright and shiny in her bank uniform. Ben trailed behind, sunburnt around his eyes. His bag rattled as he dropped it. One of his experiments – a rocket, a bomb. An animal he found in a tree.

'Why are you shouting? I could hear you in the car park.' He leaned over the couch.

'Jesus,' Jason said. 'Can't get a bloody thing done in this place.'

Mum pushed us towards the kitchen. 'Give him some space.'

'Maybe we could help him,' I said. 'If only we knew what it was he does, exactly. Crime lord? Train robber?'

'He runs his own business,' Ben said.

'We were just talking about it,' Mum said. 'How I might work for him.'

'You? But you work at the bank.'

'He reckons I'd be an asset.' Mum puffed herself out, like she'd won an award.

'Because you know so much about diamond heists?'

Jason rubbed his palm across his scalp. 'It's import–export.'

Mum stuck her hand in her top and adjusted her boobs. 'He reckons with my good connections, we could be raking it in in no time. That's what he said: good connections.' He came over to her and kissed her neck, her shoulder, her arm.

Ben said, 'Hey Jason, can I work in your business? Yiannis showed me how to make an abacus out of Coke bottle lids. Do you need an abacus? I reckon I'm pretty good at adding.'

'Nah, mate.'

Mum slipped her arm through Jason's elbow. 'Enough

questions. You'll get a job soon enough, Ben. When you're fourteen.' She slid past me. 'Maybe get one for your sister while you're at it.'

Jason went home to Port Flinders for the weekend. Mum woke up on Saturday morning and sat at the kitchen table and when I left to go to Casey's party that night, she was still sitting there with her face in her hands.

'Are you going to be all right?' I said.

'Oh sure,' she said. 'Just lonely. Without the man I love.'

I made a vomit sound. 'You've known him for five seconds,' I said.

'One day you'll understand. When you know, you just know.' She picked up her phone and stared at it. 'He's probably out of range. He said he might be out of range.'

'You should do something.'

She stretched. 'Maybe I'll watch a movie.'

'Outside, I mean.'

'Don't want to miss him if he calls.'

'Your phone can go with you, Mum.'

She put her fingers in her ears.

Casey's house was on the other side of the park, backing onto the canal. Kirrily and I walked together, her dad's beers clinking in her handbag. 'Three beers each,' she said. 'Or maybe four for me, two for you.'

'Piss off.'

It was already dark and the park was mostly empty. We stayed close together. My heart pounded in my ears.

'It's creepy here at night,' I said.

'Do you think? It's the same as during the day, isn't it? Just like, darker.'

'Murderers can hide in the dark,' I said.

'Can't be worse than that guy living at your place.'

'He hasn't even been with us for two weeks. Why is everyone so obsessed?'

'You know Jessyka said she saw him outside the sex shop?'

'No way.'

'Yeah.'

'Can we just get out of here?' Water slapped at the concrete walls of the canal.

Casey lived with her parents and big brother, but none of them were home that night. We stood at the door and stared at the doorbell. 'Is it her birthday?' I said, but Kirrily didn't know.

'Could be, I guess. You got a present?'

'Like a little kids' party? No, I haven't got a present.'

'Then I guess we'd better hope it's not her birthday.'

We stood and stood, staring at the doorbell. After a few minutes, a couple of older-looking guys came up behind us in a cloud of smoke.

'You going in?'

'Yeah, obviously,' said Kirrily. 'You can go first though.'

Casey came to the door with Jessyka draped around her. We stood dumbly behind the guys, who pushed past the door and fist-bumped another guy in the stairwell. Casey peered out.

'Kirrily?'

'Here!' she squeaked, and handed over one of her dad's beers. 'Happy birthday.'

The party was shit. We perched in a corner of the living room on a half-rotten brown couch and watched people from our classes rub up against each other. The music was bad. The food was cold. I held my beer to my mouth, whistled a little tune over it. I'd ignored Kirrily and hadn't rolled the sediment, and the flavour of piss was strong. I sipped at it, regretted it, but couldn't put it down in case it was spiked. I thought of Haylee getting her stomach pumped.

'Having a good time?' Kirrily said.

'Nope,' I said.

'Maybe we should go back to the park. Being murdered would be way more interesting than watching Lachie trying to slip roofies into unguarded drinks.'

'Especially if we can find a murderer with a decent car. He could take us to Macca's.'

She put her arm around me, and my shoulder burned again. 'KFC, even.'

'Let's not go crazy,' I said, but the words scraped in my throat and I spat them across the couch.

She was a bit drunk by then, two beers in. Her words washed around in her mouth and she chucked them out at random. We walked arm in arm back to the park, across to the playground where there were still those metal diggers from the nineties, and swings with chains.

'Let's go on the slippery dip,' she said, laughing. She tripped on the stairs and planted her face in the plastic frame, but kept laughing. At the top of the slide she stretched out her arms and said, 'I'm the king of the world!' and slipped down the slide and into the dirt below.

'Graceful,' I said.

'Go on, you have a go.'

'Nope.'

'Go on.'

'You're drunk.'

'You're drunk.' She reached for my hands and pulled me towards her. We sat in the dirt together. 'Skye,' she said. 'You are my best friend.' She took a swig of her beer. 'Like, we've only known each other for a couple of years but I feel like I could tell you anything.'

My ribs felt too big for my body. 'Oh yeah?'

'Anything. Go on, ask me something and I'll tell you.'

There were things I wanted to ask her. Questions I'd never used words for. She had this way of looking, like her eyes were too big for her face, like they wanted to break out and see every single thing there was to see, all the things they couldn't see from the prison of the head they were in.

'Skye. Ask me something.'

My throat was tight.

'That guy in the tunnel. What did he look like?'

'Gross, Skye. Don't ask me about that.'

'I'm just wondering. You know, what it might be like to go out like that.' She screwed up her face. 'Do you think he did it –'

'On purpose?'

'Right, on purpose.'

'Dad said he thought he probably did. He said people mostly don't fall in front of trains by accident.' She brought her face very close to mine. 'Unless someone pushed him.'

'Murderers.'

She squealed and pulled herself closer to me. 'I don't really come to the playground anymore. What about you? Do you miss it?'

'Nah, I bring Ben here all the time.'

'But do you miss the times when you came here because you wanted to?'

I shrugged. 'Sometimes I still want to come here. Depends how good the company is.'

Her head dropped onto my shoulder like a bag of shit. Passed out. Unconscious. She'd had two beers and she was paralytic. I waited there in the park with her, at the foot of the slippery dip in the dirt, keeping watch for murderers.

3

When I was in Year 2, Dad and I ate McDonald's every month in a C-47 plane. It was concreted in behind the playground, fold-down tables just right for Happy Meals. Afterwards we watched the footy players file onto the oval and he told me about his failed career as a centre half-back, and his failed career as a second slip, and his failed career as a point guard.

One time we reclined our seats and he said, 'Let's go to Fiji!' and pointed out the window and then said, 'Look at those people, like ants,' but they were ants and we were still just cemented into the ground.

The FOR SALE sign went up the next day. Ben and I stood in front of it on our way to the corner shop and I said, 'What the hell?' and then he fly-kicked it.

'*Spacious three-bedroom apartment*,' I read. 'Spacious? Your room is the size of a cupboard.'

'Your room doesn't even have a proper door.'

'*Great views towards the hills. Refurbished kitchen.*'

Once, Mum had decided to paint the kitchen. She'd got

some crackle-effect paint from someone at her work and she wanted to do the bench top in it. Spent a couple of hundred dollars on sponges and brushes, slapped the paint across the vinyl contact. 'Just wait,' she said. 'In half an hour the cracks will show up. Paula showed me.' We all stood and watched the bench tops for two hours. The paint dried. No cracks appeared. 'I'll kill Paula,' she said, and put all the paint in the bin. The landlord made her pay half the cost to have the bench top resprayed.

Ben kicked the sign again. 'This is so unfair.'

'We've gotta tell Mum,' I said.

Mum came running from her bedroom in just a t-shirt. 'Back already?' she said. Her face was flushed and her hair stuck out at right angles.

'You seen the sign?' Ben said.

'What sign?'

'There's a FOR SALE sign out the front.' Mum didn't say anything. 'Did you hear me? The flat's for sale.'

'Yeah, I know.'

Ben's bag of trinkets dropped to the floor behind me. 'You *know*?'

She waved her hand in the air. 'They sent me a letter last week. Don't worry, Ben. Investors.'

'Will we have to move?' I said.

'Nah. They said the new owners will let us stay here for sure.'

'They better,' said Ben.

'Nick off though, seriously,' Mum said. 'Get some fresh air.'

The corner store did pretty good hot chips. We bought the biggest size they had and drowned them in salt and vinegar. That road ended in a cul-de-sac and we took the food down a path that ran between the houses. It was quiet there, if you could block out the far-off drone of the main road.

'Yiannis says if you eat too much vinegar, your stomach can dissolve.'

'I don't care.' I shoved a few chips into my mouth at once. Last night's beer still sat piss-soaked on my tongue.

'Do you think they'll really let us stay?' He was drawing with a stick in the dirt.

'I don't know, Ben. I don't know how this stuff works.'

'I don't want to go back to the old place. Can they make us go back there?'

Right after Dad disappeared we'd spent two years in the commission flats, on the very top floor right at the back, three of us in two small rooms. Ben was three when we moved in, and I was nine. Mum banged on the walls and shouted a lot. We weren't supposed to leave the flat without her but we did, went down into the quadrangle to play with the other kids. Maron from the building next to ours had a tricycle with a seat on the back, and we took turns riding Ben around and letting the neighbourhood dogs chase us.

'Nah,' I said. 'Mum won't let them.'

He was quiet for ages, pushing chips around in his mouth. Seagulls came to squat nearby. Strutted their feathered pants around, making out as though they didn't want the chips for themselves.

'Try not to worry,' I said, and pulled him close to me.

His voice squeaked out: 'Yiannis says you can be so worried you die.'

'Yiannis doesn't know everything.'

'Yiannis does know everything. He says that his yiayia used to worry all the time, like she would go round her house turning on every light and turning it off again and putting her whole hand on the iron to see if it was hot and taking her dog to bed with her because she was worried about burglars breaking in, and then one day she worried so much she died.' He took a breath. 'And no one even found her until her dog had eaten part of her leg off.'

'He might be exaggerating a bit there.'

'He said her brain exploded.'

'I don't think brains can explode.'

'Do you think my brain is going to explode?'

'I promise your brain is not going to explode.' I threw the last soggy chips to the pack of gulls, and they blew into a cloud of white. 'Do you remember that trike from the flats? Maron's trike?'

'Sort of.'

'He rode so fast on that once that you flew right out of the back and a car nearly ran over you.'

'No he didn't.'

'He did. I was racing you guys down the driveway, running as fast as I could. And he beat me to the end but when he stopped you just came straight out. Like this' – I squeezed around his shoulders – 'pop!'

'Then what happened?'

'Then this car came around the corner and tried to pull into the driveway and you were right there in the middle of it. Crying. Like maybe you had scraped your knee, I think.'

He sat up and looked at me. 'And was I worried then?'

I pictured him on the bitumen in his green tracksuit, face torn into pieces. The howl that came from Maron as the car turned the corner at speed. The two of them afterwards, sitting on the brick wall that faced the street; Maron with his head between his legs and Ben throwing bits of grass into the air and laughing.

'I don't think you were worried then. Maron did all the worrying for you.'

'And did his brain explode?'

Maron when we moved out, crouched in the doorway of the western building with a joint between his thumb and forefinger, sunglasses on. His mum had died. Or his step-mother. Or his sister's mum. Someone had died, and he had sat that way for weeks, waiting for the days to end.

'Maybe a little.'

'Told you.'

Monday night, Jason was back and Mum had chicken drumettes on, filling the kitchen with smoke.

'Look,' she said. 'Jase bought me this grill while he was gone. You plug it in and you can have a barbecue inside. Clever, huh?'

'Yeah.'

'It'll make things easier. Maybe you can cook us something other than sausages.'

'Right, *I* can.'

She'd made a little salad, flat and limp in a glass bowl. I took it to the table. Jason had his body stretched down the couch and a man I hadn't seen before sat in the armchair, watching the football with his feet up on the coffee table. Barefoot. His toenails poked long and yellow towards the ceiling.

'Uh, hello?'

He waved with a bandaged hand. 'Watching the game.' He pointed with the other.

'I can see that. Who are you?'

'Merv. Friend of your mum's.' He had a bag of corn chips in his lap and he rustled around in it. 'Chips all gone. Got any more?'

'Mum doesn't let us buy those chips,' Ben said.

I kicked the couch. Jason groaned a little.

'Don't worry about him,' Merv said. 'Bit on the nod. He'll come good.' He tipped the last of the chips into his mouth. 'You kids got any video games?' He pulled up his shirt and rubbed his belly.

'No.'

'Might head off then.' He walked out the door and closed it behind him.

'That was weird,' Ben said.

Mum called out from the kitchen: 'Merv? Not staying for tea?' A motorbike started up downstairs.

After dinner I sat on the couch with Ben, who caught flies and glued them to the coffee table. Mum stood with her ear against her bedroom door, waiting for something. I read aloud from *Macbeth*, giving Ben the dramatic supporting lines.

'Come, you spirits
That tend on mortal thoughts, unsex me here,
And fill me from the crown to the toe topful
Of direst cruelty!'

'What does unsex mean?' he said.

'She doesn't want to be a woman anymore.'

'Why not?'

'She thinks if she can get rid of her feminine feelings, she'll be like a warrior. Strong, like a man.'

'That doesn't make sense.'

'I know.'

The smoke alarm went off in the hall. Jason's voice shot out, 'What the hell?' Then Mum, 'You're up!' I went to the linen closet, took the broom and used the handle to stop the alarm. Jason wiped a string of spit from his cheek.

'Hey, Linda,' he said, and his eyes got very wide. 'Forgot. Estate agents called before. Reminding you there's an inspection Wednesday. Four pm.'

'Shit. You didn't tell them you lived here, did you?'

'Nah, said I was your brother or something.'

'Can you help out?' she said.

'Nah, I'll be in Flinders on Wednesday. You know that.'

She rubbed her hands around his shiny head. 'Skye, I'll give you ten bucks to get the flat clean. Ten bucks.'

I put down my book. 'Twenty.'

'Fifteen.'

'Deal.'

I knew she wouldn't. A couple of years ago I'd started keeping a tally in a tiny notebook I kept in my drawer. When I reached $145 I decided to stop waiting for her to pay up, and got it back in other ways. Keeping the change at the supermarket. A faked school excursion. We were nearly balanced. For a woman who'd worked in a bank for eight months, she was shithouse at money.

My room was fine, but I pushed open the window to get the stale air moving. The flat was full of it – just a general feeling of being trapped in smog. A dull cigarette odour. A fruity, fishy smell. And a thin layer of grime on nearly every surface, which only budged when I used the proper Ajax stuff, the powder. Two of the kitchen cupboards had come loose; one of the hinges had fallen out completely. I scrubbed the bench tops with steel wool but couldn't shift the burnt patches – Ben's science experiments.

'Don't let them open the oven when they come,' I said. 'Smells like someone took a shit in there.'

'Skye!'

'*Did* someone take a shit in there?' I said.

Jason's throaty laugh came from over the couch. 'Are you serious?'

Mum laughed, too. 'Maybe it was Merv.'

Ben hovered in the doorway while I tidied his room. 'Don't look under the bed,' he said. 'I mean, you can look under the bed. It would just be really boring for you if you did. I don't want you to have a boring time when you're cleaning because it's already boring and the last thing you need is to be even more bored because underneath my bed is so boring.'

'I'm not going to look under your bed.'

'No, but I mean, you can if you really want to, it's just like I said, there's nothing there that's interesting and I know how much you like things to be interesting.'

He hopped from one foot to the other.

'Well, now I have to look.'

I leaned down and peered into the abyss below. There was a faint whiff of mould and sweat. Part of a sandwich. Socks with mud caked onto them. Some kind of electrical circuit board. I pulled out a box of shells and a plastic container with a lemon inside it.

'Yiannis is behind this, isn't he?'

Ben said nothing, just tapped his feet against the floor.

Scratching.

'Ben, is there an animal under here?' Another box, and another. I pushed them aside in search of the sound, found a shoebox with holes cut in the top. 'This had better not be a spider.' Opened it; inside, a brown shell the size of a tennis ball.

'A turtle?'

Hop-hop-hop. 'A tortoise, actually.'

'Mum is going to kill you.'

'You can't tell her.'

'Sure, I just won't tell her and it can go on living under your bed forever.'

'It's not mine. I'm just looking after it.'

'Yiannis?'

'He found an egg at the park so he incubated it and this tortoise hatched out and his mum says he's not allowed to keep it at their house.'

'Just found a turtle egg in the park, huh?'

'Tortoise.'

'How long has it been here?'

Hop-hop-hop. 'Since my birthday.'

'Far out.' I bundled the tortoise back into the box.

'Please don't tell her.'

'He can't stay here while the inspection is happening. What if someone sees him? You know we're not allowed to have pets here.'

'I'll think of something.' He frowned. 'Do you reckon he ever thinks of his family at the park? I mean, what are the chances of finding one tortoise egg just on its own? There must be others.'

'Are you sure?'

'Yiannis never lies. Maybe I should take Bilbo back to visit.'

'Bilbo?'

'Yeah. He's on an adventure. Pretty obvious.'

'Why don't you just focus on keeping him hidden for the next twenty-four hours?'

'He likes carrots the best. You know sometimes you cut them into little sticks and put honey on them? That's his favourite.'

'Great. So glad I go to all that effort for a tortoise that lives in a shoebox.' He grabbed box and tortoise from me and climbed through his window to the balcony.

We had to leave the house during the inspection, so I went down to the park and had a few goes on the spinning thing. It was warmer than it had been and kids were everywhere, all laughing until they fell over and cried and someone hugged them and they started laughing again. On the other side of the playground, some guys were hitting a cricket ball, and the laughter was occasionally drowned out by a cry of 'Howzat!' and the *thwock* of ball against bat. I walked over and leaned into the fence. Some of the guys from the party were sitting in the grandstand, fading in and out behind their cigarette smoke. From the kiosk I bought a lemonade with the two dollars I'd found cleaning under the fridge. Someone was clean bowled. The next guy went in. The ball came bouncing towards him and he hit it over the bowler's head and they ran.

I crushed the lemonade can under my foot, took it home so Ben could cash it in for ten cents. Most of the people had dispersed. A couple sat in their car with a brochure, looked from the brochure to the flat and back again. They didn't look much like investors, but I had never seen one anyway. I tapped on the driver's-side window.

'Sound investment, these flats.' The man nodded. 'Not much of a place to live, though. So much noise at night. The couple in number six fight constantly. No one gets any sleep.'

'Good to know,' he said, and slipped the brochure into the gap beside his seat.

Every Saturday for a month, people traipsed through our flat. I watched them come and go to see if I could spot the investors, see who turned up in an expensive car or wore a good tie. And each Friday afternoon Mum promised me ten or fifteen dollars (depending on her mood) and I cleaned from top to bottom before slipping Bilbo next door to hang out with Amir.

Jason went to Port Flinders most weekends, and sometimes during the week. He was always gone on Wednesdays – a weekly meeting, Mum said. On those nights she let us get a pizza from the dodgy place behind the corner shop, and it always tasted like the toppings had been dead for months but at least I didn't have to cook it.

'Are you still going to work for Jason?' Ben said, on the Wednesday before the last open inspection.

'Yep,' Mum said. 'Jason's business is booming, you know. All my connections. That's what's done it. He's going to be a millionaire.'

'There's no such thing as a millionaire,' Ben said.

'Millionaires do actual work,' I said. 'Like getting off the couch in the daytime.'

'He works at night,' Mum said. 'You don't know what you're talking about.'

The next morning he was back, sweaty and black around the eyes. Mum jumped on him when he walked through the door and his knees buckled and the two of them went crashing to the floor. Later, I heard Mum sobbing in the bathroom: 'You think I'm fat.'

She hadn't asked again what we thought of him, and his place in our flat seemed like a done deal. Even my bedroom had some of his stuff in it – a couple of plastic tubs that wouldn't fit anywhere else. I was banned from opening them.

'Do you think he's sending live birds overseas in Coke bottles?' Ben said to me one night. I was watching the people come and go from the Westfield again, trying to decide which ones I would follow home. One family had bought a TV as big as their car and were trying to cram it in around the children. 'TVs don't bend,' I said aloud. 'You're going to have to get out.' After a few minutes the mum and daughter got out of the car and waited in the car park while the dad and son drove off. I wondered if they would come back to pick them up. Probably just stay home and play Xbox for a while first.

'Or,' Ben said, pulling himself up on the bench to see what I was looking at, 'do you think he's selling something on the black market? Or the dark net?'

'What's the dark net?'

'It's part of the internet you can only get to if you have a secret password and I think you can buy human body parts there.'

'How do they ship them to you?'

'Maybe in an Esky?'

'Gross.' The mother and daughter moved to the trolley bay and leaned against the railing. A guy in a hi-vis shirt came over and talked to them for a moment, pulled all the trolleys out in one long snake. 'How does he manoeuvre that?'

'Inertia?' Ben said. 'Or, I heard about this guy in Canada who stole all the maple syrup in the country and the whole government collapsed. Could you do that here? What if Jason was stealing all the Vegemite in the country?'

The daughter was crying now, cross-legged on the bitumen. The mother tried to pick her up by her wrists but she was stubborn and they were locked like that for a few seconds, until the mother fell backwards and started crying herself.

'I reckon he's skimming credit card details,' I said.

'What does that mean?'

'It's when you steal other people's credit card numbers so you can spend the money on them. Didn't they do cyber safety stuff with you at school? Never give someone you don't know your password and that?'

'But why don't we have heaps of stuff here then? If he's spending all this money on things?'

'Why do you think he's got a whole separate house?'

Ben shrugged. 'I still reckon birds. Port Flinders is in the country, right? They have heaps of birds there. Cockies and kookaburras and those big eagle things and parrots. He could go part-time into lizards as well. Heaps of lizards in the outback.'

'Who knows? I don't think he's going to tell us.'

The car returned. Mother and daughter climbed in, still crying.

'Come on,' I said. 'I have to get the bathroom cleaned. And you have to take Bilbo next door before Mum gets home.'

At the end of May, an auction was held. We weren't allowed to come so we set up a couple of folding chairs across the street and listened. A man in a suit shouted numbers that couldn't have even been real. Two hundred and ninety thousand dollars. Two hundred and ninety-five thousand dollars. He got excited, all shiny with his mouth hanging right open. He demanded the people in the crowd give him more. 'Can I get three hundred?' and the people looked to one another and shrugged and shook their heads, but there was always another one to shout out right afterwards.

After ten minutes he said, 'Third call,' as though the words had tripped out of him without his permission, and then he rolled up his brochure and slapped it into his hand. Off to the side, a couple hugged and the woman shouted, 'I'm freaking out!'

Afterwards we sat around the kitchen table, eating salty biscuits from their box.

'Did they look like investors to you?' I said.

'Don't know what investors look like,' Mum said. Jason frowned at his phone, tapped furiously for a few seconds. 'Jase?'

'Investors.' He shoved the phone in his pocket and went out to the balcony. We listened to him pace back and forth past the front door, stopping occasionally to make a pained grunting noise. An earthy smell came in through the crack in the window and Mum stopped looking at us. Jason's phone rang. 'Give us some good news,' he said to whoever was on the other end.

'See?' Mum said. 'Investors. Nothing to worry about.'

4

THE FIRST TIME Dad took me for Chinese food, at a place on the corner near our house, we had sweet and sour pork and noodles with flat fish pieces. He said he'd taken Mum on a date there once, because she had never had Chinese food and he liked the lanterns. They ordered lemon chicken and fried rice.

They found out she was allergic to prawns that night. He rode with her in the ambulance and she swore she'd never go out with him again.

Eight months later, I was born.

Every afternoon I walked into the same flat and saw Jason counting out his five-dollar notes, and every afternoon I went to my room and thought about an afternoon he might not be there, always exactly the same. Mum had started counting the money too, after she got home from work. She was good like that, thimble on her thumb, flicking through the plastic and counting it without really seeing it.

Two weeks of these afternoons went by until something was different. Mum was home early, not even four o'clock, and

Jason stood in the window and blew smoke through the crack in the glass.

'Just stopped going outside to do that, huh?' I said, without meaning to.

'Shut up, Skye,' Jason said.

The table engulfed Mum, there in the middle of it with her head down. Her body stuttered as she breathed, a hiccup at the top and a shiver at the bottom. She'd been crying. Maybe she still was. I pulled a chair up next to her and put my face close to hers, took on her breath.

Her voice came quiet from between her fingers: 'They've sold the flat.'

'I know, I was there. Remember?'

She didn't look up. 'The flat. It's sold. They want us to leave.'

'But they said we could stay. They said people only buy these places as investments. To rent out.'

'Yeah, well.'

Jason pushed his cigarette butt through the crack. 'It's my fault,' he said. 'They don't like me.'

'Can you blame them?'

'Skye.' Mum's pinched voice. 'Can you give it a rest for five seconds?' She turned away, rode her body through the dips and crests.

'Great,' I said, threw my bag against the table. 'Where are we going to live, then?'

'Jesus Christ. Do you ever stop talking?'

'Jase.'

'I'm trying to run a business here.'

I took twenty dollars from Mum's purse and walked down to Westfield, sat on the bench at the top of the escalators. From there, the building stretched out to the new Kmart and the upstairs food court and the discount clothing store, where I'd tried and failed to get a job over the holidays. At the other end of the building, Myer and David Jones and the fancy supermarket with its own cheese shop inside. Kirrily said that was the rich end. T-shirts for fifty dollars. Chocolates imported from Europe.

I fingered the note in my pocket. I would buy sausages, beans, potatoes. That could last us for two dinners and Ben liked to make castles out of his mash.

A man and his daughter stood at the top of the escalator. She was little, not much taller than his knee, and she wore a pink dress with frills around the bottom. 'Come on, Lily,' he said, and his voice rolled around and out of his mouth. 'It's just the escalator. You've been on it lots of times.' Her hand was white in his, clenched as tight as it would go.

'I can't do it,' she said. 'I'm too scared.'

They stood there together and looked down the escalator together and he said, 'Just one step at a time.'

She took a deep breath. 'Okay, but just one,' she said, and climbed onto the first step, and that step moved them all the way to the end.

The supermarket hissed with people on their food missions. I picked the freshest-looking beans from their tub, used my fingernail to make sure the potatoes weren't green under their skins. All the sausages had gone gluten free, and they'd got more expensive at the same time. We always had the ones with beef and honey (when I looked in the ingredients list, honey wasn't there). I got a little tin of gravy powder. A chocolate koala, on special for seventy-five cents. I would say I'd lost the receipt. I would say it was my payment for making dinner when I still had to write an essay about King Duncan.

Mum was up and about in the kitchen when I got home. Smiling, even.

'Okay, what's going on?'

She nudged Jason. 'You tell her.'

'She's your kid. You tell her.'

'You're freaking me out,' I said.

She clapped her hands. 'Jason says we can move in with him!'

'But Jason lives here.'

'No, silly girl.' She took the bags from me. 'In Port Flinders.'

Breath all jammed up in my throat. She wouldn't do it. We'd been here before with the others but never seen it all the way to the end. Never actually got in the car and driven away, even when that South African guy had begged her to live in his castle. Her attention span was short. Jason would be gone in six months, the way they all were.

'Are you joking?'

'So generous of him, right? He reckons there's a great pub there, and the air's so clean. Good to get out of the city.'

Ben had squirrelled his way under the chair in the corner. I kneeled next to him, put my face in the dust. He had his toy cars again, and he drove them into head-on collisions over and over.

'Ben?'

'I don't want to move.' He'd been crying, just the hint of it when he spoke.

'We're not moving.'

Mum called out: 'We *are* moving.'

I lowered my voice. 'Don't worry. You know how this works. Mum'll lose interest soon enough and we'll find a new flat to live in. Closer to the river, even.'

'Mum says we're definitely going. In a month, she says.' The Ford careened over a cliff he'd built from cardboard, exploded into flames below. I pulled down the chair skirt. Mum had turned on her fancy new grill and put on all the sausages.

'That's supposed to last two days,' I said.

'Uh-huh,' she said. 'And my change?' I handed it over. 'Three sixty? Come on, Skye. I'm not stupid.'

'That's all there was. Sausages have gone up.'

'Where's the receipt?'

'I lost it.'

'You know the rules. Hand it over.'

'I can't. It's lost.'

'Oh well.' She shrugged. 'Then you can pay me back.'

'Yeah, I'll do that. Right after I get a job in Port Flinders. Heaps of jobs there, right? We can all work in Jason's business together.' I cut the ends off a few beans. 'Kirrily will let me stay with her. I'll get a job, get my own place. I'll be a high-school dropout like you. Family tradition.'

'You're too smart for that.'

'I'd say you can't stop me, but I know you won't even try. Why would you? You can spend all your time in Port Flinders, sucking Jason's dick.'

Hot oil splashed onto my skin before I'd had a chance to register Mum's new barbecue tongs being slammed down on the grill. 'Shit!' Pain like ant bites. And then sausages on the floor, their shiny skins picking up the dirt.

'Don't you speak to me like that again,' she said.

'Where does he keep going, anyway? Out on a job? That house on Dyson Road, right? With all the broken down cars out the front.'

'You don't know what you're talking about.'

'Right, I'm just a kid. I know.' I touched the soft welts along my arm, took a bag of peas from the freezer without meeting her eye. 'I've got an assignment to do.'

'What about dinner?' she said.

'Looks like you have everything under control.'

My room was hot. It had got dark outside, and in the car park downstairs two men were talking. An older one, bent around his body. And another one with his back to me, leaning against a car I hadn't seen before, Victorian plates on it. Their voices were hushed but I caught the inflections on the air; they were arguing. The light above them flickered, reflected in the younger man's shiny head.

Jason.

I leaned a little way out of my window, trying to catch a few words. The older guy stood to his full height, still a head shorter than Jason, and began to prod his chest. Jason's arms were up. He took a step back. Each time the man shoved, he seemed to grow a little taller. The car's lights went on and a third man appeared in the driver's-side window but I couldn't see his face, and the older man limped around to the other side and slammed the door, and the car tore into reverse and pulled out of the block with its tyres screaming.

Then silence.

Jason, in the middle of the car park with his hands in his pockets. He waited for a minute before throwing something to the ground – his wallet? – and shouting: 'Fuck you!' into the empty night.

When I looked from my window along the balcony, all the doors were open, with faces peering out.

We packed for Port Flinders almost immediately. Every day Mum seemed more frantic to get up there, and the month we'd had became three weeks and then two. We wouldn't need our furniture, she said, so I should ask around the apartment block to see if anyone else could use it. See if anyone else wanted a cheap table with peeling lino and a TV cabinet we'd found in hard rubbish.

'No one will want it,' I said.

'They're all cheapskates. Someone will take it.'

I went to Amir's flat first, where the door was wide open. Ben was already inside. The two boys were covered from head to toe in dirt and his mother was laughing, round and glossy with her hands on her belly.

'Nadira?'

'Skye,' she said, and she was smiling. 'Please, come in.' She poured tea from a blue pot. 'We were just about to have a cup of tea.'

Ben's eyes widened. 'Do you drink tea, Amir?'

'Yes.'

'But you're eight!'

Nadira laughed again. 'Won't you join us?' she said.

She seemed to be pregnant in her whole body, swollen and flushed. 'No, thank you. Mum just wanted to see if you wanted any of our furniture.'

'Don't you need it?'

'Nah, it won't fit in the new house.'

She sipped her tea. 'I heard they had sold your apartment. Where will you go?'

Ben stood up. 'Come on, Amir, let's go to your room.'

'We're moving to Port Flinders,' I said.

'Where's that?'

'North. On the Gulf.'

'Oh, my girl. That's a big move. And in the middle of Year 10?' She pulled me into her hard belly. 'You are smart. You will be just fine.' I breathed her in, her baking, tea-leaf, baby-growing smell. The flat was so tiny around her. She filled all the spaces as she moved between them. When I pulled away I'd left a damp patch on her head scarf, but she pretended not to notice.

'So, no furniture then?'

'No furniture. No tea?'

'No tea.'

The Adelmanns didn't answer their door, which was no surprise. They had two modes: arguing and screwing. I knocked a couple of times, reluctantly put my ear to the door and quickly tore it away. Those thin walls. It was amazing Nadira had ever wanted to get pregnant again.

At the end of the main walkway was the largest flat, built into the corner. For most of the time that we'd been in the block, an old man had lived there with a fish in a bowl. He had the bowl on the windowsill and in the mornings around school time he'd drop a few pellets into it. Never smiled, not at me. Said things about 'boat people' and 'our jobs' and used words I'd never heard before. The only reason anyone noticed he'd died was that the fish was upside down.

A couple lived there now, with her mother or his mother, or maybe even his grandmother. They had a stool out on the landing and now the husband sat there with a glass of brown liquid in one hand and a cigarette in the other. He had his legs crossed, one elbow on the opposite knee. It was pretty obvious he didn't want to be disturbed, but I knew that was not an option.

'Excuse me?' I said. He drank from his glass. 'Hello?'

He turned to look at me, sweaty under his eyes. When he spoke it was with a thick European accent. 'Yes, little girl?'

'Hi, I'm Skye.' Again he sipped at his drink. 'We're moving house soon, and my mum wanted me to ask if anyone wanted our furniture.'

'You think we don't have our own furniture?'

'What?'

'We work hard to buy good furniture. I got this dinner table made from oak. Handmade. Bought from antiques.'

'That sounds very nice.'

'I show it to you.'

'Oh no, that's okay. You're busy.'

'I am not busy.' He leaned close to me, breath like Christmas cake. 'I am hiding from my mother-in-law.' Then he laughed like a cartoon, mouth wide open and slapping his leg. I laughed too, partly in shock. 'But I am also hiding from the people who live there.' He pointed to the Adelmanns' door.

'Everyone is always hiding from them,' I said.

'I thought someone put hit on them. On Monday.'

'What?'

'These men arguing in the car park. I sat here on my chair like always because my mother-in-law has the dementia and I keep watch so she can't get out and go make life hell for some other family.' He laughed. 'These men looked like criminals. You know, gangsters.' He gestured with a flourish. '*Mafioso.*'

I thought of Jason with his hands in his pockets. 'I think they were just friends of my – my mum's boyfriend.'

He tipped the last of his drink into his throat. 'My friends act like that, I cut them.' I tried to read his face. He might have been joking behind his beard. 'Maybe I should be glad you are leaving, if your dad is bringing home these hit men.'

'He's not my dad.'

'So this not-dad is bringing around men in these cars with their tinted windows so we cannot see who is inside. Imagine, my mother-in-law gets in one of those cars. Because she has the dementia. And they drive off with her!' He lit another cigarette. 'Maybe that is a good thing.'

I leaned over the walkway railing, saw one of the sisters from downstairs washing her tiny dog.

'Well,' I said. 'We are leaving in two weeks. If you need a bed or a TV cabinet or this thing mum calls a sideboard, you let me know.'

He nodded. 'I will not be letting you know.'

From inside the apartment, a high-pitched scream, a crash, then nothing.

One evening late in June, with a week left in Adelaide, Jason said, 'Ben, mate. My house is small. Can't fit all those toys.' Ben didn't look up from the floor, where he'd trapped a spider under a glass. 'You hear me? You can't bring all this shit.'

'I can,' he said.

'No one took any furniture. Look at it. It's shit. We can't take it. Gonna put it on the nature strip. Burn it maybe.'

Ben moved the glass, watched the spider run with it. 'Ooh,' he said. 'One of its legs came off.'

'Maybe just a few toys,' Mum said.

Jason picked up her hand and kissed it. 'Want to make sure there's room for my girl.' She blushed. My stomach turned over. 'We got a big bed. King size.'

'Can you not?'

'Quiet, Skye. The adults are talking.' He moved his fingertips along her arm to her neck. Her whole body shook.

'What kind of house has room for a king-size bed but not a few Matchbox cars?' I said. 'Doesn't sound like much of a place.'

'It's a fine place,' he said. 'Just not full of kid crap.'

'Kid crap? Like, actual children?'

'Like shitty toy cars.'

I crossed my arms. 'Just shitty actual adults.'

Jason raised his flat hand. 'You want to say that again?'

'Jase,' Mum purred next to him. 'Jase, put your hand down.'

'That little bitch better know. Once she's eighteen, that's it. Nothing. No more handouts.' He slammed his hand on the table.

'Oh no. My plans are ruined.' I put my hand to my forehead. 'Screw you.'

In my peripheral vision, Ben slipped a piece of paper under his glass. He stood slowly, looked to me. Padded across the floor towards the table.

Dumped the spider right in Jason's lap.

'Shit! Ben, what the fuck?' He leapt to his feet, frantically brushed his jeans with his hands. 'That thing poisonous?'

'You mean "venomous". Poisonous means if you bite it, you die. Venomous means if it bites you, you die. Probably not poisonous. Dunno. Not that many people eat spiders to check, I guess.'

'Is it fucking venomous?'

'That guy? Oh yeah. Me and Amir found him inside the letterbox. Funnel-web, probably.'

And Jason – tall, bald, tattooed Jason – stripped from head to toe, shoes first, then jeans, Big W jocks, flannelette shirt, dirty old singlet. Chucked the whole lot across the room and into the kitchen and stood there in the middle of the apartment, stark naked except for his socks, screaming at the top of his lungs.

Ben exploded with laughter. And he kept laughing, his face bright, until Jason picked up the dining table and threw it into the TV cabinet.

'One less thing to worry about,' he said, and walked out.

5

One rainy Saturday afternoon, my dad took me to the local footy. The tickets were a gold coin donation and for that you also got your choice of a pie or a can of drink. Dad chose the can of drink. By the time we got to the front of the pie queue, all they had left were rabbit pies. 'You can still get a drink,' Dad said, but some part of me wanted to eat the pie.

We took our seats at the back of the grandstand and the players were dots running on a green tablecloth. At half-time, all the kids took out their tickets and one was drawn at random. A boy a couple of rows in front of us won a brand new bike. I took my pie from its bag. Bit into it. It was cold in the middle and it tasted like a bit of old fur that had been dunked in gravy.

'How is it?' Dad said.

'It's great,' I said, and he let me wear his favourite scarf.

The month we arrived in Port Flinders was the wettest on record. We drove up on a Saturday, along the highway, stopped at Port Wakefield and bought an orange juice and a sandwich to share from the service station.

Near the intersection to the highway was a school marked by a rusted sign, and a caravan park with washing lines strung between faded cabins. Nappies and granny undies like sails were thrown about in the wind. The pub was two-storeys with a wide verandah painted both red and blue, like someone had forgotten to finish it off, and at the outside tables men sat with their tall glasses and their cigarettes and we could hear their laughter even with the windows up.

When the Spencer Gulf reappeared, it had white peaks and it slammed over and over against the retaining wall. We passed a post office and a bank and a Centrelink office, a sign pointing to a lighthouse and a police station, where a couple of cops leaned against the only patrol car and their uniforms were untucked.

'Look at this shithole,' Ben said, eyes glossy, and for the first time ever, Mum said nothing because he was right, it was a shithole.

We rolled through in Jason's old Ford, saw the jetty with tugboats moored to it like they were its children, and the street was full of kids with their clothes plastered, damp with rain, to their bodies. We drove down to the water, where a marina rocked back and forth. A couple of guys in floppy hats had fishing rods in the water, but mostly they were drinking from crumpled cans and slapping their knees. At the end of the jetty, someone was hunched over, feeding scraps of food to a little brown dog. The houses along the foreshore were older, and had pretty verandahs with curled iron eyelashes. People sat on their porches. Ben waved to them; they didn't wave back.

'How many people did you say live here?' I said.

'Four thousand, give or take.' A group of guys in school uniform walked by, barefoot, kicking a footy around. 'Take, mostly.'

'Is that even enough to have a school?'

Mum snorted. 'Nah, Skye. We're gonna send you both down the mines.' Jason laughed, touched her arm.

'Out on the fishing boats,' he said.

'Funny.'

Mum's arm came into the back seat, slapped my leg. 'We're guests here,' she said.

The rest of the main street was a bunch of shops with metal signs: two chicken shops facing off on opposite sides of the road, a corner shop, a bakery, an old electrical goods store probably still selling VCRs. As we rounded the corner, a doctor's surgery. People milled around in front of it. Some of them shouted at each other. There were no traffic lights. We pulled up at a GIVE WAY sign and a car rolled along in front of us, gleaming under the rain clouds. The whole place was old. Old buildings. Old people. A man with his face screwed up walked a dog across a roundabout. Somewhere, a clock started striking eleven o'clock.

Jason's house was a fair way out of town, over a bridge and across the road from a bit of flat land that someone might have wanted to make into a park, once. Now it was mostly green and yellow spinifex. We stood in the driveway with our bags in our hands. The house was a cream brick one with a flat tin roof and a satellite dish sticking out like an ear. He had a corrugated fence with a few paint smears, and over it we could see a Hills hoist with faded towels dancing. At the back, a gum tree stretched into the huge sky.

'Get your shit out.' Jason pulled open the trailer; it creaked on its hinges. 'Gotta take this back before four or they'll charge me an extra day.'

Ben and I would share a bedroom, he told us. Ben's bed had *Thomas the Tank Engine* bedsheets. 'I'm ten,' he said. The house had three bedrooms but Jason needed the one at the front for his business and under no circumstances was he going to run it from the living room. Ours was at the back, in an asbestos extension with a sliding door out to the garden, where a sad-looking dog walked laps around the clothesline.

'Who looks after the dog when you're not here?' I said.

'My brother Kurt pops in. He's happy s'long as he's got a bone.'

'What's his name?'

'Kurt. I said that.'

'The dog's name?'

Jason spat into the kitchen sink, wiped his mouth on his sleeve. 'Murray.'

We stood in our bedroom, faced the window that overlooked the busted shed in the yard. Ben slipped a cardboard box under his bed and said he was going to have a lie down.

I spent the afternoon circling Murray. He was a wiry thing, just some bones with sinew wrapped around them. Black face with a white stripe down the middle. He might have been a Border Collie in part of him, and a Kelpie in another part, and maybe a Jack Russell in another part. One of his front legs was twisted out of shape. I threw a stick to him but he did nothing. He didn't lie down once. From time to time he walked a full lap of the clothesline and came back to where he'd started, and under his feet he'd walked a crater into the dirt. I wondered how long he had been chained there, how old he was, whether Jason ever took him to the empty lot across the road.

Over dinner – Mum burned some chops and slapped lettuce on top – I pushed him for more information.

'Where did Murray come from, Jason?'

'What's that?'

'Murray. Your dog. Where did he come from?'

'Oh. This guy out of town. Lives on a station. His dog got knocked up and he had these pups.' He chewed on his charcoal meat. 'Said they could work but I never saw any work getting done. You see him working?'

'He seems sad,' I said.

'Yiannis said dogs can live for seventeen years in captivity, if you get the ones that don't have hip problems,' said Ben. 'Does Murray have any hip problems?'

'Nope,' said Jason.

'He's going to get some pretty fast if you keep leaving him chained to that clothesline,' I said. 'His paw is all bent out of shape. Don't you think you should take him to have it looked at?'

'Vet's not in,' he said.

'What does that even mean?'

'Only one vet in town. This guy Grovey. He's gone to visit his sister in Whyalla. You want me to train as a vet?'

'I'll train as a vet,' said Ben.

It was strange to sit around another person's dinner table. It was bigger and older and its legs had been made to look like curvy women. Jason's living room was in the middle of the house, outside our bedroom, and overlooking the yard. He and Mum sat on one side of the table, us on the other, and my chair rocked when I moved. The whole time, I was forced to look out at Murray, who stayed standing with his ears down.

After dinner I washed dishes alongside Mum. It was dark outside. Murray's low whine came from the yard while I cleaned.

'Does he at least have a kennel or something?' I said.

'Who?' Mum said.

'Jason.' She slapped my arm. 'Murray, obviously.'

'How should I know?'

'Just thought you might know something about him. Maybe Jason mentioned him. Like, during your D&Ms.'

'Shut up, Skye.'

When the washing up was finished, she and Jason went out to the front porch and sat there with their heads close together. I listened with my ear against the window, itchy on the mesh curtains, but couldn't make out much of what they were saying. They held hands. Mum laughed a bit and her whole body moved.

'I don't get why she likes him.' Ben appeared next to me and I jumped. He didn't smile, just let out a deep sigh from his shoulders to the bottoms of his footed pyjamas.

'It won't last,' I said. 'It never lasts.'

Her laughter again.

'It might,' he said.

'It won't. We're a set, me and you and Mum. Jason doesn't want a set.'

Ben sat next to me on the couch. 'What if you leave, and then I'm just a pair with Mum and not a set anymore and we find out Jason doesn't like sets but he does like pairs? And I have to live in Port Flinders forever even though I don't think there's ever a Royal Show here so I can never have another Bertie Beetle again?'

I put my arm around him. 'Won't happen. I'm not going anywhere.'

Later I lay awake inside my pink sheets and listened to the noises of the house. The thudding from Jason's room, Mum's pitchy voice. And the soft crying from under *Thomas the Tank Engine.*

I pulled open the curtains, slimy in my hands. The scenery was so unfamiliar it could have been an alternate reality. I blinked at it, tried to connect it to the other parts of my brain.

'One night down,' I said quietly. Ben stirred in his bed.

I untangled Murray from the clothesline. He stood, stared. One of his eyes seemed larger than the other, bulging. I reached out with a closed fist and he stepped towards me with his nose in the air. 'Good boy,' I said. That seemed like the kind of thing to say, even though we'd never had a dog. We'd had a little cat on the sly, until it jumped out the window and ran down to Dyson Road, where its life abruptly ended.

The sliding door clunked shut behind me. Jason.

'The hell, Skye? What are you doing?'

'I thought Murray might want to go for a walk. Just down the road.'

'Oh yeah? You some kind of dog psychic?'

'No, I just thought because he's been chained up here. At least since we met you. I'm guessing longer, by the looks of him.'

'You reckon a dog like him wants walks?'

I looked back to the dog, quaking on his skinny legs. The blankness of his stare. The drooping tail. And somewhere in his face, the vague idea that he might lash out at the man who'd contained him, given half a chance.

'Who knows? I'm betting he's never been on one.'

'Know what? Take him. See how far you get.' He stood in the doorway with his arms crossed.

I sat on the ground with my face level to the dog's. He had beady eyes, the smaller one mustard yellow and the swollen one the same but ringed at its pupil in red and blue. I moved between the different lines of sight, trying to catch his gaze, but the more he looked back at me the clearer it became that he couldn't see me at all.

'Murray,' I said. 'Come on.'

His head cocked towards the sound of my voice. I couldn't find anything like a lead, so I wound the chain around my hand and tried a few steps with him. Just to the end of the yard. He hesitated, resisted the chain, limping on his bad foot. At the fence, I kneeled down to speak with him face to face and a deep growl came from the back of his throat.

'Murray,' I said again. The growling grew. A tiny thunder. He took a couple of steps back, pulling on the chain, and I let it slacken in my hands. He backed off further. Tripped on his busted foot and fell onto his haunches. Growling gave way to a high whimper. I took the chain and reattached it to the clothesline.

Jason laughed. 'What'd I tell you?'

I pushed past him, into the putrid living room. 'Your dog is blind.'

Mum rubbed her hands, the way she did when she was nervous. 'Let's do something nice today,' she said. Ben sat at the counter, eating burnt toast with brown goo on it.

'Lots of fun to be had in Port Flinders, do you think?' I said.

'I know!' Ben slammed his glass on the bench. 'I can show you how to train a grasshopper to carry a flower on its back. Yiannis showed me.'

Mum stared at him. 'Thought more like going to the beach. Or a market? Jase, is there a Sunday market?'

'Dunno.' Jason frowned at his phone. 'Can't go anyway. Work today.'

Mum rubbed his hand. 'Do you need my help? I can help.'

His face cycled through a few emotions before he settled on: 'No.'

'Right,' she said. 'No worries.'

There was a bus in our street but it didn't run on Sundays, so we walked to the bridge that led back into town. Ben's feet hurt. Ben's legs hurt. Ben's arms hurt.

'You're making my head hurt,' Mum said.

The foreshore of the original port was clean and pretty, with rows of chairs facing the water and a few people drinking from paper cups. Other people, too, leaning against the pylons of the jetty with their heads inside a cloud of smoke, shouting sometimes at each other and sometimes at the rest of the people on the beach. The day was grey, dulled, but the air was warm and Ben went wading out with his pants pulled up over his knees. Mum and I watched him together, his funny little head bouncing up and down.

'He'll be all right here, I reckon,' she said.

'Oh yeah? What makes you say that? All the other kids living in our street, coming out to play with him?'

'You don't have to be so negative all the time.'

'Maybe his dad can come to visit?'

'Shut up, Skye.'

'I thought I might take him to the library. They have this thing they get kids to do now, at school. Reading, I think they call it.'

Mum picked up a handful of sand and looked as though she might throw it at me.

'Go on,' I said. 'Can't make things worse than this.'

She threw it into the air. It came straight down again.

Ben squealed. 'I think a jellyfish swam past me!' he shouted. 'It hurts! Do you think it stung me?' He came running from the water with his thongs still on. 'Are the jellyfish deadly here? They're deadly in Darwin. Do you know what you should do if a jellyfish stings you?'

'What?'

He pulled down his pants, jocks and all, lifted one leg perpendicular to his body. 'You should wee on it.'

And so he did. Me and Mum stood there on the Port Flinders foreshore, watching Ben piss on his skinny knees.

'School starts tomorrow,' Mum said. She had her hair pinned back and the grey roots had been freshly covered.

'Can't wait.'

School was a bunch of little buildings held together by a bit of old clay. It backed onto the Spencer Gulf itself, right where the ocean ended and the sludge began, and that might as well have been the edge of the world. I crossed the dry football oval in my second-hand dress and the dirt kicked up behind me and I had never felt so alone.

My homeroom was twenty-two pissed-off kids and a young teacher with a long neck and dark eyes. As far as I could tell her plan was just to watch us until we eventually shut up and sat down. Everyone had a desk already so I sat close to the front, near the window, hoped no one would notice me. Thought of my

Lady Macbeth lines. Wondered who was reading them in my absence and doing it worse than me, probably.

'Skye Teller?' The teacher surveyed the class over her roll book.

I shrunk into my chair and raised my hand.

'New, right?'

'Yep.'

'From Adelaide?'

'Yep.'

'Great.' I was the last one on the list. While others disappeared into the hallway, she came over to my desk.

'Have you done work experience yet, Skye?' she said.

'No.'

'Everyone does work experience in Year 10. Most of the kids in your class have organised theirs already.'

'Where do I do it?'

'Up to you,' she said. 'You've got a bit of time to figure it out.'

'Okay,' I said, thought about getting some work experience at any of the places we'd driven past on the way in. Chicken shop work experience. Centrelink office work experience. Fishing work experience.

I took my new timetable into the hall, walked along the rooms in search of some kind of numbering system. Knocked on the window of the administration office, and a woman in a tight skirt came out to look me up and down.

'You in trouble?'

'A little. I don't know where I'm supposed to be.'

'But not in trouble, trouble? Not here for detention?'

'No.'

She walked back into the office and shut the door. I didn't knock again, just sat and watched the clock tick. A few times, other students got sent into the hallway. One came to the window with a bee sting and the woman in the skirt put a bit of ointment on it.

'Should I be doing something?' I asked her.

'You got a bee sting?'

'No …'

'Then this isn't gonna help you.' She disappeared again.

Third period was PE, so I took a guess and went back out to the football oval. I recognised some of the others from the morning: a blond guy with a hooked nose that looked as though it had been broken a few times; twin girls with different haircuts; the guy I'd sat next to in homeroom. He came over and introduced himself: 'Raf,' he said. 'Can't remember your name.'

'It's Skye.'

'Skye. That should be hard to forget. It's everywhere, right? Sky?' He smiled at his joke. 'You like footy?'

'Sure, I like footy,' I said.

'Should be right then. Mostly we just kick it around a bit but Mr Oates lets us have a friendly at the end of class. Mixed teams usually.'

I was so bad at it. No surprises. Mr Oates was nice enough, stopped with me for a couple of minutes and showed me how to hold the ball with the pointed bit facing out, how to connect it with the top of my foot. I learned to do a hand pass, and one of the other girls explained how to do a chest mark without getting 'whacked in the tit'. And at the end of the class, as promised, we had a friendly match, ten on ten. Raf was on the other team. I didn't know if he was any good, but the other guys seemed to pass it to him a lot, and he could kick it pretty straight. I walked up and down the side of the oval, hoping the ball would keep well clear of me.

It did, mostly. But with a minute to spare, someone 'kicked it from the side of their boot' (they shouted this loudly, so everyone knew it had happened) and it bounced at weird angles towards the out of bounds line. Towards me.

Chasing after it: Raf. I made a kind of grab for it and sort of nearly got it. Raf pointed up. 'Sky!' he shouted, smiling. Then he lunged at me, grabbed my waist with both hands and threw me to the ground. We both lay there for a microsecond, and he said, 'And this? Ground,' and laughed. When he helped me up, his hands were rough and warm. Somebody shouted, 'Holding the man!'

At the end of the school day, people gathered around the bus stop and smoked cigarettes behind their hands. Everyone did it, so it just looked like one big cloud. Like the bus stop was on fire. I waited on the other side of the road with my bag between my knees. The rain had stopped but the ground was wet and I felt it soaking into my dress.

I wondered about Ben's day. His school was walking distance, just a couple of streets. They had one of those stupid walking buses going, tie all the kids together with ropes. He'd love that. He'd be right up the front making everyone look at landmarks he'd invented.

My bus arrived. I sat near the back and pressed my nose against the window, breathed a little cloud to obscure the town I'd ended up in. Drew a little heart in it with my finger, to remember where I'd been.

6

One summer, Nonno bought an outdoor setting and put it on his back verandah and I ran in circles on the grass while Dad barbecued chicken wings. The smell was amazing. After a few minutes his neighbours from down the road turned up, their singsong 'Hello?' at the side of the house and the rattle of their bottles.

'Time to christen her!' someone said, and there were kids running everywhere, blurry with their legs pounding the grass and their squealing bouncing out into the valley, and my dad had his arm around me and he was smiling.

It took all the guts I could muster to get on the bus for day two. Ben was still on the couch in his pyjamas – 'School's so close I don't have to get dressed until five minutes before the bell!' – and Mum's door was closed. Mum and Jason's door. Jason's door, with Mum behind it.

There were a few other kids from school on the bus. Heads down, curled over their phones. I didn't have a phone. Who knew anymore whether it was because Mum couldn't afford it or because she just plain didn't want me to have one? Even a bad one without a camera. Just so I could have something private. Searching for stuff on the internet on Jason's computer made my skin fizz.

The bus stank. A kid next to me blew his nose into his arm. The driver shouted at the guys in the back seat. At the front of the bus an old lady started banging her walking stick on the floor and the sound bounced in my brain until all I could hear was the walking stick and I wasn't sure why I was even on the bus. Finally, the driver shouted, 'Mrs Nerington, stop it!' and the bus was silent for a split second before the laughter.

We pushed through the school gate as one mass, popped out the other side. I stood by the office for a while, thought about asking them to call the mayor of Adelaide to tell him I would need a lift home; stood at the bottom of the stairs a while longer and thought about smashing my foot with a brick so I wouldn't be able to walk up there.

Our homeroom teacher – Miss Fan, I had learned – gave me another copy of my timetable and sketched out a map of the rooms I would need. Raf had sat next to me again. He took one look at it and started laughing.

'The only rooms you need to worry about are the science labs and the ones downstairs near the gym. That's where we have everything else.' He scribbled his own drawing over the top. 'So many subjects to fail!'

'I've never failed any subjects,' I said.

'Figures,' he said.

'Why?'

'No reason.' When he smiled, his left cheek cracked into a deep dimple. 'Other important things: at recess we go across the oval and get the good spot at the top of the pipe; Mr Tostini is the most hard-arse English marker in the whole school; everyone plays footy; never get the chicken rolls from the canteen, because they're secretly made of camel meat.'

'Um, gross.'

Raf laughed. 'It tastes okay. Like, for an animal that's mostly bones and can run faster than a car. Tough as shit. Better than turkey, not as good as crocodile.'

'You can eat crocodile?'

'If you can catch one.' His breath was hot on my skin. I pulled away.

'Don't think I'll try.'

'Whatcha got first? Maths?'

'Maths.'

'Then we're going the same way.'

He walked right next to me, down the stairs and out into the quadrangle. Everything had a thin layer of damp covering it, but the rain had broken and we walked to class in the sun.

'Are you doing work experience?' I said.

'Yeah. My brother's doing an apprenticeship at the mechanic so I'm just going to hang there with him. He can show me how to change some oil or something.'

'Oh, right.'

'Good free child labour. Where are you doing yours?'

'Dunno.'

He was quiet for a second. 'Footy is my dream job, though,' he said. 'It's not just guys playing here, either. There's a girls' team that goes on trips around the coast.'

'Did you see me yesterday? I'm really more of a "read books in bed" kinda girl.'

'You just need a bit of training. Maybe something one on one.'

God, how did his skin stay so warm all the time? He wasn't even that close to me, but it burned my own. We got to Maths just in time, before I could say something ridiculous, or worse. I sat at the front, next to a girl I'd never seen before. Raf went to the back, someone passed him a footy over another guy's head.

Nothing was much different about sitting in a classroom, trying to understand trigonometry. The numbers and letters were the same, and the dickheads in the back row were the same. Our teacher paired us off to do some kind of problem-solving exercise. The girl I'd sat next to was also from Adelaide. Her dad had come up to work on the mines two years ago. When I asked her if she missed it, she just shrugged.

'I like it here. Hardly takes any time to get back to town anyway. We go there about once a month usually, so we can go to Myer and get a decent coffee.'

'Right,' I said.

'We get the train down most times.'

'That's cool.'

We tried to figure out the lengths of some lines with some angles next to them, but my lack of ability frustrated her and she said she'd do them herself. I stared out at the footy oval, the expanse of yellow grass. Felt a pang of homesickness for the cricket oval down the road. Even missed, for a second, the guys hitting balls around in their stupid white costumes. The air dripped thick and wet around the window frames and slipped across our desks. My hair stuck to my forehead. Fans on the ceiling just pushed it around from one of us to the next, until we were swimming in a pool of teenage guy stink.

When class ended I went out under the building and through the toilet block. I had History after recess, but I didn't have the book and the woman at the front desk told me they were out of photocopier cards.

'You can go into town and do it at the post office,' she said. 'Go early. Usually a pretty big queue there at lunchtime.'

'How will that help me for the class I have in fifteen minutes?'

'Not my problem.'

I thought about Raf spending recess at the 'pipe'. I didn't know what the 'pipe' was. A football thing? Something to do with skateboarding? Other kids cast long shadows across the grass but I didn't follow them; found a spot under a gum tree instead and leaned my head against it. The bark was smooth and cool. Noises from the yard bounced in and around it, so my ear became a kind of conch shell in reverse. Hold your ear to the tree and listen to the sounds of dickheads shouting in the middle of nowhere.

I ate my chips. We got the individual packets, now that Mum was working with Jason. Not the brand name ones, but still.

In History I read over someone else's shoulder. We learned about Franz Ferdinand and the beginning of World War I, history so ancient I couldn't relate it to my current world at all. Someone said: 'Who fights over countries the size of Tasmania?' Someone else said: 'Why can't white fellas be happy with the land they already got?' A little cheer went up in the back row.

The History teacher, tiny inside his grey jacket, closed his textbook. 'We'll get to that later. We're doing World War I right now.'

'Sounds about right.'

The bell rang.

I glazed my way through the last three periods. Geography: places are close to other places. Science: things explode when near other things. Drama: some people like attention more than other people. By the time I walked through the gate, I had forgotten all of it.

'You okay there, my cloudy friend?' Raf had flakes of sausage roll around his mouth. 'Finding your way around?'

'It's not the Louvre,' I said.

'The what?' A football came flying at his head and he caught it without even looking. 'Dickheads.' He turned and kicked the ball back; someone shouted 'Modra!' and they fell in a pile on the grass. 'I can help you, you know,' he said. 'If you want.'

'Why would you?'

He shrugged. 'It's hard to be new.'

'Has someone asked you to look after me?'

'Nope.'

'Then why?'

He swung his bag over his shoulder. 'I liked your ball-handling skills.'

'Are you for real?'

He smiled, crushed me in his solitary dimple.

I thought about getting onto the other bus, heading south as far as it would take me, hitchhiking into Gawler and out the other side. Maybe there would be a boat there that could take me to Kangaroo Island or somewhere, and they would never find me.

For a moment, I felt relief.

Then I thought of Ben in his walking bus with all the other shitty kids, imagined him arriving to home to find me gone, just him in the rotten house with Mum and Jason and Murray, who couldn't see him anyway.

I crossed the road. Sat on the ground with my knees to my chin. Someone at the other bus stop shouted: 'We can see your undies!' but I kept sitting. The wind was cool against my legs and more than that, I just didn't care a single bit.

It rained all afternoon. Ben took his cars outside and made the mud into jumps, and Murray lunged at him a couple of times but the chain held firm. Jason's dead lawn drank in the water and became a bog; Ben had already lost a shoe in there. The dog stood with his one busted paw in the air. Sometimes he put it down again, but it flicked up again almost as a reflex. As the storm washed through he lifted his nose and sniffed the air.

The water running outside the house made a sound like dragging a couch along the floor. The gutters were full of grass and weeds, little trees growing all along the roofline, and there was no room for water with all of that greenery so it just gushed right out. In one corner of the kitchen the water came in through a crack in the ceiling, and it sped so fast down the wall that you couldn't even tell it was moving.

'I wonder if Bilbo would like the rain,' Ben said.

'You're doing a good job keeping that secret. Where is he?'

'Can't tell you. What if Mum tortures you and you have to tell her so she doesn't cut off your ears?' He looked at me, straight-faced.

'I feel like those are pretty long odds.'

'Maybe. She's done some weird stuff.'

'Fine, you don't have to tell me. You should bring him out for some fresh air though. I'll make sure Mum's not looking.'

Mum was on Jason's computer. 'You cooking anything?' I said.

'Too much work to do, Skye. Can't you do it?'

'Did you get any groceries?'

'Nope.' She didn't look at me, just clacked away on the stained keyboard.

'Great. Well done.'

Murray's bark broke through the typing, a serious guttural sound starting right in his guts and punching the air, punch-punch-punch. Ben's laughter, a light squeal. I ran out to the yard, saw Ben walking Bilbo along the porch right in front of the dog's nose. Murray threw his head around, yanking on the chain, hunting for the source of the smell.

'I dipped him in the mud,' Ben said. 'Look, his feet are covered. He's leaving a trail.' He pointed at the prints on the concrete, laughed again.

'He'll eat him, you know. If he gets off that chain, Bilbo is dead meat.'

'Don't say it so loud.' He grabbed a clump of dry grass and made a nest on the pavement. 'Tortoises lay eggs in nests like this.'

'So there was one like this at the park?'

He looked at me. 'I wasn't there. Yiannis didn't tell me if there was a nest.'

'Sorry.'

'Don't make fun of me.'

Bilbo stepped into the nest, left his muddy prints in it, stepped out again. I got down on my knees to look at him face to face.

'Hello, Bilbo.'

He had a short neck and a look of permanent frustration, and his legs had squat little knees in them, as though this tortoise would one day need to jump hurdles. I touched my finger to his skin; it was soft and rough all at once. Murray barked behind me, pulling again on his chain. The Hills hoist groaned under his determination.

'Seriously though, you need to get him away from here, or go out the front with him or something.'

'He'll be okay. How is a dog like Murray going to bite through a tortoise shell?'

'He looks pretty angry.'

'He can't get off his chain.'

I brought my homework out to the porch and sat in a chair that was more rust than metal. History: Write three hundred words about the catalyst for World War I. Maths: Find the size of all these angles no one gives a shit about. I threw out a few lines from *Macbeth* under my breath. We were doing something else in English at the new school. Thomas Keneally. Something about a blacksmith.

I scribbled a few lines about Franz Ferdinand, and Gavrilo Princip's sandwich. Heard Jason's computer chair bump across the floor.

'Ben!' I hissed. 'Mum's coming.'

He wiped Bilbo's feet on the grass and shoved him inside his t-shirt. Mum appeared at the sliding door, holding a couple of glasses of juice.

'What're you two up to?' She smiled, a bit of her regular self spilling out.

'Homework,' I said.

'Ho– homework,' Ben said.

'Homework? In Year 3?' Mum drank from one of the glasses, handed the other one to Ben.

'I'm in Year 4,' he said, and took the glass in one hand. The lump in his shirt moved.

'Are you?'

He squeaked. His face flushed red. 'Ben?' I said. He made a fist, unfurled it and stretched out every finger, made a fist again. 'You okay, mate?' He squeaked again.

Mum blinked at me first, then at Ben. 'No one has homework in Year 4. You guys are up to something.'

'Yeah, that's it. We're the ones who're up to something.'

'Well, stop it.' She grabbed Ben's glass and the juice still in it sloshed over the side. The sliding door clunked into its latch behind her. Ben's eyes had filled with tears.

'What? What's wrong?'

He shook out his t-shirt, frantic, and Bilbo clattered to the cement. Ben doubled over. Hyperventilated. Tips of his ears bright red. I grabbed the tortoise and sat him on the step. Finally, more fuchsia than ruby, Ben put his hand on my shoulder.

'He bit me.' A red circle seeped through his t-shirt. 'In the nipple.' Tears in his eyes. 'Maybe I *should* feed him to Murray.'

Dinner was a few more dried-out sausages and bread. I poked at mine and the skin cracked open.

'Are these even made from actual animals?' I said. Mum had a vacant look about her. 'Are these the ones that were in our fridge in Adelaide?'

'Yep.' She pushed her food around the plate. 'Big day at work. Right, Jase?'

'Right. Huge day.'

'I thought you worked at night,' I said.

'Night, day. I work all the time.'

He'd grown a little moustache, like a bit of dead insect crawling across his lip. I stared at it. It moved as he ate.

'Isn't anyone going to ask how school was?' Ben said.

'How was school?' I said.

He grabbed his bag from under the table and pulled out an exercise book. 'Mrs Johansson told us about how she used to work for the School of the Air. That's how kids learn when they live really far away from everything.'

'Like here, you mean.'

'No, like really far away. Did you know some kids live on camel stations? That's a big farm where they breed camels.'

'Why?' Mum said.

'I guess they eat them,' he said.

'They do eat them.'

Mum looked at me. 'How do you know?'

I thought of Raf's hand in mine. 'I read about it.'

'Anyway,' Ben said, banging his fork on the table, 'in the old days people from other countries came and brought their camels with them so they could ride in the desert, and now there are heaps of feral camels just roaming around everywhere. So the camel farmers shoot them.'

'Gross,' Mum said.

'Maybe then they make them into these terrible sausages, and people like us are forced to eat them,' I said.

He frowned. 'I mean, I guess they could be made into sausages. I think they can make them into pretty much anything. Steaks. Chops.' He shoved half his bread in at once. 'Mrs Johansson says the kids who live on stations have the best manners of any kids she knows.'

'Is that right.'

No one asked me how my day was, so I didn't tell them. Mum cleared her throat a couple of times, but no one asked her either.

After dinner I washed the dishes while she and Jason curled up on the couch together. He had his arms around her and his moustache moved up and down as they whispered. Mum's body had collapsed into his. Every couple of minutes, her leg muscles spasmed. I put the dishes away and went to read in the room I shared with Ben.

When I came out two hours later, they were still there on the couch. Mum asleep. Jason counting five-dollar notes out onto the coffee table.

Ben and I got into a bit of a routine. Mum and Jason ignored us, and we fed ourselves and in the afternoons we walked across to the empty block and threw rocks at stuff that moved in the shadows.

One night before it got dark we went down to his school and he showed me where he'd cut his leg on the swings, and where he spent his lunchtime alone in the doorway of his classroom. He crouched down in there and crossed his legs. 'I sit like this,' he said. 'I have to get up before the other kids get back because they step on me when they go back into the classroom.'

I sat next to him.

'I don't know why they don't want to play with me but I guess that's their decision.' His skin and bones buzzed next to me.

'You'll make friends,' I said. Hollow promise.

'I tried showing them some of the things Yiannis taught me. I wanted to start with the one where you give Panadol to a bird and make it explode, but I thought that might freak them out so I just tied a balloon to a bee.'

'Did they like it?'

'They got bored of waiting for me to tie it on so they just left.'

'Did the bee like it?'

His face lit up. 'Yeah, bees love being tied to balloons! They can fly even higher than Mount Everest but there's hardly any nectar up there so mostly they don't. So when you tie a balloon to them it's like they get to go back to their true calling.' He leaned against my arm. 'I'm glad you came with us.'

'To school?'

'Nah, here to Port Flinders.'

'I was always going to come with you. Where else would I go?'

'Dunno. Just Mum said you might not be coming. That you might stay in Adelaide.'

'I don't know why she would tell you that.' I put my arm around him. He was hardly anything, like hugging a stick. 'What if tomorrow I take you into town, just the two of us, and we get a vanilla slice?'

He nodded quickly. 'Did you know vanilla slices were originally from France? They had heaps of pastry and sometimes they made them into whole cakes of vanilla slice. I reckon I would like a whole cake of vanilla slice.'

'Don't know if they do those in town.'

'I guess they might not. Maybe we can go to France one day and have one.'

'Let's do that. But tomorrow, we might just go to the bakery on the main street.'

'Maybe you can show me your school, since I showed you mine.'

'Nothing much to see at my school.'

'Do you have any friends?'

Raf and his grinning, his always-warm skin. 'Dunno yet.'

'Yeah,' he said. 'Sometimes it's hard to tell. Like when I tied the balloon to the bee, Braydon came over to have a look but when I gave him the special close-up, he told me the bee would die.' He curled closer to me. 'But I only do it to bees that have already lost their stingers. They're going to die anyway. It's like their last big adventure.'

We were a team, Ben and me. I felt it then more acutely than I had ever felt anything.

Mum and Jason got home late, after Ben was already in bed. I'd found a movie on the shitty regional stations we got, watched it while I waited for Jason's car in the driveway. They were fighting before they got inside. I could hear them through the window. Jason's voice raised. Mum's voice low and short. A car door slammed. Jason: 'You fucking liar.' A thud. Jason shouting, not even words but just sounds. Gravel hitting the window as the car tore off again.

I went to the door. She was there, folded, on the ground. Knees drawn up to her chest. Her body moved rigidly, statically, and her shoulders slumped as though the air had been pulled right out of them.

'Mum?' I said.

Nothing. The streetlight above her flickered. She stared into the empty space where the car had been. I sat on the ground next to her and put my fingers to her cheek, under the bone where the red birth of the bruise began.

'Come on. I'll take you inside.'

She leaned into me and her hair smelled of cigarette smoke and something unfamiliar but putrid, and I half-dragged her into the house and dropped her on the couch. Her eyes remained half-focused, hands folded together in her lap. Inside the bruise, a paper-thin cut stretched from her lip to her cheekbone. Her breath came in quick bursts, as though trying to escape.

I wanted to find Jason, to push his head through a window. I watched myself parent my parent, got her a drink in a scungy plastic cup, washed her face with a warm towel.

'Where were you?' Silence. 'Is Jason coming back?'

She shook her head slightly. I took her hand and tried to think of a time we had been together this way, with our selves right open. Hadn't ever practised the words to say to her. I sat there with my mouth half-open, waiting for the right things to come out.

The movie roared in the background. Headlights flashed across the wall and Mum flinched, but they continued down the road. I turned her face towards mine.

'You're all right now,' I said. She rolled her eyes. My chest tightened. I looked for other words, better words, ones that would take us from Jason's rancid living room and back to the flat and the TV cabinet before it had a table in it. 'I don't know what to say. Okay? I don't know.'

Then we were just there for a while, in the glow of the TV, and Nicolas Cage was on a plane with some other guys, and still we sat there and Mum didn't say a single word. During the ad breaks I watched her face. It moved in and out of shadow; sometimes the bruise was there, and sometimes it wasn't.

Ben appeared in the doorway, stood there in his dinosaur pyjamas and rubbed his eyes. 'Mum?' he said, and her head snapped up. 'What's wrong?'

'It's nothing. I'm fine.' She wiped her face with her sleeve. 'Turn the bloody TV off.'

I didn't turn the TV off. She sat there with me for another thirty minutes while I watched *Con Air* and thought about my own days, one after another. And every so often her whole body shook, until her breathing eased and she was asleep with her hand curled around mine.

7

One weekend, Dad took me on the O-Bahn bus, pushed his face up against the window like he'd never seen it before. And I squeezed up next to him because I really had never seen it before.

It stopped off in a place called Paradise, which was actually just concrete paved into a couple of palm trees, and a bus depot someone had graffitied from top to bottom. We got out there, and Dad said, 'So this is Paradise,' and we sat under the PARADISE sign and he made the joke a few more times before he took me back to Mum's house.

Jason didn't come back for two days. I took Ben into town but no one sold vanilla slices, so we got a stale finger bun each and one for Mum. She stayed on the couch the whole time he was gone, only moving to go to the toilet and stare out the front door for a minute. I brought her cups of water and asked if she wanted toast, but she didn't. By the end of the first day, half her face was purple. I couldn't stop looking at it.

'Could you stop?' she said, and pulled her hair over it.

'He shouldn't have done that.' It seemed so obvious a thing to say.

She rolled her eyes. 'You're fifteen.'

'I'm sixteen.'

'Whatever, sixteen. You don't know anything about adult relationships.'

I pointed to the bruise, the way it curled around her cheekbone, sent blue flushes down the side of her nose. 'I know that shouldn't happen.'

'You wouldn't understand.'

'Try me.'

She sighed. 'It was my fault. I pushed him. I know he's done it tough with his dad. He was an alcoholic. Did you know that? 'Course you didn't. He only came home to beat him. I should have known better than to ask questions when he was already tired. Okay?'

'No?'

'Well, that's all you're getting. I've got stuff to do.'

'Right.'

'Business is crazy. We need to make it easy for Jase when he gets back, try not to overwhelm him.' She held out her empty glass. 'We've all gotta do our bit.'

'We *all* do?'

'He'll be back soon and there'll be more work than ever. He's just so busy. I've gotta support him.' The conversation was over.

Ben and I ate toasted sandwiches in our bedroom.

'My sheets feel funny,' he said.

'They're dirty,' I said. 'I'll wash them for you.'

'Oh.'

'Your other clothes, too. Has Mum washed your uniform?'

'Nope.'

'Sorry,' I said.

'It's okay.'

I opened the window to let the air in but it was still and wet. Somewhere in the room, Bilbo was scratching.

'Where is he?' I said.

'I told you, I can't say. What if we become worst enemies and you tell Mum to get back at me?'

'We'll never be worst enemies, Ben.'

'What if the Gestapo comes and says they'll take you away unless you tell them where Bilbo is? What if Yiannis changes his mind about letting me have him and his dad comes and makes you give him Bilbo at gunpoint?'

'I mean, none of that seems very likely.'

'Yiannis says we live in a multiverse and there are infinite other universes with every possible outcome playing out all the time.'

'Can't argue with that.'

I took a blanket to Mum and she drew it around her into a cocoon.

'You're welcome,' I said. She grunted. Her face now had shades of yellow and green in it; I pointed to it. 'You should've used an icepack.'

'Mind your own business.'

When I got home from school the next day, Jason's car was in the driveway. He and Mum had the blanket over both of them, and they were watching a *Biggest Loser* repeat with the blinds closed. Mum had her hair pulled over her face again; Jason sat on the other side of her. She glanced over as I walked past, but didn't say a word.

'I'm not making tea tonight,' I said. 'One of you is going to have to get off your arse and go to the supermarket.'

'Pizza,' Jason said, waving me away.

They didn't move for that, either, not even a courtesy walk to the front door to pay for it. Ben and I sat on the floor in front of the TV and we all ate from the boxes with our hands. Mum and Jason had their faces as close together as physically possible and he whispered, 'I'm sorry' and 'It won't happen again' to her until she was glowing almost in rainbow colours. Listening to his apologies brought out bugs on my skin.

'This pizza is so bad,' said Ben. 'The ones from the freezer are better than this.'

Jason's whisper: 'It was an accident.' Mum's whisper: 'I know.' And she rubbed his head with her oily hands and they were both smiling.

When we were finished, there were rings of grease on the carpet.

I took my last slice outside, sat on the concrete and watched Murray sniff at the air. 'Storm coming?' I said. He didn't lie down. I put my hand out to him and he shoved it with his nose and the low growling came from the back of his throat again.

'Want some?' I tore off a bit of cheesy crust and he snapped it out of my hands. 'Great. Good manners.'

Yellow light burst from our bedroom; Ben's silhouette moved behind the curtain, shoulders down. I tapped on the window and the fabric parted.

'You okay, buddy?'

He shook his head.

'What's happened?'

He wound the window open and stuck his head through, looked at me upside down.

'Mum yelled at me.'

'What did you do?'

'Nothing! I was just telling her about how you can't bury toads alive because they can get oxygen out of the soil and when it's raining they can even suck it out of the water, which is part of the reason there are so many cane toads in Queensland and now they're even going to the Northern Territory, as if it's not scary enough there already.' He took a deep breath.

'Is that true? They can suck the oxygen out of the water?'

'Yiannis says it is.'

'Then what happened?'

'Then she shouted at me. She said, "BEN DON'T YOU EVER SHUT UP EVEN FOR TEN SECONDS SERIOUSLY

I HAVE HAD AS MUCH AS I CAN TAKE" and then she said some words I don't want to say.'

He pulled his head inside and wound the window closed. I threw the rest of the pizza at Murray and slammed the door, stormed into the living room. My throat burned with the words that wanted to pour through it and I pulled myself up as tall as I could and stood over the woman and her dickhead on the couch.

'Ben's in his room. Crying. Because of you.'

She took her mouth away from Jason's ear and looked at me.

'He wouldn't shut up.'

'He's ten. He's trying to tell you something he cares about and you can't even give him one minute to listen to what he's got to say.'

'I told him, I've got a headache.'

'He's in there right now crying himself to sleep. Do you even give a shit? Happy just to let him grow up to be a loser like you?'

She shrugged. 'He won't. He's so smart.' Jason snorted.

I yanked the blanket, their naked bodies twisted underneath it, threw it across the room. 'This is fucked. You are both fucked.'

'Settle down,' Jason said, still laughing.

I squatted next to him, looked him right in the eye. 'If you touch my mother again, I will call the police.'

And I went to our room, pushed my bed against the door, and turned off the light.

In the morning Mum and Jason were sitting at the kitchen table together. Both of them on the same side like it was a job interview.

'Sit,' Mum said.

'I have to get ready for school.'

'For Christ's sake, Skye. Sit down.' Jason. His face was all lit up, eyes flicking everywhere. Jaw clenched in one flat line. I sat.

'What?'

He put his hands palms-down on the table. Jason the Godfather. He stared right into me with his eyeballs bulging. 'No one threatens me. In my own house.'

'Is that a threat?' I said. 'Because I mean, that would be pretty ironic. Threatening me not to threaten you.'

'I'm not mucking around.'

Mum put her hand on top of his hand, pushed her fingers between his. 'Look, Skye. If you're going to be in this house, throwing your weight around, acting like you're the bloody adult' – I laughed – 'you need to get a job.'

'What for? Jason earns so much money.'

'So you can learn some responsibility.'

'*Me?* Are you actually serious?'

'You can pay bloody board, that's what,' Jason said.

I rose slowly from the table, keeping my eyes on Jason's. 'Fine. A job? No problem. Maybe then I'll be able to afford whatever it is you two are selling.'

Raf was waiting for me by the front gate.

'What's up?' he said.

'I have to get a job.'

'A *job*?'

'Mum says. Bitch.'

He wrote his name in the dirt with his shoe. 'Now you'll never have time to come to footy training.'

I rubbed his name out with my own shoe. 'I can try.' He frowned. 'Maybe next week.'

'Fine. At least come and meet some of the guys.'

'Do they want to meet me?'

'They want what I tell them they want.'

'That seems like a good deal.'

'When you're the captain, these are the kinds of decisions you get to make.'

'When?'

'Come to the pipes at lunch. We can go halvies in a pie.'

I thought about the pipes all through English, and all through History, and again through Geography. I learned nothing about topography, or the lines we use to indicate changing altitude, or how to read a mountain on a map. Instead, I watched the oval, tried to zoom with my eyes to see the pipes. I couldn't place what made me so nervous about it, except that I'd never been asked to go anywhere with footy guys, or any guys, really, and the way Raf had asked me made my legs ache right into my knees.

He was waiting for me by the tuckshop. 'I told them you were coming and they had to be nice to you.'

'Would they not be nice to me? If you hadn't?'

'Nah, they're a pack of wankers.' He smiled in his one-dimpled way and took a huge bite out of the pie. 'Fflrfing hoooooot!' Threw the rest of the pie to me and fanned his open mouth.

'Hot?' I said. He nodded furiously.

The pipes were not a footy thing, or a skateboarding thing. The railway tracks ran the full length of the school and these guys were sitting right on them like some kind of dare. Some girls were there too, sitting on the fence, laughing with each other and squealing each time the lights changed from red to green.

'Fellas,' he said. A couple of them came up from the tracks and hugged him, slapped him across the back. 'And ladies.' He curtseyed to the girls on the fence; they laughed, pushed their hair behind their ears.

'Rafferty,' one of them said.

He pushed me forward. 'This is Skye. Like, you know.' He pointed up. 'She's new and we are going to be nice to her. Okay? That means you, Ellen.'

I knew Ellen from my Geography class. She had been anything but nice to me. 'Hi,' I said. She ignored me. One of the other girls tapped the railing next to her.

'Where you from?'

'Adelaide,' I said.

'Oh, the city. Nice.' She pulled a cigarette from her pocket. 'You like it up here?'

'Bits of it.'

'Lucky you got Raf here to show you round. He knows all the best stuff to do, don'tcha, Rafferty?'

He shrugged. 'I can hook you up with a pretty good art gallery. If you're into that kind of thing.' Ellen snorted a laugh. The other girl turned back to me.

'The guys on the pipes are all dickheads. The fat one is Hamish. You're gonna want to ignore him best you can. If you haven't seen him yet – good.' Hamish let out a huge burp and they all laughed. 'The two sitting on the sleeper are Seb and Al. They're twins, in case you couldn't tell. Identical. None of us know which one's which.'

'I do,' Raf said. 'Seb's dick is smaller.' Ellen laughed again, slapped Raf's arm.

'One on the end is Yardy. Not a bad bloke if you go in for the kind who'll love you with his fists.' She blew a cloud of smoke in my face. 'And I'm Renée.'

'It's nice to meet you,' I said.

Ellen leaned across Renée, took the cigarette from her hand and inhaled. 'You don't know that yet,' she said. When she smiled, I counted three different colours in her teeth.

Raf came back to sit with me. 'What do you do here, at the pipes?' I said.

'This.' He gestured as though to his kingdom. 'Sit here, eat a pie, back to class.'

'Why are they sitting on the train line though? What if a train comes?'

'Trains do come,' he said. 'Gotta get your kicks somehow.'

I thought of Kirrily then, hundreds of kilometres away studying *Macbeth* in the air-conditioning. The man in the tunnel, how he had jumped in front of the train on purpose. The way she described him with his legs sliced right off. I watched the twins on the sleepers, watched them waiting for the light to change.

'Is it safe?'

'Pretty safe,' he said. 'No one's died yet.'

Seb or Al called out: 'Nah, Gary did.'

'Oh yeah.' Raf nodded. 'Yeah, Gary did die. But no one else has died.' An in-joke I wasn't part of.

Ellen walked down to the tracks and blew smoke right into Yardy's mouth. He pulled her into his lap and she moved her hips against him.

'Should we be watching this?'

'Don't be so uptight,' Renée said, but she had her eyes half-closed too.

The lights changed from red to green. 'Get up, dickheads,' Raf said. Ellen kept grinding. Seb or Al yanked on her arm. Yardy shoved his tongue in her throat. Down the line, the boom gates sounded. 'Seriously, get up.' Ellen gradually untangled herself. Yardy smiled up at her, pants pulled tight across his crotch. The train sounded its horn at the other end of the tunnel and four of them scuttled up the embankment, leaving Yardy standing right by the tracks with the train rushing right past his nose.

'Nearly hit my boner, man.' They all laughed.

Ellen pulled a glass tube from her pocket and grabbed Yardy's hand. 'Time for the tunnel?' He lifted her over his shoulder and they disappeared into the blackness.

'What's that about?' I said. Raf shrugged. He ate a banana. Some kids kicked a football around on the oval and I watched it, yellow against the sky, pinging up and down like they were trying to get rid of it, but failing. 'What's the deal with Ellen anyway?'

Renée laughed. 'Slut.'

'Oh.'

'She leads Yardy on but everyone knows she's in love with our mate Rafferty.' She ruffled Raf's hair. 'That's right, isn't it, Raf?'

'Nope.'

'You're gonna take her to the Year 10 dance, she reckons.'

'Yeah, nah.'

'Says she's got a pretty dress picked out just for you, the way you like it. Big slit up the back.' She laughed again. I shifted uncomfortably on the fence. A bit of metal stuck into my leg. It stung, but I was afraid that if I jumped off, my dress would tear right open.

'Just shut up, Renée.'

'Bitch stole my last ciggie. You got any more, Rafferty?'

He shook his head. 'I'd never get to play for the Crows if I smoked. You know that.'

'Right. The Crows.'

'Shut up.'

'Have it your way. I'm going to find the others.' She hopped down from the fence, slapped Seb or Al's arse as she slipped into the tunnel.

'Sorry,' Raf said.

'I might just head off,' I said, tried to unravel myself from the fence without cutting myself open. I failed. The metal scraped right along the back of my thigh. 'Shit!' I reached behind with my hand; it came back red.

'What've you done to yourself?'

'Just a little scratch.' It pricked and punched. 'Argh, it hurts.'

'Had a tetanus shot lately?'

'No idea.'

'Better get you down to the nurse then.'

He walked me back across the oval, grabbed the yellow football from one of the younger kids and kicked it over their heads. They all jumped for it at once, collided and collapsed in a puddle on the grass. In the distance, I heard the boom gates ringing.

The nurse had to lift my dress to see the cut, so she shooed Raf away and closed the door. 'Where'd you do this?' she said.

'Over the back oval.'

'The train line, right? You kids aren't careful 'n' that rusty fence is going to kill one of you one day.'

Raf lurked in the hall.

'So, uh . . .' I said.

He shoved his hands into his pockets. 'Sorry.'

'Not your fault. Just probably not my thing.'

'What is your thing, Skye?'

'Reading, I guess. Going to the park.'

'I'll tell you a secret.' He leaned so close to me I felt the pulse of his breath. 'Those are my things too.'

'More than playing chicken with a train?'

'Way more.' He bumped me with his shoulder. 'We could try doing them together one time. If you want.' My stomach flipped over. He was so earnest, looking at me with his whole face. His body radiated. The muscles in his arms tensed and flexed. What did he expect me to say?

'You probably wouldn't like my books,' I said finally. He kept staring at me. Smiled. Rubbed his hair with his hand flat.

'Got my own books.'

We stood like that in the hallway for a minute or more. Him staring at me. Me trying to escape into the centre of the earth. When the bell rang, he touched my arm with the tips of his fingers and said, 'We could start a club.' Disappeared down the hall and around the corner.

I walked home along the train line. It went almost from school to Jason's house, running parallel to the highway. The sleepers were dry and bloated, and they broke away in parts as I stepped along them. I would hear the train coming. The road was so flat it was impossible to miss, after it came out of the tunnel. The boom gates would tell me, anyway. I hoped.

Across from the train line the land was flat and dry. Wheat grew in its thin stalks, green and immature and thrown a bit in the wind. A chorus of wheat, an audience. I skipped along the line, slipping a bit on the rounded tops of the tracks, watched the way the wheat came with me. Beyond the fields the ranges started: rocks that shot out where the tectonic plates had smashed together, spewing these new mountains out of the old ground.

Maybe I would go there sometime. Get a car, drive out there with Raf and Ben for a picnic.

I reached the train station. No one was there but a skinny conductor with blisters on his face, and he sold me a cold lemonade for a dollar so I stood in the sun and drank it in three gulps, crushed the can against the brick wall.

All the roads met the train tracks in cul-de-sacs, brush fences rubbing up against the wire of the line. Each time I passed one I peered over. Tried to get a sense of who was down there, who lived there. In one street, a couple of kids kicked a footy, lost it over the wall to someone's backyard. In another, a man and a woman stood on the footpath and shouted very close to each other's faces until they were so close they were kissing.

Near Jason's house, the train line went over the top of the creek along a narrow bridge. Some of the railings had come loose so I sat in the hole they had left and let my legs swing in midair. I could see Jason's house from there, down the road a few blocks, on the corner opposite the empty block. The street was empty. A few shitbox cars without people in them. No kids coming home from school. It was like the whole street was poison, like no one wanted to be seen in public in Jason's street.

The air came up from the creek cool and perverse, shoving its fingers under my skirt. I wished I'd worn tights. The winter hadn't been too cold, but when the clouds lifted they took the blanket with them. I shivered. Thought about how nice it would be to sit here on the bridge with Raf. Let him kiss me behind my ears. Kiss his hands one at a time.

A person came out into the street; a little girl in a yellow jumper, and then a woman who might have been her mother, wheeling two bikes alongside her. They went across to the park. Even from the bridge, I could hear the little girl's laughter. Like cymbals. It came sprinting down the road and went under the bridge and out into the wheat fields.

I had a memory like that, somewhere. Couldn't quite grab it.

In the distance, the crossing signal sounded. Across the flat ground I could see the train hugging the coastline, headlights glossy in the low afternoon sun. I thought of Yardy and Ellen near the tunnel, their grabs for immortality, pulling up at only the very last instant. The carriages disappeared into the tunnel. I stood slowly, pulling myself up with the metal barrier, walked a little closer to the end of the bridge. Thought again about coming here with Raf, dodging fate with him. The train emerged from the tunnel. It was a kilometre away, still, and it had to stop at the station.

The little girl and her mother rode their bikes back across the road. She had picked a bunch of flowers, purple ones, and she stuck them in her basket.

A horn sounded. The train came curving around the bend, close now; the thump of its wheels shook the bridge. I slipped through the cracks where the railings had fallen out and held tight to the handrail with one hand, stretched the other out into the path of the train. It rounded the corner. Its horn sounded again. All the wind building up under its wheels came rushing at me and I grabbed the railing with both hands and leaned my head back over the water and the train rushed by with its horn blasting the whole time, just a metre between me and the certain death of its wheels.

When it had gone and the bridge had stopped shaking, I turned around and the little girl was waving.

*

Ben was in the backyard, digging a hole with one hand, Bilbo in the other. 'We're trying to find water,' he said. 'Tortoises are very good at sniffing out water.'

'I thought they only lived on land,' I said.

'They do.' He rolled his eyes. 'That's why they need to be able to find water.'

'Where's Mum?'

He dropped Bilbo into the shallow hole. 'Dunno. She went somewhere with Jason. In the car.'

'And just left you here?'

'I'm not a baby.' Bilbo walked in circles in the hole, apparently more interested in climbing out than finding water.

''Course you're not. I got you a finger bun,' I said. 'On the bench.'

He leapt to his feet, wiped his hands on his shorts. 'With sprinkles?' Face ablaze.

'Of course with sprinkles.'

He disappeared inside, leaving Bilbo floundering in his hole. Murray cocked his ear, pulled gently on his chain, testing the resistance. He put his nose close to the ground. Bilbo rocked and dropped back into the hole, shell-side down, stumpy legs kicking the air. Murray's throat rumbled. Ears went down. Bilbo made a throaty cry and Murray went off, barking and kicking at the ground, yanking at his chain until the line was almost bending under the force of him and Bilbo was bouncing around in the hole like a mercury droplet.

'Murray!' I scooped the tortoise from his almost-grave and propped him upright on the concrete. Ben returned with his face covered in icing. 'Murray nearly ate your stupid tortoise.'

'Dogs can't eat tortoises.'

'He was giving it a pretty good crack.'

Ben sat next to me on the concrete. 'I can't believe you got me two finger buns. One would have been enough. I've only got a little belly.' He rubbed it.

'One of those was for me!' He pulled the other from behind his back and handed it over. When he smiled he had hundreds and thousands between his teeth. 'Did Mum say when she would be back?'

'She said we should get our own dinner,' he said.

'Big surprise.'

He was quiet for a long while, then, all curled up in his little body with the tortoise in his lap. He put Bilbo on the ground next to him, and the animal pulled all of its limbs inside and stayed that way.

On Friday night, Mum and Jason had some people around for dinner. Local dickheads and his brother Kurt, all pulling up in their Holdens with the engines practically dragging along the road. Mum sent us to the front room with bowls of pasta she'd cooked too long, and we watched some garbage on the TV but mostly listened in to their conversations from under Ben's blankets.

'Must be nice not to be alone anymore!' Kurt was saying, banging his hand on the table. He coughed loudly. 'Linda, you would not believe how long it's been since Jase brought a woman home. How long d'you reckon, Jase? Five years? What was her name – Destiny? Harmony?'

'Liberty.' Jason's voice was low and serious.

One of the women, then: 'Liberty! God, she was such a slut. Used to come into Joe's when I's working there, y'know, after I had the kids and I had'ta get out the house so I didn't go total farking insane. Remember, Tony, when I worked at Joe's? He tried to molest me, y'know. In the storeroom.'

Tony hollered: 'Explains why I got no action at home!' They roared with laughter, Jason joining in when the joke had shifted to someone else.

'She was a slut, though,' he said thoughtfully. 'You know I met her at the Paddington Hotel. In Richard Creek? Took her home and she made breakfast stark bloody naked.' More laughter. Through the door, I saw Mum in the kitchen, her face screwed up over a pot of whatever her next course was. I went to get a glass of water, brushed up next to her for a second and she flinched.

'Get back to Ben,' she hissed.

'You guys were together for ages though, right?' That same woman.

'Four years I reckon, Rach,' Kurt said. 'Got engaged for a bit, didn't ya?' Mum's body grew rigid at the stove. 'Yeah, must have. Asked if you could have the wedding in my front paddock.'

'You're right.' Rach scratched her bleached head. 'Dodged a bullet there, angel. She was loony bin material.'

'Gotta check this stuff before you get your dick wet.' That was the guy opposite Jason. Tattoos around his neck, words I couldn't make out. He had his arm around a tiny brunette woman who kept her eyes down while she said something too quiet to hear. 'Piss off, Cheryl,' he said.

Mum dished out her main course, took plates of it across to the table with a big smile sewn into her face. Jason grabbed the first one. He used his cutlery like a caveman, holding his knife and fork in clenched fists.

'Linda, babe, what d'you call this?' Rach said, poking her plate with hesitation.

'Corned beef,' Mum said.

Jason gave a big *whoop!* 'Well, it's fucking disgusting.' The other guys hooted, pushed their plates into the middle of the table. Mum had her back to me and she stayed there, still as boulders, while the others went out to smoke on the deck.

'Never get a missus 'at can't cook,' Tony yelled. 'Oi, Murray! How's that foot going? Taught you a good lesson, didn't we?'

Mum collected the full plates into a pile in front of her.

I watched as she tipped a full pavlova into the bin under the sink, went back and cleared a space for her under our blankets. 'What are you guys watching?' she said, but she'd already sat down before I could answer.

For days afterwards, Jason ignored me. I watched him working, tried looking for clues, tried to figure out where he kept going. He was still out on Wednesday nights, sometimes until three in the morning. I heard him come back most of the time, the door slamming and Mum's soft voice and his belt buckle hitting the floor. Most afternoons, Mum went for a walk to Kurt's place a few blocks away, and I tried the handle on Jason's door but it was always locked.

The weather turned foul. The block across the road was a mud pit and the spinifex turned from green to yellow to brown. I walked through it in the mornings to the bus stop on the other side, tired of waiting at the same bus stop in the same street with the same shitty house staring back at me.

Every day I went to school and every day I found a reason to leave a little early to get to Ben, until the teachers stopped asking and I stopped offering. Sometimes I got there in time to walk him home without a rope holding us together, and every day Mum and Jason were on the couch with their eyes bugging out of their heads, watching repeats of *The Biggest Loser*, Jason counting five-dollar notes into a metal container.

After a week, I applied for a job at the supermarket in town, and I didn't have any experience but the owner didn't seem to mind. He shook my hand with his sweaty one and told me he could offer me six hours a week. He spent most of his time in the Port Pirie store, he said, but he called in sometimes and would be delighted to have me on board. I could start on Tuesday and he'd pay me $12.36 an hour.

'I got a job,' I said over dinner. Mum put down her fork.

'Why?'

'Because you told me to.'

'Didn't think you *would*, though. What doing?'

'Working at the supermarket.'

'Good for you. Ten bucks in my hand every week.' She went back to her macaroni. Jason gave her arm a squeeze.

Raf cornered me after school before my first shift. His face was bright. 'Footy tour soon. We're going to Port Lincoln.'

'Sounds fun.'

'Join the girls' team and you can come too.'

'Can't now. I've got a job.'

'I forgot about that.'

'Might save up for a phone though,' I said. 'At least you can call me.'

I changed into my uniform in the toilets, where a couple of girls were bent over the sink and talking loudly to one another. One of them had a boyfriend who'd cheated on her. They were going to find the girl who'd done it. I crouched on the toilet and listened to their voices, the flick of their cigarette lighters, their heels on the tiles.

I found a payphone in the main part of town and reversed the charges to call Kirrily. It had been ages since we'd spoken and when she answered she sounded very far away.

'It's me,' I said.

'Who?'

'It's Skye.'

'Oh, hey.'

The line crackled. 'Just thought I'd see how you are.'

'Uh yeah, I'm fine. How are you?'

I took a deep breath. 'Yeah, fine.' A second of static; Kirrily's voice buzzed in and out.

'What?'

'Not really fine, I guess. Not totally fine.'

'Sorry, Skye, the line is really bad.'

The call dropped out. I hung the receiver back into place and stared at it for a while. Shoved my fingers into the dispenser in case someone had left change behind. Traced the graffitied window with my fingertips even though the words were meaningless. I picked up the phone again, called directory assistance and just listened. The man at the other end said 'Hello? Hello?' and hung up.

I knew I was avoiding the supermarket. My stomach flipped, and I could feel bile rising in my throat. 'Totally normal,' I said aloud. 'Everyone's nervous on their first day.' Raf's voice in my head: *It's hard to be new.*

The supermarket was in a strip of shops almost on the water. I stood in the entry and let the automatic doors shudder behind me.

My boss was a bearded man in his thirties, whose eyebrows met in the middle.

'Skye, welcome,' he said, and when he spoke the words only came from one half of his mouth. 'Looks like they've got you stacking shelves. Pretty girl like you should be on the register.' He put his hand on my shoulder and left it there even after I'd tried to duck away from it.

'Stacking shelves is fine,' I said. 'I'm a hard worker.'

'Even so. Get a few more sales this way.' He led me to the registers, guided me with his arm across my lower back.

Jeannie would train me. She was much older than me, grey and folded in her face, but she seemed very happy to be there. 'The new system's so easy!' she bleated. 'You just press these ones and these ones and swipe the thing and pow! You're all done!' She wore her hair long and curled, and it had been pinned over one side of her face with possibly the world's entire supply of hairspray.

'Is it true that if a product scans at a lower price, you have to honour it?' I said.

'Nah. Some tightarse made that up and went round saying it to everyone. We do it anyway though, saves having a punch-on.' A customer appeared at her register. 'Good afternoon,' she said. 'Nice day we're having. Oh, good choice on the chocolates. A pressie for someone special? They'll love that. Fourteen twenty. Cash out? No? Can I PayPass your card? Not a worry at all, you pop your PIN in there. Pleasure. Have a lovely night.' She smiled with the collection of teeth that remained, turned to look at me. 'Next one's yours. Let's see if we can't find you a badge.'

She rummaged in her drawer. Pinned a TRAINEE label to me. 'There you go.'

The next customer was a younger woman with several bags of cat food and an orange lipstick in a plastic packet. I fumbled with the buttons, didn't look her in the eye, couldn't remember how to say have a nice day. And she left without her receipt. Scurried, really.

'That was terrible,' I said.

'Listen, lovie.' Jeannie pushed my chin up to look me in the eye. 'You do what you gotta do to get the bills paid. You don't love it? No one cares.' The line moved. 'Mrs Lee! So nice to see you. Your son's leg better? That's no good. What about Tina's exams? All done? Thirty-six exactly. Pop your card on the whatsit, that's the way. Receipt's in the bag. You have a lovely evening.'

And so the line continued to move, one customer after another receiving Jeannie's sincere and open enthusiasm. People known to her, and unknown, equally welcomed. I muddled my way through a few transactions, helped her put away the plastic coathangers for recycling. The boss came over a couple of times to see how I was getting on; Jeannie lied and told him I was brilliant, whispered to me afterwards that he would take whatever I was willing to give him and I wouldn't necessarily have to be willing.

It was only at the end of my shift that Jeannie's hairspray gave out. Revealed the purple bruising underneath.

8

DAD AND I STAYED once for a couple of nights in a caravan park by the Murray River. It rained. After it had finished raining, Dad took me to the pub, which was the only building in town and was also the post office, corner store and bank. Above the bar someone had mounted the mouth of a Murray cod, and the bartender told us the story of Ngurunderi.

After dinner we went down to the river to see the pelicans and the banks had broken and the fish were throwing themselves at the sand.

'Why are they doing that?' I said.

'They're lost,' Dad said.

After school Raf crossed the road and waited at the bus stop with me to head west. He had to visit his auntie, he said. She lived somewhere near Jason's house, he said, even though he didn't know where Jason's house was.

'Shouldn't you be at training?' I said.

'Gotta mow her lawns before it gets dark,' he said. 'She pays me fifteen bucks a month to keep the snakes out of them.'

'Lots of snakes in winter?'

'Yeah, heaps.' He grinned.

'She's getting a bargain,' I said.

'Probably.' He looked away from me. 'But when the company's this good, I'd do it for free.' My face burned. 'Where's your place?'

'Near the … park?'

'That big empty block? Nuclear dump site, I heard.'

'That would explain a lot.'

'They were going to turn it into, like, a theme park, I think. Waterslides, rollercoasters, the whole shebang.'

'Much demand for theme parks around here?'

'Zero. Hence the picturesque bit of dead land you see today.' He shuffled closer to me. Our legs nearly touched; the centimetres between them hissed. 'Anyway, that's right near my auntie's place. I can walk you home.' He nudged me with his shoulder. 'If you want.'

'I –' My mouth was full of jelly. 'Okay.'

'Can we go by mine first though? Gotta get changed.'

Raf's house looked just like Jason's, if Jason had ever bothered to take care of it. Yellow brick and a corrugated fence, Hills hoist spinning in the backyard. But the front was landscaped, neat little rows of ferns and grasses, and a couple of roses in pots by the door. Instead of hanging on one hinge, the front door swung open with a little squeak, and a woman wearing actual clothes was on the other side, not shouting at anyone.

'Oh,' she said.

'Mum!' Raf pulled me in front of him. 'Mum, this is Skye. God, shit.'

'Nice to meet you, Skye-God-Shit.' She smiled, like a mother might.

'It's Skye. This is Skye.'

'Hi, Skye.' She gave me a little hug.

'Hi,' I said.

'Claud.'

'Hi Claud.'

Raf shuffled nervously. 'Didn't know you'd be here.'

'I live here.' She took his school bag from him. 'Getting changed before Hazel's?'

'Yeah.' He ducked past her and into the house.

'Sorry,' I said, the only thing I could remember how to say.

'No need,' she said. She looked tough, kind, patient. I hardly recognised those things in another human.

'I've never met my … a boy's mum before.'

'We're just like regular mums, but really tired.'

'Oh,' I said.

'And, you know, dirty, a lot of the time.'

'Ha ha.'

Raf came rushing back down the hallway.

'Okay,' he said to me. 'We can go.'

Claud squeezed him as he moved past her. 'Your pants are on inside out,' she said.

'I'll fix them later.' He pushed her away, but she was still smiling.

We sat together on the bus, though it was hardly full, and the chair was just big enough to fit both of us without our bodies touching but they touched anyway, his leg against my leg, my arm against his arm. He smelled of sweat and dirt, but not in a bad way. Like he'd been running through a rainforest. I felt it through my collarbones, my shoulderblades, just wanting to be close to him.

'This is my stop,' I said, and he stepped aside to let me out.

'Lead the way.'

We met Ben on the corner, where he was waiting with a box in his hands and his face all dirty. 'Look! Skye!' He held it out. 'Today I found a mouse.' He looked up at Raf. 'Your pants are on inside out.'

'Raf, this is Ben. My brother.'

'Hey, mate. Rafferty. Pleased to meet you.' Raf extended his hand; Ben put the box in it.

'I think it's a hopping mouse. It's got big feet and this tail that looks like it's covered in feathers and I looked it up on the internet and that's exactly what a hopping mouse looks like. A, uh' – he stuck out his tongue, frowned – 'spinifex hopping mouse. I think.'

Raf opened the box. 'That's a hopping mouse all right.' I peered around his arm.

'Look how big its eyes are.' I replaced the lid. 'What are you going to do with a mouse? You're already keeping a fugitive tortoise.'

'A tortoise?' said Raf. 'Ben, are you planning to race these animals?'

Ben laughed, bright and easy. 'I thought I might take it to the empty block,' he said. 'There's spinifex there, I looked that up too. Spinifex hopping mice must live in places where there's spinifex.'

'Good thinking. Let's get this little guy home.' Raf handed the box back to Ben, hooked my brother's bag over his own shoulder. I watched him as we walked, watched the way he talked to Ben instead of me, bent right over with his ear close to my brother's face so he could hear everything.

'Skye, get this,' Raf said to me. 'Did you know that if you leave a chimpanzee on an island with wood and ropes, it will build a raft?'

'Is that right?' I said.

'Yiannis says he saw them do it with his own two eyes when they went to Africa,' Ben said.

'Lots of islands in Africa?'

Raf prodded me in the ribs. 'At least one island, by the sounds of it.'

Ben held tight to his box. 'Mice can chew through cardboard,' he said. 'So I couldn't keep him in here anyway. I would have to buy an aquarium and then I would probably have to get a permit and I don't have any money. And anyway, he would probably be sad in an aquarium.'

'Where did you find him?' I said.

'He was hiding in the dirt under the bench. In the corner near the tennis courts.' He dropped his voice low. 'Mrs Johansson said I can't sit in the doorway anymore, so I go there at lunch now.'

Raf put his arm around Ben's shoulders. 'How old are you? Eleven?'

Ben laughed again. 'Eleven! I'm ten.'

'Ten! You're so tall. Going to play footy one day? You could be in the ruck.'

'I don't know how to play.'

'Maybe I can teach you.' Raf mimed catching the ball, dropping it onto his foot. 'When I was ten, the only friend I had was this parrot my mum bought at the market.'

'You had a parrot?' Ben's eyes went wide.

'Yep. Our house was behind the school so the parrot just came over the fence to hang out with me. It was super tame. When I didn't feel like listening in class – which was pretty much always – I could just look out the window and my parrot would come and tap on it.'

'Wow,' Ben said.

'At recess he helped me find worms and stuff in the grass.'

'It sounds like he was a pretty good friend.'

'Haven't seen him for a while. Probably still goes over to the school looking for me, I bet.'

'Do you miss him?'

'I've got lots of other friends now. Happens when you get to be old like me. Find the people you really like, people who like you.'

'I miss Yiannis. He was my friend.'

Raf shrugged, gave my brother a gentle shove. 'Maybe you can come and visit my parrot sometime.'

Ben skipped ahead to the park, holding his box above his head. 'You're nearly home, Mr Hopkins!'

Raf put his arm through mine. I felt like I might stop breathing at any second. 'Beautiful story,' I whispered, which was the maximum volume I could manage.

Raf whispered back, smiling: 'Mostly true.'

Ben found a spot with big clumps of dead grass, picked through it to clear out any spiders. 'I don't know if spiders bite hopping mice,' he said, 'but it's important to be careful.'

'Better safe than sorry.' Raf crouched down with him and they opened the box together. The mouse took a tentative step, lifted its nose.

'Go on, mouse,' Ben said. He gave the box a rattle. The mouse sprint-hopped away in a blur.

'See ya, Mr Hopkins,' Raf said.

My brother skipped ahead of us, rambling about something called the Bloop and picking up bits of rock and grit as he went.

I hadn't been so close to a guy since Henry from next door to Dad's house when I was six (his mum made us run under the sprinkler together, naked, insisting the photos would be perfect for our eventual twenty-first birthdays; Henry died in a car accident the next year). Did I stink? Had I even showered today? I smoothed my hair with a sweaty hand. Tried to find my voice, pluck it back from where it had slipped down my throat.

'Thanks,' I croaked.

'What for?'

'You know what for. Helping Ben.'

'No biggie.' His legs were longer than mine and I had to step faster to keep up with him.

'He hasn't really made any friends. The whole time we've been here.' My heart raced. 'Like, at least I've got you.' *Oh God oh God, shut up, mouth!*

Raf stopped and turned to face me. 'Is that right?'

'Helping me, I mean.'

'Right, helping you.' Without warning, his hand was in mine. Rough, hot, like that first day he'd picked me up off the ground.

He leaned in. My hands stuck to my sides. Every part of me froze and exploded at once. His breath was pie and chewing gum. Warm on my face. Would I spew? I closed my eyes. His hands were on my hips. Oh God, was Ben watching?

His lips were soft on mine. Softer than I expected. His mouth opened a little. I tried not to spew into it. He pulled away and my face flushed hot and then cold.

'Come to footy training. Meet some of the guys properly. Then you can have them, too.' He scratched his head. 'I mean, not like that. Not like this.' He lay his hand flat on my collarbone. I tried to kickstart my body back into breathing. Nodded. Couldn't remember how to do anything else. 'Really? It's tomorrow. Wednesday. Don't forget.'

'What about Ben?'

'Bring him. I'll show him a few of my moves.'

'Okay. I guess.'

He grabbed my hand. 'Let me walk you home?'

Jason's car wasn't in the driveway. Mum wasn't home either; her dressing-gown was strewn on the couch and her shoes were by the door. Ben had pulled Bilbo from his hiding place and he was walking across the kitchen table.

'Ah,' said Raf, 'the tortoise.' He pulled up a chair, ran his fingers across Bilbo's shell. 'A fine specimen indeed.'

'I don't know what kind he is,' Ben said. 'Yiannis found his egg in the park so he incubated it and after a while, Bilbo hatched out.'

'Bilbo, huh?'

'He's on an adventure.' Ben held out a piece of lettuce but the tortoise walked past it. I took a couple of glasses and poured juice for each of them.

'See you got a dog there, too.' Murray, standing under the clothesline, looking at nothing.

'He doesn't belong to us,' I said. 'You can blame Mum's boyfriend for that.'

'Sad.'

'Wanna see my room?' Ben leapt up, grabbed Bilbo with both hands. 'Well, it's both of ours, technically. But most of it is mine.'

'That's only because you've got more stuff.'

Raf scratched his head. 'You guys share a room?'

'The adults need the other bedroom for their business,' I said. 'That's more important than my privacy, apparently.'

'I like it,' said Ben. 'A lot of nights I can't sleep because I'm worrying – did you know you can die from worrying? It's true – but it's okay because Skye is right there in the next bed and sometimes I climb in with her but I don't think she notices.' Sometimes I noticed. Always pretended not to. 'I might even show you where Bilbo sleeps. Even Skye doesn't know that.'

'Yep,' I said. 'It's Port Flinders's best-kept secret.'

Raf let his fingers slide between mine, went with Ben to see Bilbo's hiding place. I poured myself a glass of orange juice. Dragged the filmy bit off the top with a spoon. Thought again about Raf's mouth as he leaned in, how soft he was. His hands on my waist. I couldn't remember where mine had been. Where were you supposed to put your hands when you kissed someone? I imagined it happening again, me running my fingers through his hair, him kissing my neck.

A car door slammed in the driveway.

'Ben! Ben, they're back!' I threw open the door to the bedroom. Ben held Bilbo above his head.

'Don't look!' he said.

'Mum's here. Raf, you need to leave.' The front door opened. They were shouting, Mum first, in her high-pitched screech, and Jason responding with his low grunts. 'We're going to have to sneak you over the fence,' I hissed.

'Not allowed to have friends, huh?'

'Not ones that kiss me.'

I opened the window and he climbed through; I went out after him. 'This is ridiculous,' he said. 'How bad can they be?'

'Seriously?'

'Parents from the city are never as bad as the ones out this way.' He jumped up to the fence, swung his leg over. 'Do you need a hand?'

'I can't come with you.'

Mum's voice from inside: 'Where's your ratbag sister?' and Ben making naïve murmuring sounds.

'Sure you can. Come on.' He reached down to grab my wrists, pulled me almost clean over the brush.

We walked down the road to the next bus stop, empty as always. My heart raced. Alone together in the street, just the seconds dancing in the spaces between us. No bench to sit on; we crouched close together on the footpath with our feet in the gutter.

'Your auntie is going to be mad, isn't she? Weren't you supposed to be there like, an hour ago?'

'Oh, nah, all good. It's getting too late now anyway. She'll understand.' He kissed my cheek. 'See you tomorrow' – pointed up – 'Skye. Wednesday. Footy training.'

He got on the bus, went right to the back where he always sat. Waved through the window as it drove away, and my heart crashed through my ribs and out into the night.

It didn't matter, that night, that Mum didn't ask about my day. It didn't matter, that night, that Jason snapped my bra strap in the hallway. It didn't matter, that night, that I had to lie down in the bedroom I shared with my ten-year-old brother and listen to my mother and her boyfriend having rank, angry sex down the hall and shouting at each other afterwards.

It didn't even matter, that night, that I was hundreds of kilometres from home with my face in a dirty pillow.

I replayed it again. The waiting. The fear and excitement building in my guts. His face next to mine, his mouth on mine, his hands on mine.

'Ben,' I whispered. He was sleeping. And then I was sleeping.

Raf was there by the gate when I got to school. Was he waiting for me? I tried to play it cool: 'Hey.' He took my hand and we walked in together. I imagined the people behind us watching our fingers swinging, noticing how close our bodies were, noticing how much we were enjoying each other's company.

We went to Maths and he led me to the back row to sit next to him, kicked Seb or Al out of his seat so I could be there. I was royalty, in my tiny square of the world. Worthwhile. Adored. At the front of the class, the girl whose name I'd never learned said, 'Ugh, miss, my partner has absconded,' and her hair flicked into the eyes of the kid behind her. We laughed, in the back row. All of us together. Raf reached for my hand under my desk; when we linked our fingers, we made a barrier for anyone who wanted to get between us.

At recess we stood in the line at the tuckshop, me facing forwards and him with his arms draped around me. When I walked, he walked, awkward and bumbling, his body hot against my back. Sweat pooled where our clothes touched. The other kids in the line all looked at us, at how magic it was to have a guy who couldn't stand to be away from you, even in the tuckshop line.

Someone's mum was working the till and she looked us both up and down and said, 'Hands off, Rafferty. This is a schoolyard.'

He laughed. 'Iced coffee please, Mrs J. Two muffins.' He kissed the side of my head. 'Freddo for this one.'

Overnight I had become part of him. An extension. I was almost certain I liked it. It was easy to forget what was happening at home. Easy until I had to catch the bus on my own, watch

Murray from the kitchen table while I did my homework, wash Ben's uniform and cook dinner all at once.

That day, though, I intercepted Ben's walking bus. 'Hey mate,' I said. 'Got a surprise for you.'

He picked up his bag, bounced alongside me. 'Is it a snake?'

'What? No! Why would it be a snake?'

'Oh. I guess it wouldn't be.'

'Nah, I'm taking you to Raf's footy training. Show you around my school, too, if you want.'

'But football is boring.'

'I'll take you down to the back of the oval. I heard someone found a baby eagle there once. And Raf will be there. He likes you.'

He kicked the footpath. 'No he doesn't.'

'He told me he does.' I grabbed him and pulled him under my arm. 'You heard what he said yesterday. You're just too awesome for the other kids. They're too stupid to realise.'

'Ydri and Hannah are pretty smart.'

'Come on. We need to catch the bus back again.'

He sat right at the front with his bag on his lap, looking straight ahead. The old woman with the cane was back and she thumped it against the floor until he turned to her and said, very politely, 'Would you mind not doing that, please?' She stared at him for a moment, then pulled out a tiny album from among her many bags. 'This my daughter Cheryl,' I heard. 'This Sammy our dog. He died.' Ben looked at all of the photos, nodded at each one, sympathised with the old lady when she explained that she was now all alone.

At the school stop, Ben patted her hand and said, 'Feel better soon, Mrs Nerington,' and she said, 'Thank you, Ben.'

Footy training was already underway; we could hear the shouts from the street. Maybe twenty guys from my grade thumped the yellow balls into the sky. Across the oval, a group of girls did the same. We took a seat on the sidelines with our backs against the fence. I had a packet of chips I'd saved for the occasion; Ben scoffed half of them before I'd even opened them properly.

'Hungry?'

He didn't make eye contact. 'Someone took mine.'

They were tough, the guys. Each time a ball came at them they grabbed it clean out of the air, or dived head-first into the dirt. It was a kind of ballet, or a circus. These guys all synchronised. Choreographed. Each one predicted the next one's move. They ran ahead of the ball to where the ball would be, not where it was.

I thought about being where the ball would be.

I thought about Ben on his own in the playground.

I thought of Kirrily and the man in the tunnel with his legs chopped off.

'Hey, Ben.' It was hard to know if he was watching. His face pointed in the general direction, but he had his knees against his chest and he crumpled the chip packet in his fist, let it unfurl, crumpled it again. 'After this, d'you want to get a pizza? We could go into town.'

'Don't have any money.'

'My pay should be in now, I think. Weekly, they said.'

'Okay, yeah!' His voice came from all the way inside him.

'What do you think of the football? Maybe you could play sometime? Raf said he would teach you.'

'I would be horrible at it.'

'You wouldn't.'

The chip packet crunched in his fist. 'Yiannis says that you can tell if someone used to play football by all the bruises in their brain. He says they do scans when they retire and their brains are full of bits where their brain cells have been injured and died.'

A shout went up from the guys. Two of them were on the ground with their fists in each other's faces and the rest of them went between trying to pull them away and cheering them on.

'I'll fuckin' take ya!' That was Yardy, right in the middle. He threw a punch at the other guy, someone I didn't know. 'Say that again. I dare ya.' The other one shot right back at him, shoved Yardy's face in the dirt. Then Raf was shouting: 'Stop it, you dickheads. You wanna get benched so close to the tour?'

Yardy stood up and dusted himself off. Ben stared at them, frowning.

'Want to go for a walk?' I said.

'Yeah.'

We went around the back of the oval and found a eucalyptus with a nest in it. Huge, maybe a metre across and stretching between the two main branches of the tree.

'You should climb up and have a look,' I said.

'Never do that!' Ben put his hand over his mouth, dropped to a whisper. 'Never do that. A mother bird with a nest that big could eat you in one bite.'

'What kind of bird is it, do you think?'

'I bet I can figure it out.'

He ran to another tree a bit further along, swung his little monkey legs over the branches and pulled himself up. He was pretty high, five metres at least, crawling out on a thin branch to get a better look.

'Be careful!' I said.

'Shhhh.' He pointed to the nest, and then to the sky. Above us a huge silhouette went around and around. He beckoned me over. 'It's an eagle,' he said. 'I can see its baby. They have fluffy white babies. They look like huge baby chickens.'

'Can I see?'

'You'll have to climb up.'

'But I'm wearing a dress.'

'Then you'll miss out.'

I held the fabric between my legs, tried to hoist myself up to the lowest branch. Nothing doing. I scratched my arm on the way down.

'No one's looking,' Ben said. 'Just put your legs over.'

I tried it, scaled the trunk and stood on the low branch. Went for the next, one leg after the other. Like monkey bars. Hooked my legs over the low branch and pulled my arms up. Failed. Swung from the branch with my legs still attached, dress over my face. Fresh air on my bum.

'Ben!'

He was laughing. I pulled my dress away and there was Raf, at the bottom of the tree, smiling with his entire face. 'Nice undies,' he said.

'Kill me.'

'Let me help you down.' He took my hands and I jumped down to him, fell flat against his chest. He wrapped his arms around me. Leaned close to my ear. 'I want to kiss you,' he whispered. The world sped up, my heart thundering.

'Here?'

'Anywhere.'

Ben came tumbling from the tree, one branch after another the way only ten-year-old boys can. He came to an abrupt stop at our feet. Looked up, waved. 'Hi Raf!'

'Hey, mate.' Raf pulled away from me. 'You enjoying the footy?'

'To be honest,' Ben said, 'I have really liked this eagle nest much better.'

Raf smiled. 'Fair enough.' And to me: 'Training's finished. And uh, my mum is here. Said she came to cheer us on.'

'That's so nice.'

'Yeah. I mean, embarrassing but nice, I guess.'

Claud was flushed red from cheering. 'Rafferty, who's this strapping lad?'

Raf put his hand on Ben's head. 'This is Benjamin. Ben, this is my ma, Claud.'

'Hi.' He put out his hand and she shook it.

'Hi, Ben,' she said.

'And you know Skye.' He was smiling with his one dimple flashing. He turned to me. 'You coming to Yardy's?'

'I told Ben I'd take him for a pizza.'

'Sounds pretty good.'

'You can come, if you like.'

He looked back to the pack of guys, stretching and punching on. Looked back to me. 'I would really like to. We've just got ... we've got something we need to do at Yardy's first.'

'Raf!' Yardy waved his hands in the air. 'Put your dick away and hurry up!'

Claud coughed loudly.

'I'll see you tomorrow, yeah?' Raf said.

'Yeah.'

Ben and I walked up the main street into town to a pizza shop. It looked almost closed down, with boards across the windows, but when we pushed the front door it gave a little tinkle. We were the only people in the restaurant. I ordered an Aussie and we took a seat by a mock fireplace. Red gingham tablecloths. Paper napkins. Mismatched cutlery.

The pizza was surprisingly good and we chewed on the bacon until it dissolved in our mouths. I wondered if the fireplace had ever been real, or if they had put it in with the full knowledge it was fake. I wondered if the blonde woman by the cash register had somewhere else to be. I wondered if she had someone else to be. I wondered what Mum was having back at Jason's.

'Thanks for taking me to see the football,' Ben said finally, his mouth full of pizza.

'Oh. That's fine.'

'Sorry Raf saw your undies.'

'It's not your fault.'

He stared at his plate. 'It is my fault. There wasn't even a baby bird in the nest. I just wanted to see you climb the tree.'

'Seriously?'

'I thought it would be funny because you had a dress on and girls aren't very good at climbing trees anyway even if they have jeans on.'

'Girls are good at climbing trees.'

'I don't know anything about girls.' He looked sad about it, for a second, until he filled his mouth with pizza again.

'You're ten.'

'I'm a mature ten.'

The man who looked like the owner and the girl who looked like his granddaughter went behind the bar and poured themselves a couple of beers. I wondered what they saw when they looked at us. A red-headed girl who can't climb trees without flashing her undies at a boy she thinks she likes but might not because maybe he's just leading her on. I had spent so many hours trying to figure it out, the reason he had ever taken notice of me to begin with. His face on that first day in homeroom, squeezed out of hiding.

'You going to finish that?' I said to Ben.

'If I don't finish it, what do you think they'll do with it? Do you think they give their food to the homeless? I saw a man when I was having lunch who looked like he was homeless. I couldn't see him very well because I was in the school grounds and he was over the other side of the road but I'm pretty sure he was homeless. He didn't have any shoes on. And like, his hair was all crazy and sticking out everywhere.'

'Dunno.'

'What if I just put this bit of pizza in your bag and we can give it to him if we see him on the way home?'

'Okay. That's a nice thought.'

He looked to the bar as he did it, but the owner didn't look back at us once.

9

I LOOKED FOR Dad. For ages, I looked for him. I would leave school and go the back way past the canal and catch a bus down to Marion shopping centre, wait at the bus terminal for the other buses to come and go, for the people to climb off them and find the people they were looking for.

They all had different ways of finding. Some of them peered over all the other people, as though the person they needed might be inside the throng, like a kid hiding in a clothes rack. Some of them shouted with their arms in the air, as though it were volume that would reunite them.

And some of them just knew exactly where to look. Walked over to a bench or a doorway without hesitating. Knowing who to expect when they got there.

The next afternoon, Jeannie set me up on her register again. 'Now, remember what I taught you.' She adjusted her polo shirt. 'Mr Gleeson. Fine afternoon, no? Saw you walking down with that little dog of yours before. What's her name again? Candy, beautiful. She looks like a funny thing. Oh sorry, of course, your items.

Just these? I've tried this myself, good choice.' She paused. 'Ooh, we haven't taken cheques here since the nineties, Mr Gleeson. You got a card I can use? Don't worry, I'll keep your stuff here behind the counter while you go to the bank.' He limped out. Jeannie stowed his bags on a shelf under the checkout.

'Tries that every time,' she said to me. 'Cheque always bounces. Next customer?'

After an hour another girl showed up. She didn't say anything, just pinned her tag – ELLIE – to her shirt.

'Ellie,' Jeannie said to me. 'Never says a word. You won't even notice her.' The break room wasn't much more than a cleaner's cupboard, so she took me out the back, where we could get the sea air on our faces. She took out a cigarette, blew the smoke through her nose like a dragon.

'That's pretty cool,' I said.

'Filthy habit,' she said. 'But it's the only way you can get a decent break in your ten hours.' She pointed the cigarette at me. 'Never take it up.' Then she lit a new cigarette with the end of the first one, drew it in as though she'd been ten years clean. 'So, Skye,' she said. 'What's your story?'

'Don't really have one.'

'You're new in town, right? Where from?'

'Adelaide.'

'Ah, the big smoke.' She tapped her cigarette on the edge of her milk crate. 'My first husband had family in Adelaide. Not much of a guy, but he took me to the … what's that place? At the beach?'

'Glenelg?'

'Right, Glenelg. Took me there for a buffet breakfast. Sausages the size of your little finger. Ever wrapped one of those babies in a pancake? Nothing better.'

'I've never been in that hotel. Just got out at the end of the tramline a few times. Kirrily likes going there for frozen yoghurt.'

'Kirrily is your friend?'

'Right, my friend. Kirrily is my friend.' I tried to pull the sound of her voice, but it just came out as echoes of my own. 'She still lives in Adelaide.'

'What brings you up this way then? The call of the outback?' She laughed, a wracking, phlegmy laugh.

'My mum had to come here for business.'

'Ah, business.' She lit another cigarette with the dying embers of the last.

'You're really getting through those, huh?'

'You'll learn,' she said, and pulled a can of energy drink from her handbag. 'If you're gonna front up to these people day in, day out, you'll need some moral support.'

The door to the break room flew open. 'Jeannie?' The bearded guy. What was his name? Darren? Wayne? He pointed at me. 'You brought her with you? Who's on the registers?'

'Ellie,' Jeannie said.

'Ellie's back? I thought it was next week. Anyway, she' – he pointed at me – 'is here for three hours. No breaks. What am I even paying you two for? To sit around and get high on milk crates?'

'You can't get high on milk crates, Daryl,' Jeannie said with a laugh.

'Just get back to work.'

She adjusted my TRAINEE badge. 'Hop on the register next to mine,' she said.

'By myself?'

'I'll be right here. Remember, just press the buttons. Distract them by making them talk about themselves and they won't even notice you've made a mistake. If you do, and you won't.' She squeezed my shoulder.

My line moved, gradually, one customer at a time. A woman bought a box of cookies and a pink t-shirt. A couple bought a striped cat bed and a stick with a feather on the end, and they smiled at each other and at me until one of them shouted, 'We're getting a kitten!' Jeannie showed me how to process a return, an older guy who'd changed his mind about a pair of shorts. The fluorescent lights bore down on me. I wondered what the weather was like. I thought about taking up chain-smoking.

A familiar face appeared next in my line.

'Skye,' he said. 'You got a job.'

'I told you I did,' I hissed. 'The next bloody day I went out and applied.'

Jeannie looked over, still scanning her customer's crap.

'Good afternoon,' I said loudly. 'Thank you for shopping at Foodplace. How's your day?'

Jason rolled his eyes.

'Would you like a bag? They're ten cents.'

'Ten cents for a bag?'

'We try to encourage reusing and recycling. So, a bag?'

'No bloody bag.'

I took note of each item in his basket: a couple of boxes of freezer bags; permanent marker; a couple of new baking trays. I piled them up on the counter, took his card. Shoved the receipt into his hand.

'We won't be back for dinner,' I said.

'So?'

'Didn't want you to starve without me cooking for you.'

'Your mum didn't even notice you were gone.' He walked off, juggling his items in his hands. When the line had died down I excused myself to go to the bathroom, slipped into the break room and out the back door. Daryl came barrelling out, chin-first.

'What did I just say, Skye?' he said, his face gleaming with sweat and anger. 'You're here for three hours. You don't get a break.'

'I'm really sorry.'

He huffed and stomped across the car park. 'I don't think this is working out.'

'What do you mean?'

'It's your second shift and you're already taking liberties.'

My chest tightened. 'It was an emergency. Really.'

'I have to give you a written warning. If that's how you're going to be.'

'Shit.'

'Three warnings and you're out, Skye. I don't make the rules.' He slopped his way over to me, put his hand on my shoulder. 'I just enforce them. You understand?' His hand slid lower, across my back, sweaty. Warty. I shifted on my crate.

'I need this job.'

'Maybe we can work something out.' His breath smelled of food court curry and peppermint gum and every part of his face that crinkled ran in rivers of sweat.

'It won't happen again.'

He sat on the crate next to mine. His other hand went to my knee, bare between my skirt and my socks. Face close to mine. Curry breath hot on my cheek. 'There are always other ways.' Sweaty fingers on the outside of my thigh, the hand on my back moving lower, trapped between these arms like jellied tree trunks. My breath stopped. I felt in there, caught in the space below my throat. Not moving. Afraid to move. It stuck there and it stayed there and my face was numb.

Fingers on the inside of my thigh. I froze. Watched the sea bang against the retaining wall. Watched the people walk past it, fifty metres away at most, walking with their children and their dogs and their husbands and not knowing I was on a milk crate in a car park with a hand inside my skirt and no one to tell me what to do next.

Daryl grabbed my hand. Acid rose in my throat, pushed past the bit where my breath was caught. Moved it for me, with his burning, blistered fingers. Pants pulled tight across his crotch. He pushed my hand to his dick, pressing hard against his leg.

I choked on my spit. My body shook and froze all at once. Closed my eyes. His hand was so greasy on top of mine, moving my palm in his lap.

'What do you say? Can we get rid of this silly warning?'

His lips on my neck. Wet. Air hissed through his nose. Beard on my skin like a cheese grater.

'Don't.'

'What did you say?'

'Please don't.'

He groaned in my ear. 'You filthy tease.' He got to his feet, heaved his massive body in front of me. Grabbed the back of my head, got my hair twisted tight around his fingers. Shoved my face into his crotch, held it there while I fought for air. 'Written warning. You don't get a break when you're only here for three hours.' He let me go. The door slammed behind him, and the lock clicked.

I sat. The crate rocked beneath me. Still people walked, safe with their people. Watched out for. I sat and sat and my shift ended and still I sat.

I found my legs again sometime after the sky had turned pink but before the mozzies came out, and went back inside. Daryl stared at me while I spent most of Mum's money on chocolates in different shapes and flavours. Threw in a couple of pre-made Caesar salads as an afterthought, mostly so Ben wouldn't go hungry – or worse, actually eat any of the mouldy junk festering in Jason's pantry. Jeannie looked me up and down. Passed me my bag and put her hand on top of my hand, gave it a little squeeze. Like we were in a club together.

We had a test at the end of the day and finished early.

'Come to mine,' Raf said, but I wanted to get home, be there when Ben got back. I was quiet coming in and Jason had his door wide open. He sat on a scratched up leather couch next to a desk stacked with containers. Mum sat next to him with her head down. They hadn't heard me.

'Just do it,' he said. He had a bit of glass in one hand, thin like a straw and with a bulb at the end, and a blue lighter in the other. 'They're gonna think you're a narc. Someone'll rat on you.'

'I don't want to,' she said. He slammed his hand into the desk and the glass smashed under it.

'*Fuck*, Linda,' he shouted, shoving his bloody palm in Mum's face. 'Fuck!'

My heart raced. The credit card skimming, the parrot exporting, stealing Vegemite. Any of that would have been better. I slipped into the bathroom, put my forehead to the wall and listened to my breaths slam against the cool tiles.

Mum came to the bathroom door. 'Skye, Jesus.' Her hand went to her throat. 'How long've you been there?' Her hair had got thin, crispy at the ends like paintbrushes hanging off her head.

'Just finished.' She didn't move as I pushed past her, stuck firm in her own ground.

She rummaged in the bathroom cupboard, went back into Jason's room and didn't come out again.

Later, I made a few pork chops and dropped them on a plate with a bag of salad I'd got at the supermarket. Jason ate the chops with his fingers, one hand bound in sloppy bandages, left the salad behind. We sat around the kitchen table and he stared at us, at me first and then at Ben.

'We're learning about the First Fleet,' Ben said to me. 'I borrowed a book from the library.' His face was greasy, 'It didn't have all the information though. D'you know how many Aboriginal people died when we brought our boats? I found that out on the internet. Ninety per cent. That's almost all of them.'

'Like hell,' Jason said. Wiped his mouth on the back of his bandage.

'It's true. They called Australia *terra nullius* but actually there were heaps of people here and we didn't even count them as people until 1967.' He chewed on his chop bone. 'I have to know this for my presentation.'

There was silence for a minute. 'Where's Mum?' I said, in the end, with nothing else to say.

Jason's voice was quiet. 'Got a migraine.'

'She was okay before,' I said.

'Well, now she's got a migraine.'

Jason scraped his fork across his porcelain plate. 'Funny.' He dumped his cutlery in the sink and disappeared out the front door. Murray barked at the car starting, and Ben stared through the window until the noise stopped.

'Yiannis's mum sometimes gets migraines,' he said. 'She stays in her bedroom, too, like Mum. But they have sixteen pillows on their bed. Square ones and rectangle ones and triangle ones. Yiannis showed me. He said the square ones are the best because you can build them into a pretty good fort, but I told him triangles are the strongest shape there is so we tried it my way and I was right.' He looked over at me. 'Are you sad?'

'Nah,' I said. 'Not sad.'

He came and sat next to me. His feet barely touched the floor. 'You look pretty,' he said.

'Thanks, mate.'

We got an old blanket from the cupboard in the hallway and sat in front of the TV. Nothing was on so we just flicked through the channels. After a while we were watching the ads instead, picking out Christmas presents for people in town. Vegetable slicers and magic cleaning balls and things for microwaving eggs. Ben reckoned we could set up a stand in town, with him dressed up as Santa and me as his elf, handing out this crap I knew no one would ever use. He had something picked out for his teacher and the lady at the canteen and the sleazy grandpa at the pizza shop. He tore the back off a magazine and started writing them down, everyone's name and the infomercial garbage he would buy for them.

'Maybe I can get you one of those *cyclonic* vacuum cleaners to help with the cleaning? Is that what they said it was? Can you rewind it?' He wrote *SKYE* and next to it, *VACCUM (CYCLONIC)*. 'Do you think Jason is nice to her?' he said.

'To who?'

'To Mum. He seems like maybe he isn't nice to anyone. Maybe if they got married he would be nice to her. Yiannis said husbands and wives have to be nice to each other because it's in the marriage constitution and the police will come otherwise.'

I stroked his hair. 'Yeah mate, I reckon that's how it works.' I flicked over to another ad break. Thought of the apartment again, for the first time in ages, the dining table jammed in the TV cabinet.

Ben wrote *MRS NERINGTON (FROM THE BUS)* and *SHOWER STOOL* on his magazine.

'Sometimes you have to go, though,' I said. 'You remember how the Adelmanns always argued? Whenever you walked past their door they were always behind it shouting at each other?'

'Kind of,' he said. 'Sometimes I saw them kissing through the window.'

'Yeah, but sometimes people are only kissing because they're trying to stop fighting.'

He wrote *MUM (LINDA)* and *HELICOPTER DRONE*. 'Do you think Mum would like a helicopter drone? I was thinking maybe she could use it to send me messages when I'm at school. Maybe you can get ones with two controllers so I can send messages back to her. Like if I forget my lunch I can just zoom the drone over to her with a note that says *Mum, I forgot my lunch!* and she can make me a sandwich and send it back on the drone.'

'I guess so.'

'I might have to teach her to use it though. I got a radio-controlled car once and she tried to use it and drove it into the street and a truck ran over it.'

'Really?'

'Yeah, but she said sorry for like, an hour, and then we got McDonald's. I think. That might have been a different time.'

'Uh-huh.' I grabbed the pen from him and wrote *BEN*. 'What do you think Ben would want?'

His eyes widened. 'Out of every single thing?'

'Anything at all.'

'A dolphin-shaped speedboat.'

'A *what*?'

'It goes over the water and under the water and it's shaped like a dolphin so it goes really fast through the water. That's how they were designed. Not the boats, dolphins. Their beak cuts through the water so their body can come up behind it. That's aerodynamics. Did you know it's called a *rostrum*?'

'The boat?'

'Not the boat! The beak. A dolphin's nose is called a rostrum.'

'You're like an encyclopaedia.'

'Nah, I'm just good at organising stuff in my brain. I pretend it's like a library and everything is in alphabetical order, and then when I need to remember something, I just go to that part of the library. Like just then, I went to D for Dolphin, and then I found the thing I knew about rostrums.'

'Tell me something else.'

He closed his eyes and his fingers moved like they were typing. 'Emus and kangaroos can't walk backwards. I found that under C for Coat of Arms. That's why they're on there, because they can't go backwards. So it's like Australia can't go backwards.'

I flicked the channel again. A man shouted at us, hair so black it was like he'd drawn it on with texta. '*Someone in your life need cheering up? This frypan is for them! Make delicious pancakes with your custom message cooked right into them. Specially designed to put a smile on any dial!*'

Ben took the magazine from me and wrote *JASON*. Next to that he wrote *PANCAKE FRYPAN*.

10

Dad had a brown notebook he carried in his top pocket, next to his cigarettes. A pen, too; a certain kind of pen with a round lid and blue ink like a river. He said he couldn't write anything unless it was with that pen.

Sometimes he took them out while we were on adventures. Watched me and wrote notes, laughed and wrote notes, frowned and wrote notes. I wasn't allowed to open it. He would slip it back into his pocket and it would be hidden, like it had gone through a wormhole.

Once, he was in his favourite chair in the lounge room, music on, and I was quiet on purpose so I could sneak up on him. He had the book open in his hands, eyes closed, music playing, and on the page he had written: Vanilla milkshakes – Skye's favourite.

On Saturday morning I dragged Ben from bed and stood over him until he'd eaten all his Cornflakes. Mum and Jason had gone for a drive out of town. She hadn't spoken to me again, even when we were together in the kitchen in the mornings, but she knew I would make sure Ben went to school, that he'd have an apple in his lunchbox. I'd tried the handle on Jason's door twice but it didn't move. I was almost grateful.

It was cool and clear that Saturday. No clouds for miles, but it meant the warm air escaped. I showed Ben how to walk along the train line to get into town, and we blew dragon clouds as we walked, steam from our warm bodies.

'You can hear it coming,' I said, 'so you don't have to worry. Just need to make sure you get out of the way in time.'

'I'm scared,' he said.

'You'll hear it. See how flat everything is? It can't sneak up on you.'

'What if the wind is blowing the wrong way?' He looked behind us, looked around me to see in front of us. 'What if it's blowing so hard it blows the sound of the train all the way in the other direction?'

'It won't. Here's the bridge. Sometimes I come and sit here so I can look at the whole neighbourhood.'

'Why would you want to look at the neighbourhood?' he said.

'Makes it seem further away, maybe.'

We stuck our legs through the gaps in the railings. He swung his and they bumped against mine.

'Stop it,' I said.

'You can see all the way down the street from here.' He started pointing at things. 'There's the park and there's the beach and there's the tip. I can smell it. Do you know they sometimes set the tip on fire to get rid of some rubbish, even though there's plastic in there? Plastic fumes are poisonous. They probably shouldn't do that.' He looked both ways down the train line.

'You'll hear it,' I said.

'Yeah, I know.' He didn't look at me. 'There's the girl who lives down the end of the street. She goes to my school. I guess all the kids my age go there though, don't they? Because it's the only one.'

'Maybe. I think there's a school in Port Pirie that some kids go to.'

'That's a long way to go. They must really hate my school.' He picked a bit of enamel from the railing and flicked it to the canal below. 'My teacher is leaving. She's going to have a baby.'

'That sounds nice.'

'I guess. I like her. I kind of wish she wasn't going to have a baby. Is that mean? I don't want her to think I don't like her because I don't want her to have a baby.'

'Nah.'

'She's always nice to me. You know, like when the other people aren't. Sometimes in the playground they ignore me and she comes to sit with me. We have a spot together near the monkey bars and sometimes she sits with me all through lunch.' A few more leaves of enamel flaked away.

'Hey,' I said, standing up. 'You hear that? The train's coming. I thought it was further away.'

He leapt to his feet. 'You said I would hear it! I didn't hear it!' He started running, throwing his skinny legs along the line, jumping over the sleepers.

'It's still ages away. Don't run, you'll trip over.'

But he went, running for his life across the bridge. 'It'll get us, Skye! Trains are fast! Yiannis said there are trains in Japan that go more than three hundred kilometres an hour. That's nearly as much as a Formula One car.' He was at the other end of the bridge. The train had rounded the corner before the station. We had a few minutes. I chased after him, wishing I'd tied my shoelaces, hoping they wouldn't catch in the bolts.

The horn sounded. Ben squealed, tore away from me.

'Slow down!' The wind was blowing the wrong way and my voice came crashing back into my face. 'Ben, seriously!'

The train wasn't slowing. It was going to skip the station. It was going to skip the station and come straight for us, all those passengers charging right at Ben, who was running and tripping along the tracks like a gazelle.

'Ben!' I lurched for him, grabbed him around the middle, dived for the embankment. His whole body shook inside mine and we fell to the grass. I reached for my breath but it shot away from me and over the field. He got to his knees, started taking in gulps of air with his whole body. After a minute, his breathing slowed, and then mine did. The train slipped away into the distance.

He sat next to me, frowned. 'Never make me do that again.' His face was so serious I nearly laughed, all the lines folded in.

'Okay, I promise.' I grabbed him in a headlock. 'We were safe, though. Like I told you, you'll hear it.' But he hadn't, and I'd almost missed it.

We went the rest of the way along the road, past Ben's school and into the main street. There were people everywhere, finding their way around their Saturdays. Families, some of them. Mums with bags of groceries and dads wearing kids on their shoulders, and every kind of combination. Ben watched them, and I watched him watching them.

'How about we get a milkshake?' I said.

The place on the first block did a ripping milkshake. It was a corner store like any other, but the guy running it had a chest freezer full of ice-cream and three milkshake makers that ran pretty much all the time. And he'd bought a deep fryer, so you could get chips as well, and dip the chips into the milkshake. That was a thing Raf had taught me. It was disgusting, but in the way things can be disgusting and delicious at the same time.

Ben looked up at the sign. 'JOE'S STORE,' he said. 'Not very original.'

'You've never been here?'

'Who would take me here?' He pushed through the plastic curtain.

'What'll it be?' Joe said. He looked at Ben. 'You look like a caramel, to me.'

Ben grinned. 'Yes, caramel! Thank you, Joe.'

'Vanilla for you, young lady?'

'Right.'

We took our metal cups into the street. Joe had set up a rusty table there, with two folding chairs that would catch your skin if you moved a millimetre the wrong way. We perched at the edge of them, as close as we could get to not being on them at all without falling off.

'My milkshake is really good,' Ben said.

'Told ya.'

'Thanks for saving my life before.' He swirled his straw around until it stood up on his own. 'I should wear a lifejacket or something. Maybe I can build a bubble and live in that. Yiannis says there are kids who actually live in bubbles because they're allergic to everything in the whole world. Do you think that's true?'

'Yeah, I think I read about that.'

'I feel like I'm starting to forget the things Yiannis told me.' He took a long sip of his shake. 'Maybe this is what it's like to get old.'

'Why don't you call him?' I said.

'*Call* him? What would I say?'

'You could start with "hello", I guess. Go from there.'

He jumped from his seat. 'How do I call him? Can we find his phone number?'

'I bet we can. We can call the directory assistance people.'

'Now?'

'Sure. Finish your milkshake first.'

He drew it through the straw so fast his eyes crossed. We went across the road to the payphone, chucked two dollars in the slot. The number was listed. I passed the phone to Ben and he jiggled his feet, sucked his lip through his teeth like he was waiting for an old girlfriend to pick up.

'Yiannis?' His face was alight. 'It's Ben. Teller. It's Ben Teller.' Feet jiggling. 'I'm in Port Flinders. Yeah, that Port Flinders. I know! I forgot to tell Skye about the guy who drowned in the wheat silo here. Do they call that drowning, or something else?' He took a deep breath. I could hear Yiannis's squeaky voice on the other end of the line.

'Yeah,' Ben said. 'It's cold sometimes here but we're two degrees higher latitude than you so it's not as cold. And the desert is right near us. Nah, I haven't been there. We might go fishing. Did you know jellyfish aren't actually fish, even though their name has *fish* in it? Oh yeah, I did too. Nah, yeah, of course I did.' He was smiling and frowning at the same time. His voice dropped. 'How is my old school? Is anything different?' He looked over at me, moved his hands for me to go away. 'Have you got other friends now?' Pause. 'Yeah, me too. I showed them how to tie balloons to bees but I guess they already knew how to do it.' Pause. 'Oh yeah, sorry. I have to go as well. Skye's taking me on an adventure today so we better get started I guess. Okay, bye, Yiannis.'

He dropped the phone into its cradle and stared at it for a bit.

'Yiannis doesn't have any new friends either,' he said finally. 'Can we go and look at the water?'

We went down past the pub, between the post office and the doctor's surgery and behind the supermarket.

'Is that where you work?' Ben said.

'Yep. That's where I work.' I thought of the conversation with Daryl. The thought of his spit-filled mouth made me want to puke. 'Maybe soon I can buy my own phone,' I said. 'Then you can call Yiannis whenever you want.'

'Oh,' he said. 'Maybe.' We walked past the sign to the motel. Ben jumped up and punched it.

The water was clear, small waves breaking over the rocky reef. Ben flattened a bit of sand and we sat together for a minute just watching. People went past. They were always going past. None of them stopped.

'Reckon there are crabs here?' I said.

'I hope not,' he said. 'Maybe there are blue-ringed octopuses. They kill people. If they start to turn blue you have to run away as fast as you can or they will chase you and kill you.'

'Terrifying.'

'Let me bury you.' He scrambled to his knees. I let him throw sand over my legs until they were buried in a mound. He went up and down the shore, looking for shells to make my leg mound into a castle, brought back a colourful pile of them.

'These ones are from cockles, I think. We have them in Adelaide. I mean, we did have them in Adelaide. I guess the people who live in Adelaide now still have them.' He pushed one into the sand castle, splayed open like a butterfly. 'And I found some mother of pearl. It's like an opal from the sea.' He put that one on top. The sunlight caught it and bounced into my eyes. 'And this is a cowrie. Hermit crabs live in them. They move out when they're too big and go and find another shell.' He added a few more. 'All done.'

'I make a pretty sandcastle, don't you think?'

'Yeah.' He sat next to me again, took a lot of fast, small breaths. 'Will *you* move out when you get too big?' he said.

'What do you mean?'

'When you're too old to live with Mum. Will you leave?'

He frowned, went all bug-eyed, panicked. Like I was going to leave him right at that second, not wait another minute there with him on the sand.

'Where would I even go?'

The tide was starting to come in. Kids gathered along the shoreline and dug trenches for it, squealed as it ran through.

'Want to go build some canals?' I said.

He'd tucked his body over and rested his chin on his knees. 'They're called aqueducts.'

'How do you know all this stuff?'

'I dunno. I just know it.' He let out a spherical breath. 'Can I tell you something?'

'Yeah, 'course you can.'

'I'm scared about Mum.'

'You are?' The newly black circles around her eyes, the late nights counting five-dollar notes into a locked tin.

'It's pretty obvious Jason isn't trafficking birds in tubes, which means he must be doing the thing you were saying.'

'What did I say again?' I thought of Mum with her hand curled around the arm of the couch, Jason's hand bleeding right through its bandage.

'You know, the thing with credit cards.'

'Oh. Skimming?'

'Yeah. I'm worried because Jason seems like he doesn't like us very much and what if Mum goes to jail?'

'She won't.'

'How do you know?'

'She's an adult,' I said. 'She's . . .' God, his sad eyes. Eyelashes all stuck together. 'Hey? Look at me. Everything's going to be fine. Okay?'

'How do you know?'

'Mum's not going to jail and even if she did, they wouldn't let Jason look after us.'

'So *no one* would look after us?'

'Not no one. No, they would . . .' What would they do? Take us away? Put us in an orphanage? 'They'd send us to Nonno's house.'

'Your nonno?'

'Yeah.'

'Why?'

'He has a big, safe house. And goats.'

'I wish we were at Nonno's house now.'

'We could be,' I said. Just like that. Cogs turning in my head, imagining the three of us on his farm.

'What do you mean?'

'We don't have to stay here.'

'Yes we do.'

'What if we don't? What if we can take Mum and go?'

'How?'

'We can make a plan. I've got a job now, so that's a start.' At $12.36 an hour, six hours a week, it'd take three years to get us out of Port Flinders.

Ben was sitting straighter. 'I'm good at making plans.'

'The best.'

'We're going to need a good one,' he said. He grabbed my hands, tried to pull me from the sandcastle. We went up to the post office and bought a tiny lined notebook and a pen shaped like a flamingo. The people in the line bought their things with their eyes down. The guy served us with his hands flapping all over the counter, shoulder twitching. He dropped the flamingo a couple of times. Didn't charge us for the one he broke.

We sat on the kerbside. It was after lunch; people were starting to go home to their Saturday afternoon families. What did people do on Saturday afternoons? Watch TV? Play board games? Wash their dogs? Some of them had paper bags with bread and vegies sticking out of them. Maybe they were having people around, making a roast. I knew how to make roast. Couldn't afford to buy the ingredients though, and Mum didn't like the way it heated the house up.

A couple of older men shouted in the street. Walked down the middle of it, just shouting to one another, shaking brown bottles in the air and throwing empty ones into the pools of old rain. I watched as the bus did its u-turn and came back up the road again, watched the driver lean out the window and shout, 'Get a job, Kenny!' Ben watched, too.

'That's the guy I was telling you about.'

'What guy?'

'The homeless guy. Is he sick?'

'He might be.'

The bus drove on. Kenny dropped to his knees on the bitumen, then to his face, and lay there with his eyes on the chicken shop and his hands behind his back, laughing.

Ben tugged on my arm. 'The plan is,' he said, showing me where he'd drawn a crude map on the first page of the book, 'we sneak out in the middle of the night. Jason can't see us leaving or he'll make us stay.' He looked up at me. 'Or he'll make Mum stay, I guess.' He pointed to some dotted lines, an arrow. 'We could go out this way. The train line would be the easiest but I don't know if it's safe unless it's easier to hear the train in the middle of the night. Is it easier to hear in the middle of the night?'

'I've never tried it in the middle of the night.'

He made a *hmm* noise. 'We should test it out before we go. Then we can hide at the station until the first train comes. Do you know what time that is?'

'Nope.'

He frowned. 'Tell me your plan then.'

Daryl again, his sweaty neck rolls. I could get some more shifts. Go in every day and be close enough to him to hear the hair growing from his earlobes. And to Jeannie, who'd never done anything except stand behind that counter with her smile pasted on.

'I had only got as far as going to Nonno's farm.'

'Where *is* Nonno's farm?' he said.

'I don't know exactly, but it's in Happy Valley.'

'That sounds nice,' he said, closing his eyes. 'Happy Valley. It sounds like the kind of place they would make juice, don't you think? Happy Valley Juice.'

'Nonno used to make orange juice with me,' I said.

'How will we find him?'

'If his number's not private I'll find it in the White Pages. Or I think maybe you can sometimes get people's addresses from the electoral roll.'

'Maybe the police can find him.'

'I'm not going to ask the police.'

'Oh.' He nodded. 'Because of Jason's credit card skimming.'

'Right.'

Ben ran over to the payphone and pulled out the White Pages.

'What's your nonno's last name?' he said.

'Same as my dad's last name,' I said. 'Esposito.'

He ran his stubby finger down the pages. 'How do you spell it?'

'E-S-P-O-S-I-T-O.'

'Oh, here they are. Espositos. There's a bunch of them. What's your nonno's name?'

I had the picture of him so firmly in my mind. His crooked nose, the way his eyebrows kind of shot out from his face like they were trying to escape him. Big hands, dirty from working on the farm but the kind of dirty you couldn't wash off, so dirty the skin underneath his skin was dirty. But his name. His name.

'Claudio?'

Ben frowned at the page. 'There's one C Esposito but they live in Modbury. Is that near Happy Valley?'

'Nowhere near.' He had one big jacket he wore all the time, with wool folded over the ends of the sleeves, and it smelled like his pipe and oranges. He tucked me under it in the afternoons, let me use his silver letter opener to unpack his mail. 'It ends with an "O", I'm sure.'

'Okay, but the phone book only has the letters names *start* with.'

'I remember! Gino.'

'Two G Espositos in here. It says this one lives in somewhere called Reynella. Is that near Happy Valley?'

'Yeah. Yeah, I think so.' I went to take the book from him but he pulled it away.

'The other one is in Seaford Downs! That can't be Nonno, he would have come to visit you if he lived in the same suburb, wouldn't he?'

I frowned. 'It's a really old phone book.'

'What was your dad's name? You told me once but I can't remember. That hardly ever happens. I always remember everything. Was he a G Esposito?'

Greg Esposito. My dad, Greg.

'I don't want to talk about him.'

'Maybe you should call both of these. Maybe you should call them right now. I guess it could be a woman, couldn't it? Gin-*a* Esposito. I feel like I've said Esposito so many times it doesn't make sense anymore.' He peered into the book.

My throat felt like someone had put Glad Wrap over it. I couldn't get the air in properly – it stuck to the film at the back of my mouth.

'Let's call them. There's only two. I can call the one in Seaford Downs if you're worried. You seem worried.' My windpipe full of stones, lungs tightening. 'Are you worried?'

'It's expensive to call from the payphone. Anyway, I can search for them online at home.'

He chewed on the flamingo's fuzzy head. 'I guess that's a good start. Maybe we can blend our two plans together.' He handed the notebook to me. 'I don't know what happens after we get on the train. You might have to figure that bit out.'

'I will,' I said, and wrote *EARN MORE MONEY* at the top of a new page, put the notebook in my pocket. 'I'll put the book back.' I tore out the page of Espositos and shoved that into my pocket too.

Clouds had clustered together down past the highway, wind blowing around an empty can in the street. Ben crossed his arms and brought his bony knees underneath them. 'I thought we were going on an adventure,' he said. 'We haven't even had any lunch and now it's going to rain.'

'Why don't we go down to the oval? Sometimes they play footy there on a Saturday afternoon.' He wasn't convinced. 'If they're playing, the sausage sizzle should be going.'

We could smell it before we even turned the corner, the fat meat burning on the grill. Some days you could get your sausage and bread with onions and even bacon, depending on who was cooking it. Two dollars, and a dollar for a can of drink.

The guys were on the oval. I heard Raf's voice from the gate, not the words he was saying but the way he was saying them. Ben jumped over the fence, caught his shorts on a bit of loose wire. We lined up for a minute, bought two sausages and drowned them in homemade barbecue sauce. I got a lemonade, cracked it open and let the bubbles spit at me.

Claud had a seat in the grandstand, away from the wind. She waved us over. Ben sat between us with his head on her knee and ate his sausage sideways.

'Hey, kiddo,' she said.

'Hi,' he said, without lifting his head. 'I hate football.'

'Oh no,' she said. 'At least this is the last game they're playing here before they go on their big tour.'

They'd got all dressed up in their proper guernseys, all matching. It was getting dark so early. The oval lights were on – the two that worked, anyway – and the seagulls had already gathered around them to pick off the moths. Cold air came up from the sea and into my shoes. I tucked them under my legs.

Raf always started on the wing. The captain would never start in the ruck, he'd said. If he really wanted to inspire his team, he had to be everywhere. Forward line, back line, chasing down the ball. He was easy to spot, even though their tops were identical. The whistle blew and he came running down the south side, where I was sitting, his hair shiny in the gloomy afternoon and the artificial light. Grinning. Taking the mark. Pointing to his teammates as they swarmed the field like pack animals, each one vying for the best spot, to be the open man. It started to rain, just a little.

They moved as one. A living organism. The ground got slippery but they used it, sliding back and forth across the oval to the music of the whistle. Time after time they got it out of the centre, passed it to the guys on the flank or to the centre-half forward, and they kicked it on past the fifty-metre line and each time the ball went between the posts they gathered together on the grass, twenty of them in a laughing, gasping heap with their red-and-white stripes like a snake.

The siren blew for half-time, and the players all huddled together in the middle of the oval.

'They must be cold,' Ben said.

'Nah,' said Claud. 'That's a team huddle. Rafferty's going to give them a half-time pep talk.'

He had their attention, stomping around the outside of the group, pointing his finger into the air a lot, then shoving it into his palm. He looked across to the other team, brought his guys in close and said things we couldn't hear. And then he looked to the grandstand. Saw me. Smiled, pointed to the clouds.

Claud squeezed my knee.

The siren went again. Ben was restless, jiggling his knee up and down. 'I need to go to the toilet,' he said.

'You're just bored.' I gave him a shove. 'You know what they say about being bored. Only boring people get bored.'

'I'm *not* boring. This is the worst adventure I've ever been on. I was thinking it would be like Shackleton or the *Titanic*. *Action*. It's so cold and football is so boring and my sausage is all gone.' He sighed deeply.

Claud pulled some biscuits from her bag. 'When I'm bored watching the footy, which is always' – she winked at me – 'I eat these bickies. They've got the time on them, see? You gotta check the time before you eat them, so it makes them last a bit longer.'

Ben took one. 'Five past one. This is easy.' Claud handed him another. 'Nine thirty.' He sighed. 'I wish it was nine thirty. Then I could be in bed instead of watching this.' I kicked him in the shin. 'What? It's true.'

'You don't normally complain so much. You've been listening to Jason.'

His eyebrows clenched into his forehead. 'No I haven't.' He took another biscuit, eyes still on me. 'Quarter-past six,' he guessed, then looked at the clock face and shouted, 'Ugh, ten ten!' He shoved all the biscuit clocks in his mouth at once. Claud smiled down at him.

'You remind me of my little boys,' she said.

'Hey,' he said, crumbs spilling everywhere, 'I didn't see Raf's parrot when we were at your house.'

My heart clicked over, started racing.

'What parrot?' Claud said, looking into her own hand. 'Ooh, twelve o'clock! It's good luck to get twelve o'clock.'

'Who says?'

'I do.'

Ben looked through the packet for another twelve o'clock, found one right at the end and held it above his head. 'Yes!' The yellow icing cracked between his teeth. 'Is the football over yet?'

When the final siren went, Raf came up to the boundary, hair slick with sweat. They'd won by eight goals. Yardy had kicked six and got man of the match. Ellen had stormed the field and was rubbing herself all over him while he shook hands with the guys from the other team.

'Come to Yardy's, yeah?' Raf said. 'Party of the year before we leave.'

Murderers in the park the man with his legs cut off in the tunnel Haylee having her drink spiked.

'I can't,' I said. 'I've got Ben.'

Ben appeared next to me, like I'd queued him up. 'Hi. Football sucks. And we're in the middle of the worst adventure in all of history.' I elbowed him.

'An adventure, huh?' Raf pulled a towel from the back of his shorts and rubbed his head with it. He looked at me. 'I hope the adventure involves Trey getting us some beers and you coming to Yardy's.'

'Trey?'

'My brother.'

Claud clicked her tongue. 'No drinking, Rafferty. You think that's going to help you on the trip? Not bloody likely.' She grabbed Ben around his middle. 'I can watch this fella for you, though.'

'Oh,' I said. 'That would be ...'

'Great?' Raf said.

Claud smiled. 'How 'bout it, Ben? I've got that new movie downloaded. The one with the panda?'

Ben clapped. 'Can we have popcorn?'

'Of course, treasure.' She took his hand.

'You shouldn't download movies, though,' he said. 'You can go to jail for downloading movies. You wouldn't steal a car.'

'That's true.' She began to lead him away from the grandstand.

'You wouldn't steal a handbag,' he said.

'No, quite right.'

His little voice fading into the sounds of the ground: 'You wouldn't steal a ...'

*

Yardy's place was out behind the caravan park, towards the highway. A big house, two storeys. The music was loud and the whole street seemed to be vibrating with it, right down under the bitumen.

A couple of guys from our class sat on the front porch and passed a cigarette between them, called out to a girl on the lawn to show them her tits but she was too busy puking. The front door was open. People spilled in and out of it. Someone dropped a beer on the tiles and it shattered on the doorstep. One of the guys spotted Raf, called out – 'Yewwwww!' – and went to grab him around the waist. Raf laughed.

'You're fucked,' he said.

'Yep!' And the other guy laughed as well, coughed a bit, spat into his hand. We stepped over the broken glass, pushed our way through a couple with their hands in each other's pants. People were everywhere, on everything, mouths open, legs open. The music pounded in my skull. I wanted to be back with Claud. Just a bit, for a second. An arsehole dropped half his beer on my shirt, licked my cheek in apology. I smelled vomit and beer and something else; a chemical smell.

'I've never been to a party like this,' I said, and wished I hadn't. Raf squeezed my hand.

'Just say "fucking lit" a lot and get drunk with me.' He threw his hands in the air. Shouted at a guy across the room. Cracked the lid off his beer on the edge of the kitchen bench. He led me out through sliding doors to a patio with a spa built right into it like it was part of the house. Yardy had his arm around El and Renée, Hamish smoked across from them with his legs hanging over the edge. Al, at the barbecue, was burning sausages and throwing them at some girls on the lawn.

'Raffertyyy.' Yardy stretched it right out at the end in a weird American drawl. His knees stuck out of the water and he balanced a shiny pipe on one of them. Hamish passed over a bamboo bowl, the kind everyone's mother had inherited from her mother (except mine, who bought all of hers from the plasticware aisle at the supermarket and then fried them in the microwave). Yardy tipped out the stuff inside, packed it tight into the end of the pipe. Renée took a lighter from the edge of the built-in spa and set it alight, and it breathed out its pungent animal smell.

'You getting in?' Yardy said.

Raf laughed. 'I'm not going anywhere near this orgy.'

'Your loss.'

They clinked their beer bottles. El grabbed the pipe, took a long drag on it. She passed it across to Raf, who passed it to Hamish.

Raf pulled me over to a spot by the fence, sat down on the wall around the garden. So much of it was the same as that party at Casey's house – people passed out on the grass, girls with their hands over their drinks. But then there was Raf. I finished my beer, swished the warm liquid around before swallowing, took another from his sixpack. He edged closer to me. Put his hand on my hand, skolled his beer with the other. A girl slapped some dickhead in the face and the guys around him cheered.

Yardy came over, yellow towel around his waist. His body was big, arms bursting with tight muscles. Like he was twenty instead of sixteen, like he'd been working out at the gym every day of his life. It was hard not to look, the trail of dark hair running from his bellybutton to his – 'Raf, my man,' he said. Burped. Laughed into his hand. 'Nah, but seriously.'

Raf sighed. He turned to me. 'You wanna come upstairs? This idiot is about to try to fight me.' And then he smiled, lopsided. 'Or we can have a go in the spa.'

'It's winter. And I don't have any bathers.'

'Upstairs, then?'

My head was full of music and beer, the two things banging together, spinning around. 'Okay. If it's quiet there.'

We went up to a little landing with a balcony around it. 'Yardy's sister might be here. That's her bedroom.' My heart pounded. 'That's his parents' room. You *definitely* don't want to go in there.' He stopped in front of the last door. 'Yardy's.' He grabbed my hand, and his was shaking. 'You sure?'

'About what?'

He laughed, a bit more nervous energy exposed. 'Yardy's room is pretty much nuclear waste.'

I opened the door, ignored the smell that shot out. Tried to tell myself we were just getting away from the noise downstairs. Tried not think about Daryl and his fingers in my hair. Raf closed the door, pushed a pile of clothes to the floor, and we sat together.

'Hi,' he said.

'Hi,' I said.

'We don't have to do anything.'

'Yeah.'

'We can just sit for a bit.'

'Okay.'

His arm slid around my hips. 'Is this okay?'

'Yeah.'

It moved up my back, to my shoulderblades, to the bare skin near my neck. 'And this?' He was whispering.

'Uh-huh.'

He shifted his other hand to my collarbone, down to the neck of my t-shirt. 'Tell me if you want me to stop,' he said, and I wondered if he could feel my heart beating out of my chest, if he could feel the sweat between my boobs, the beer in my throat.

The door burst open. I snapped upright, suddenly sober. Yardy stood in the doorway, laughing.

'*Get some*, Rafferty.' He reached out to shake Raf's hand.

'Fuck off.'

'Very sorry to interrupt.' He walked in and sat on Raf's other side. The others came in after him, hair still wet from the spa. 'Got some business to attend to.'

Yardy opened the drawer next to his bed and picked up a glass pipe with a bulb at the end, and I gasped. Couldn't help it, saw Jason again with his fistful of glass.

'Okay, Skye?' El said. 'You look freaked out.'

'Me?' She looked at me sideways. They all did, all their faces aimed right at me. 'Nah,' I said. 'Nah, I'm good.'

Yardy unwrapped a foil packet, took out a couple of crystals and dropped them in the chamber. Raf was uneasy next to me, leaning from one side to the other, pushing his fingertips together. 'We can go,' he whispered. 'Right now, if you want.'

'Oh Raf,' Yardy said. 'My hero.' He kissed Raf hard on the cheek. 'She said she was good.' Someone screamed downstairs, then laughed. Raf squeezed my hand.

'It's fine,' I said.

'Where'd that lighter go, Renée?' Yardy took it from her, held the flame close to the glass and rolled the pipe between his fingers until it filled solid with smoke. One breath in, another out in one creamy snake, and the plume curled into the skylight. He handed the pipe across to Raf, who shook his head and passed it along. Hamish grabbed at it like a hungry child. It went around a couple more times before Yardy clinked it on his bedside table and left it there, still hot.

'So, Skye,' he said, and all five of them pointed upwards in unison and laughed. 'How you liking your first Port Flinders party, huh? Not bad at all, right?'

'Yeah.'

'Fucking *lit*,' said Hamish, and Raf elbowed me.

'Yeah, fucking lit,' I said. The glass bottom of the pipe had been burned black. Yardy picked it up and put it in his drawer.

'You guys coming downstairs? Jez got fireworks from somewhere. Thought we'd aim them at rabbits.'

'No thanks,' Raf said.

'Whatever.' They all left. El closed the door behind them.

'Sorry you had to see that,' Raf said. 'And sorry about before. Like, if you weren't into it. Don't want to pressure you.'

'Nah, you didn't.'

'You want another beer?'

'No thanks.'

He pushed his hands under his thighs. Something moved under the pile of clothes. Through the window, a white flash streaked across the backyard.

'You wanna go?' he said.

'Yeah.'

Raf walked me out to the jetty. The wind was strong and it snapped at our faces. Waves crested over the old wood, went crashing down on the other side.

'Is it safe?' I said.

'Nah,' Raf said, and grabbed my hand. 'But what is?'

'Being home in bed?'

He coughed out a laugh. 'In your bed? Doubt it.'

'Piss off.'

'Nah, yeah, I know.' He pulled my hand towards him, so it was almost in his pocket. 'What did you think of the party? Good, right? Those dickheads were off their heads.'

I didn't want to tell him about the only other party I'd been to. Me and Kirrily hiding in the playground so murderers wouldn't find us because we'd had two beers. The kids from school who didn't want me there in case I started reciting Lady Macbeth or telling them something Ben had taught me about lizards. How I didn't know if the party was good. How would I know? And then the man with his legs cut off in the tunnel again. The train. It shot past in the distance, rolled its quiet rhythm across the wheat fields.

'Yeah,' I said, not knowing what else to say. 'It was cool.'

'They're usually better,' he said. 'Yardy can be such a dick, though.' We reached the end of the jetty and he swung his legs over the railing, pulled himself up so he was sitting right on the end, staring out at the dark water.

'I'm not into that stuff, you know.' His voice was quiet.

'What stuff?'

'The stuff the other guys are doing. Yardy and them.'

'Oh, yeah, I know.' I thought of Mum bent over the bed, Jason's face right up next to hers. Wanted to ask Raf for more, things I needed to know about what was happening at Jason's. I saw Yardy's face afterwards, eyes like the backs of spoons. Did Mum have eyes like that? I should've helped her, not just hidden in the toilet like a little kid.

'Seriously though.'

'I don't know what you want me to say,' I said.

'Nothing, I guess. I just wanted to make sure you knew.' He tapped the railing next to him. 'Get up here.'

'No way.'

'Go on.'

'You saw those waves. What if one of them knocks you off?'

His smile was wide and bright under the jetty lamp. 'Then I'll swim back to shore. Come on.'

I pulled myself up next to him. On the water, the fishing boats slammed into the waves, and vice versa. Far out to sea, someone shouted and a flare went up.

'Those people at the party … what do they *do*?'

'What do you mean? Go to school, play footy. Couple of them have cars so we go to Port Pirie sometimes, see a movie, go to the mall.'

'But what will they do after? You know, in life? Like Yardy. What will he do?'

Raf frowned. 'He'll go down to the smelter, like his dad. At the end of this year, probably.'

'And the others?'

'Guess El and Renée might marry farmers. Or move to the city. El's brother moved to the city this year, got a job in an office. Maybe she'll get a leg up that way.' He ran his hand through his hair. 'Al and Seb and Hamish'll be deros like their old men, sit at the bar at Heysen and spend their dole money on greyhounds.'

'Is that what they want to do?'

'Why wouldn't they want to? Beats doing real work.'

'What about you?'

He shrugged. 'Play footy, of course. I'd even play for Port, if they had a spot for me.'

'You're so good. They'd be mental not to take you.'

'It's expensive to get in, you know. Not enough to just be a good player anymore. You've gotta do programs and media training and learn how to be good in interviews. Especially if you want a career off the field. In front of the camera, on the boundary. Would've been good to get work experience doing *that* and not this bullshit mechanic stuff.'

Work experience. 'When does that start again?'

'Monday. You figured yours out? Too late if you haven't, I guess.'

'Yeah,' I said. 'Yeah, of course.' *EARN MORE MONEY.*

'What're you doing?'

Marking down meat in the freezer. 'The Foodplace.'

'But you already work there.'

'Yeah, but like ...' Watching Jeannie blow smoke through her nose in a car park. 'In the office. Ordering ... stock.'

'Sounds shithouse.'

'Really does.'

He swung his legs. 'No more shithouse than changing car tyres though.'

'Never tried it.' We were quiet. I thought about how I could convince Daryl to give me more work. How I could disguise it as *work experience.* I'd done the maths, figured out how many hours I'd need to work. Watched the clouds come shooting across to hide the stars. 'Hey,' I said.

'Yeah?'

'Do you ever feel so small you want to explode?' I said.

He shook his head. 'Nah. I feel so much bigger than this place I want to explode.'

'You'd make a huge mess.'

He was silent for a while, then, 'No one ever stays on purpose,' and we sat wet and lost at the end of the jetty, waiting for the boats to tip over.

11

THE SECOND TIME I saw Nonno after Dad left, I went by myself in a taxi. Mum was working at the school, then, and she seemed to have money all the time. Nonno had a woman living with him. Not a girlfriend, but someone who could take care of things around the house so he could do the outdoor work.

He had a new goat. Gerry, the goat. Gerry lived in a fenced-off area by the house, and he was pressed right up against the fence, bleating loudly into the orange grove. Nonno watched him from the kitchen, turning over handfuls of feed in a glass bowl.

'Why's he shouting?' I said.

'He hasn't had any breakfast,' Nonno said.

'Don't goats need breakfast?'

'He must pay his way,' he said, and tipped the feed into the tray.

In the morning I walked into town, watching for other kids or teachers who might see me, and went into the Foodplace. Jeannie was at the checkout already, not even nine am and she was there with her big smile on and her hair in front of her face. I grabbed a chocolate bar from the shelves, went over to her counter.

'Daryl around?' I said.

'Yeah, he's out the back. What do you want with him? On your day off? Would've thought you'd want to keep as far away from the likes of him as possible.'

I passed her a gold coin. 'I need to ask him a favour.'

She folded the coin into her hand. 'Chocolate bars are three bucks, my sweet.' I reached into my pocket, found nothing. 'Don't worry, I'll cover you this time. Your shout next, yeah?'

'Thanks, Jeannie.'

She smiled, the same way she did for every other person in her line. 'Next customer?' she called, right over my head.

Daryl was in the freezer room, crossing out the best-before date on pre-packaged meat. Everyone knew he did it. He was totally open about it, slapping a huge SALE sticker over the top of two days ago, keeping the meat half-frozen so the edges didn't go grey. There was that smell of him. I was barely in the door and I could smell it. His stale BO.

At the sound of my footsteps, he spun around. 'You're not supposed to be back here!' He squinted at me. 'Skye? You're not rostered on today, are you? Penalty rates?'

'No, I have a favour to ask.'

He put down his scanner. 'I'm not big on handing out favours to kids who've already had an official warning.' His jowls wobbled as he walked towards me.

'We've had a family emergency. I need more hours.'

'That right?'

'I'd really appreciate it.'

'How many more hours?'

'As many as you can give me. Daytime. Monday to Friday.'

'You want to wag school so you can work in a supermarket?' He laughed. 'Why don't you just drop out?'

'My mum can't know either.' I thought of Jason counting five-dollar notes onto the glass table. 'It's a secret. A surprise.'

He rubbed his sweaty jaw. 'And what's in it for me?' A smile crept in at the corners of his mouth. He had a bit of food stuck there, maybe toast. Stomach acid rose into my throat.

'Sixteen-year-olds are cheap,' I said. 'You can pay me less than Jeannie and I can stay on my feet longer. And no more breaks with Jeannie.'

He slid closer. Old-man aftershave, mouldy-clothes smell like when they've been left in the machine for a couple of washes. 'And?'

'And what?'

'What else are you gonna give me?' When he smiled the gaps in his back teeth showed.

'Whatever you want.' My stomach turned over. That settled acrid smell between his fat rolls. He drew his sweaty mouth along my cheek. They were just words. I'd be finished and on the train before he cashed in anyway. 'Deal?'

'Nine o'clock tomorrow. Don't be late.'

I ducked out through the back door, slammed it behind me and hyperventilated into my hands. I heard a man shout out across the docks, *Hey, dog!* and then just the sea birds calling for their breakfast.

On Monday morning, I put on my school uniform and took Ben down the road to the school's morning walking bus. He liked it better when I took him to school, he said, but I had to be at the supermarket when it opened at nine and it was right across town. He looked up at me like his face was stitched on, those sad eyes and his drooping mouth.

'You'll be all right, mate,' I said. 'It's just the walking bus. You've done this heaps of times. Hang on to the rope.'

He made a little bleating sound.

'I have to go to the supermarket every day this week, for work experience. Wait for the bus home after school, by the main building, okay?'

He nodded. He'd drawn a picture of a tortoise on the back of his hand in biro. The other kids started arriving to walk to school but none of them talked to him. The woman leading the bus didn't even talk to him, just fussed around the other kids, asked them about their lunches and their dads.

It was still cold, just a bit of spring breaking through. I thought about getting the school bus – it was just a couple of blocks from the oval to the supermarket – but I couldn't risk being caught. Not on the first day. Daryl would never give me another chance. Instead I went around the main road, slipped in behind the weird shopping centre at the main roundabout, walked in short steps through the sand. The beach was quiet. Wind picked up the granules and flicked them in sharp slashes on my skin. A couple of boats hung out in the marina with their sails down, beat a slow rhythm into the jetty pylons.

I thought about Ben in the walking bus. Couldn't stop thinking about him, for a minute, filled up my whole head with thoughts of him going to school and the other kids ignoring him.

'Stop it,' I said. 'Stop it.' A bird looked at me with its one red eye. 'Just piss off.'

At the corner I stepped over a guy with his hand inside a paper bag, eyes closed into his head. He didn't move. Grunted a bit, breathed out in one long stream.

Daryl had the front door open and was scrawling some specials on a whiteboard.

'You're a girl,' he said. 'Your handwriting's probably better than mine.'

'Yeah, that's how it works,' I said. The back of his head had rolls of fat with hair coming out of them. Rivers of sweat already, not even nine in the morning and the middle of winter. When he breathed, the sides of his body expanded. He was bagpipes. I laughed at the idea and he shoved the texta in my hand.

'What's this? School uniform? Gonna sneak in a Maths class at lunch?'

'Habit,' I said.

'You can get changed in the freezer room. Don't be long, though. Someone might need to come back there.' He wheezed his piano accordion sides.

For a while I just sat there, in the freezer room, on some plastic crates with the sides broken off. Took out my bit of paper with the plan on it, but it still just said *EARN MORE MONEY* and nothing else. We *could* catch the train back to Adelaide, find Nonno on his farm. I could pick fruit there, walk Ben down the hill to school in the mornings without a rope. He had orange trees and the neighbours had apple trees and some of them sold them from stands right on the road. Mum could get a job at the bank again. Happy Valley had to have a bank, didn't it?

I pulled on my work uniform. Adjusted my badge, which had been upgraded from TRAINEE to LISA. Someone else's badge. It didn't matter; no one was going to have a chance to learn my name anyway. In six weeks I could earn three thousand dollars, which was more money than I could even think about in one go.

I thought of school, struck for a second by how good it had felt to learn my lines for *Macbeth*. I could catch up. Once we'd got out, I could catch up.

The door to the freezer room croaked. Daryl stuck his head in, pulled the door right open and shoved his body through it. 'Get a move on,' he said, in a spray of spit. 'Need you to get those specials written up before the oldies get here. Monday is scenic-route day on the community bus, you know.' He slid next to me as I left, put his body between the exit and mine. His whole body throbbed, like his heart was trying to escape.

I pulled the sweaty texta across the whiteboard. Apples: $2.99 a kilo. Homebrand cheese slices: $4.95. Plastic-wrapped mince: $6. I drew a picture of a cow next to it, put a bell around its neck. Some of them were actual bargains and I planned a couple of good meals, imagined pulling a proper dinner from the oven instead of a pizza with bits of pig gut frozen to it. Thought again about Ben and the walking bus. He would be there by now, if the clock above the exit was right. Ten past nine. Tired and sad at the front of his classroom, waiting for someone to talk to him.

Jeannie blew in. Her hair was newly dyed, dark and shiny at the roots, and she'd pinned it away from her face. Dark red lipstick, circles of blush the way women wore it in pictures from the eighties.

'You're late,' Daryl said, but only for show. She clipped on her name tag, set herself up at her regular station. She had a bit of knitting stored in the cash register, for the quiet times. I watched her nicotine-stained fingers work the wool around and around.

'What are you knitting?' I said.

'Skye!' She put her hand to her chest, like she'd seen a ghost. 'What're you doing here? It's Monday, right?' She looked up at the clock as though it knew the answer.

'Yeah,' I said. 'I'm doing some day shifts. Got a bunch of frees at school.'

'Gotcha.' She touched the hooked rows of wool. 'Daughter's having a little'un. Up in Darwin.' She turned it over in her hands. 'Guess they don't need much knitting in Darwin though, huh. Never been there myself.'

The oldies filed through. Jeannie talked to all of them, told them something they already knew about themselves: 'Dave Cheng, your daughter is having a baby! Klaus, we're all getting older, aren't we? Ha ha. Lou, look at that shirt.' They stopped to listen. Turned their hearing aids up and down, depending on whether they liked the conversation. Pushed their way along the day, found something to keep them busy in the supermarket. They came through my line, too, with their faces all done up and their hair nice and asked me about one thing or another as though they were all my grandmothers. Not all of them, of course. Some put a pack of gum on the conveyer belt and paid in ten-cent pieces while I ignored their bulging pockets. I had a lunchbreak, pushed a milk crate against the concrete wall and stared out at the ocean because I didn't know what else to do with my thirty minutes. Kicked a couple of stones. Ate a Kool Mint I'd found in my cash drawer, turned it over with my tongue until the chewy part had got hard and then dissolved.

That first afternoon, I waited for the bus under the clock tower and listened to it chime for five thirty. I stood there in the dark, thought of Ben getting himself home from school, finding his own afternoon snack, talking to wherever he kept Bilbo. My feet ached in my cheap shoes. Knees, too, trying to bend under my tired weight but fixed rigid. No wonder Jeannie had a stool.

The bus was due at twenty-to. School had finished hours ago, no one would see me. But Ben, alone in the house. I decided instead to walk up to the chicken shop, get one of those rotisserie ones with their backs all burned. Peas and gravy. Ben loved peas and gravy, loved stacking them all up on his fork to see how many he could balance there.

The guy at the chicken shop looked me up and down, the way they always did. Grunted a bit from behind his greasy moustache, boiled and slobbered inside his skin. They had a family special and I bought it with the money I had left from last week. Tried not to think about the name of it – 'the family special' – the people I would take it home to. Let myself picture, for a second, the way the three of us might have eaten it around the table together, before Jason, with the light coming in from the train station and the Adelmanns arguing down the walkway.

A family special was the chicken, large chips, peas and gravy, a couple of sad wedges of pumpkin. He said he would throw in a Greek salad, or a pasta salad. Or I could take a 1.25L bottle of soft drink, it was up to me.

'Greek salad,' I said, then, 'Actually, Coke.' Ben would snort it out through his nose and squeal and laugh because according to him the bubbles felt like setting your nostril hairs on fire.

'Fifteen ninety-five,' the chicken man said, coughed a bit of phlegm into his fist. I tapped my card on the machine. The money ran out of my bank and into their bank, just numbers tripping along from one computer to another. I'd earned a hundred dollars at the supermarket in just one day. Enough to buy a ticket from Port Flinders to Adelaide, but only one.

I took the plastic bags back to the bus stop. Five forty-eight. I watched the bus do its u-turn at the end of the main street. It was like a morose merry-go-round, making its way up and down the main part of town all day long, as though it had actual places to go. It sighed to a stop at my feet. The doors folded open in that way they had, with a kind of reluctance. I said hello to the driver and without looking up took a seat by the door. The bus croaked away from the kerb, bundled itself along the main road.

A voice at my side. A bolt of warm skin and hot breath.

'How'd you go?' Raf said.

'Pretty good, I guess. Ordered some stock. Did some … inventory.'

'Oh yeah? I pulled bugs from the front grille of an old ute.'

'Wow.'

'Life skills, huh.' He yawned. 'I'm knackered.'

'Same.'

'Would it help if I got us some hot chips?'

'You ask a lot of questions.'

'With gravy?'

'I've already got some.' I held up my bags. 'They call this a family pack. I'm taking it home to my family.'

He smiled a bit, just with the narrow part of his mouth. 'Are you okay?'

'Yeah.'

'Okay.' The bus filled up with the chicken shop smell. Not just the chicken, but those styrofoam packets and the gravy seeping into the pores of them. Plastic and permanent. I pulled a couple of chips from the foil bag; they were soggy in the middle and they drooped into my mouth. Raf grabbed one. He pulled a face as he ate it.

'You went to Sad Tom's,' he said.

'I did what?'

'Sad Tom's is the worst chicken shop in the world. I can't believe you went there. Everyone knows you go over the road to Roosted.'

His voice had laughter in it, and my chest was heavy with the weight of the bags but he didn't notice. We were at his stop, anyway; his neat house with its people inside.

'I'll see you tomorrow, okay? After "work".' He pulled a face at 'work'.

I watched him through the window, watched Claud hug him at the front door and the light was all yellow behind her. I'd had forty-two dollars in the bank and now sixteen of it was sad chicken wrapped in non-degradable plastic.

At the spinifex block, the bus stopped its last stop before its next u-turn. I took the bags inside. Ben sat alone at the table, writing on a bit of scrap paper with the flamingo pen. He took the family pack from me and got us a couple of plates and a spoon for the peas. Stacked his high on his fork. They tasted of nothing – lumps of flour and crushed bugs. He shoved the leaning tower into his mouth, grimaced for a second, swallowed it down.

'Thanks for getting this great dinner,' he said.

I told him about Sad Tom, owner of the worst chicken shop in the world.

'It's not the *worst* chicken in the world,' he said. 'The worst chicken in the world would be poisonous and maybe even still alive.'

'Where are Mum and Jason?'

He shrugged. 'They yelled at me a bit before because I had the TV too loud, then they went out the back and shouted at each other. And now Mum's in the shower.'

'Good.'

'How was work?'

'Fine. Working on the plan.' Hiding from Daryl in the meat freezer and working on the plan. Standing out the back of the supermarket in the cold wind and working on the plan. Soon I'd have enough to get all three of us to Adelaide and – Nonno's? Maybe Mum could find us another apartment. Either way, Port Flinders would be far behind.

'Oh, good,' Ben said. 'I've been working on my part of the plan.' He pushed across his scrap of paper. 'Did you know the train station has a really old section where bushrangers used to hide out? I found a book about it in the school library. There's a trapdoor and you're not supposed to go down there because the government decided to protect it, but I reckon if we went in the middle of the night no one would notice. And they wouldn't be able to find us. We could wait there until the train came.'

'That's a good thought,' I said, chewed on a bit of chicken skin.

'I'm just so worried Jason might try to come after us. Because he misses Mum.' He flipped the paper over. 'So I've got another plan as well, in case he tries.' He had a picture of the three of us together; Mum and I with suitcases and he with a tortoise on a leash. 'Mum told me about someone in her family who lives in the hills too, like Nonno, but they live near a chocolate factory or an alpaca farm. Do you know they sell broken chocolate for cheaper? Even though broken chocolate tastes exactly like normal chocolate?'

'Ben.'

'Jason wouldn't be able to find us. I bet they would let us all come and stay with them, if she told them what was happening.' He took a quick breath and was quiet, hand shaking over the paper.

I spoke in the lowest voice I could find, the least demanding. 'What *is* happening?'

'You know. The credit card thing you said.'

'Yeah.'

He picked at the skin around his fingernails. 'And the yelling. I don't know why he's always yelling. If people yell too much they can get a thing called polyps in their throat and sometimes cancer.'

I pointed at his reversed paper. 'What's this part of the diagram for?'

'That's the beach,' he said. 'I don't know how far it is from the hills but I thought we could go there and visit the apartment, maybe, in case the people who bought it want to move out. I want to meet Amir's new baby. Well, his mum's baby.' He paused. 'Do you think we should tell Mum about the plan? I don't want her to find out and not have any time to pack. Maybe we need to tell her enough in advance so she can decide whether to come or not. So we're not just leaving in the middle of the night without her knowing.'

I pushed the paper back to him. 'Just let me worry about that bit, okay? How's your chicken?'

He shoved a bit more into his mouth. 'It's good,' he said, but it was hard along the edges, like it had been sitting in the bain-marie for days.

*

In the morning, I dropped Ben at his walking bus again and went back the long way to the supermarket. I wrote on the specials board, pinned Lisa's name tag to my shirt, took the sharpie out to the meat freezer. On Tuesdays we did a package deal on sausages made from pigs' arseholes and yesterday's bread. Bargain. I drew a little pig on the specials board, drew a knife sticking into it. Rubbed it out.

It was the same, all day, as the day before. The old people examining every single apple before they chose one. Their yelling at the deli counter, the processed meats all too colourful. Children around the lollies, the way they tugged at their parents' clothes until they found some substitute for actually bothering to listen to what they had to say. A packet of Smarties. The end of a sesame bar. The main door slid open and shut like peek-a-boo hands, keeping me from the near-empty car park beyond, and at lunchtime I sat at my milk carton picnic table and ate cheese sticks from the packet.

Daryl groaned around me, eyes always going. He watched me go to the bathroom, watched me clock in and out of my thirty-minute lunchbreak, counting every second I was late. And each time I marked down the meat in the freezer, he was there, appearing as if from nowhere in the dark corners where no one would see him. Tapping his watch. Pointing at the clock. Always, always hurrying me along, as though he had somewhere to be besides looking me up and down in my work uniform.

At five thirty I took the sale-priced sausages and a few vegetables and caught the bus from its u-turn stop. I saw Raf there again, waiting for me in the middle row with a big smile. I sat next to him. Didn't put the bag of sausages too close, in case they got hot against his skin.

'I got sent out to get pies for the guys today. You?'

'An old lady peed in the cereal aisle.'

'Shit.'

'Not this time.'

He laughed a bit, rode with me back to my house and didn't say anything, just waved from the window as the bus turned around. Ben had his knees around his ears, watching TV half upside down, all the blood rushing into his face.

I cooked for him and made a plate for Mum as well, left it by the bedroom door and knocked on it. She came out later, sat on the couch opposite and we watched the news together, sort of, her barking at the many-faced politicians and me watching the weather in case I needed an umbrella. Down the hallway, Jason shouted into his phone. He went outside a couple of times, slammed the door so hard the walls shook. Mum changed the channel and we watched a couple with drawn-on faces renovate a house they had bought after his parents died.

I thought about my parents dying. Not for very long, just while the ad break was on. In the kitchen, Ben's pens scraped against the lino table.

'Go to bed!' Mum shouted. 'It's half-past bloody nine.'

Our bedroom door closed. I could tell it was that door because it stuck at the last second, like it was resisting. You had to force that door.

On Wednesday I did it all again. Only this time, Raf wasn't on the bus. I rode it a couple of times, in a loop, all the way to Jason's house and then back to the u-turn, around again. We went past his house, all lit up, me and the bus driver on our way to somewhere worse. And I kept doing it on Thursday and Friday, no Raf on the bus, just me and the supermarket and the plan in my pocket that still just said *EARN MORE MONEY.* I got off at his place and left a note in his letterbox – *Miss you* – then took it out again. Wrote on the specials board, fetched bits of chewed-up food from under the shelves in the lolly aisle, broke up fights between the old people and the deli manager. Stood across from Jeannie and watched her hair change from one day to the next, sometimes pinned across her eyes and sometimes loose around her ears. Sometimes the skin underneath it was pink and sometimes yellow. She wore big gold earrings and small glass earrings and the people came through her checkout and didn't listen to her questions.

I had a regular, by Friday. A man trapped inside clothes far too big for him, face all bunched into clumps of dirt. One of his hands was bent into a claw and he used it to hold money, coins that smelled like he'd been keeping them in his undies. He bought the same thing every day: a can of homebrand cola and two twiggy sticks in butcher's paper. He never took a bag, just shoved it all in the pockets of his oversized hoodie and went out the back way, where the path went out to the jetty.

Jeannie told me to watch out for him. She said he was her regular, once, but didn't elaborate.

'Is he … homeless?' I said. I'd thought a homeless person would ask for a dollar but he'd never asked me for a dollar.

'Probably,' Jeannie said.

In my lunchbreak I went out through the freezer and sat on the milk crates by the door. The jetty was empty except for some old buckets rattling around, and my regular sitting on the end with his hood up, legs dangling over the edge. Next to him was a dog the size of a rat. Its legs shook, knees knocked together. He broke off bits of his twiggy stick and the little dog did tricks for them. Rolled over, played dead, shook hands. My regular's laugh busted out dry and hoarse. He rolled a cigarette, cupped his hand around it while he tried to light it. The wind was strong. He put the white stick in his pocket and rubbed the little dog's head.

I had a bit of bread and some ham so I ate them together and pretended it was a sandwich. Thought of the money I'd have in the bank on Monday. Five hundred dollars. No one I knew had ever had five hundred dollars. I wondered if Raf would wait for me on the bus again. I only needed a few more weeks without questions and then we'd have enough to do whatever the next part of the plan was. I had the weekend to think about it and then on Monday I could take the five hundred dollars and get it started.

My pay went in on Monday morning. I checked it at the ATM outside the supermarket, saw all those numbers staring back at me. The first thing I did was go to the cigarette counter and buy a pre-paid phone. A cheap one. Chose one with a phone number I thought Ben would remember, with lots of zeroes in it. Daryl ran the counter, of course. He only trusted himself with all the important stuff like lighters and razor blades and newspapers.

'Gonna call your boyfriend, huh?' he said, mouth right up near my ear.

'My mum,' I said.

I charged it on the power point in the meat freezer until lunchtime, then took it out and activated it. The box had a pair of earphones in it. I shoved them in and listened to my heart beating back at me.

'Whatcha got there?' Jeannie said.

'A phone,' I said. 'I've never had a phone.'

She had her hair curled at the ends, and it flicked underneath her chin like it was holding her head up. 'You're a proper grown-up now, huh? A proper grown-up who doesn't have to go to school, right?' She smiled a bit, teeth ringed brown around their edges. I started to tell her why she was wrong, but the old lady with one leg came through Jeannie's checkout and she turned away from me. I sent a text to Raf so he'd have my number and he texted right back: *welcome to the 21st century, Sky!* I tapped Kirrily's number in. Sent her a text with my name at the end. Put it on silent so I could imagine her replying.

My regular came through with his paper-wrapped sticks.

'Good morning,' I said.

'Morning.' His voice was all tied up inside his throat. I scanned his cola and it came up on sale, fifty cents off. 'Wait a minute.' He left his stuff right there on the belt but there was no one else in the store, so I waited. Pulled open the drawer – no message from Kirrily. I thought about asking her if we could stay. Just for a couple of days before we went up to Nonno's. Maybe her brother could drive us there, if his house was a long way from the bus stop. I couldn't remember. Couldn't even remember how old I'd been when I was last there. Eight?

'Thanks.' The belt started moving again. An extra twiggy stick.

'What's your dog's name?' I said.

He looked at me, but like he didn't know how to look at people, eyes going from side to side. After a few seconds he said, 'Why?'

'Just curious.' I took his handful of coins. 'She'll probably be pretty excited about the extra twiggy stick, right?' Jeannie was watching me then, spun around on her stool. Daryl, too, sweaty behind the cigarette counter with his priceless razor blades.

'Yeah,' he said. 'She loves them.'

'You know you can tie her up by the door. She doesn't have to wait way over the other side of the car park.'

He snatched his receipt from me. 'I know.' And then he was gone, clipping his hand on the automatic doors on his way out. Jeannie turned her stool again. She had a magazine open to a crossword but none of the answers were filled in. Sometimes she twisted her hair into a bun and stuck the pen through to hold it there. I'd have to ask her to teach me how.

A customer came through and she ran her spiel. 'Mr Greenslade, so nice to see you. New shirt? Get in to Port Pirie much? Got the big Target there. Heard they had a sale on. Ha ha, yeah, I guess they always have a sale on! Five bucks for a shirt? You're joking. Well, have a nice morning. Ooh, not sure I'll make it to church this week. I know. Okay, bye.' The old man pulled his little cart along, paused for a second to watch the doors open and close, like it was magic.

At ten o'clock, Ellie arrived and Jeannie took her first break of the day. She told me to come with her, that Daryl was on a work call and wouldn't see me, so I slipped out through the meat freezer and sat next to her while she chain-smoked. At the end of the jetty, my regular sat with his little dog and the boats went past.

'Gotta watch out for Simmo, Skye. All the ones like that.' Jeannie pushed one still-lit cigarette into the next. 'Show them a little kindness and they'll be all over you. Waiting for you at the bus stop. Finding out where you live.' She breathed, a tobacco dragon.

'Simmo?'

'Your new fan.'

'That doesn't make any sense. Why would he bother?'

Her laugh came out in one gasp. 'Pretty young thing like you catches his eye. He's lonely, you're locking up by yourself one night. Just saying, it's not unheard of.' The paper crackled as she inhaled. 'He's been coming here a long time. Never seen him make a beeline for a new girl the way he did you.'

I watched him tear off bits of twiggy stick, watched the dog stand up on its back legs to take them. Not aggressive. Not like Murray, who'd take off your whole hand, but gently, one paw bringing the food closer to her mouth. When the food was gone, he put his arm around the dog and pulled her closer to his body. The wind was cold. Her legs banged together like trees in a storm.

'I think you're wrong,' I said, but Jeannie had gone back inside.

Daryl cornered me in the meat freezer. 'Better not take up that filthy habit,' he said.

'None of your business if I do.' I tried to squeeze past him.

'Don't go thinking I'll sell them to you. You're sixteen. Disgusting. It'll make your skin like an old handbag and then who'll want you?' His breathing was laboured. He could have been eighteen or forty; it was impossible to tell from looking at him, with his skin pulled so tight around his face.

'Is there something you need?' I said finally.

He took a hanky from his pocket and blew his nose into it. 'Yeah. Someone here to see you.'

'Someone, who?' My heart beat faster. The school principal. The police! Could they arrest you for not going to school? No, I was on work experience. Everyone was. They wouldn't be asking about me yet.

'Little kid. Says he needs to speak with you.' He pushed beside me, let his body brush up against mine for a second too long.

Ben had his school hat on inside, but it was easy to see his face anyway. Blotchy. Puffy. He'd dropped down in front of the cigarette counter and had his knees pulled up to his chin. On the floor next to him, his school bag, covered in paint and something that looked like yoghurt.

'Ben?' He looked up, took a huge breath in, let it all out again in a shudder. 'What's going on?' I kneeled next to him, put my hand on his shoulder.

'I rang … your school … from my school.' He was half-sobbing, trying to get his words out around the air going in. 'They said you weren't there. Went there. Went to all the classrooms but everyone said it. No Skye. Haven't seen her.'

'But I told you I'd be here this week,' I said. 'Work experience. Remember?' My ears burned like I was in trouble, like I'd been found out. There was paint on his shoes as well. Laces all frayed at the ends.

'I was too worried to remember so I went to the front desk again.' He let go of the sigh in his throat. 'The lady there said about work experience and after *that* I remembered.'

'How did you get here?' I said.

'Walked.' His head fell back to his knees. 'Walked down the train line, like you showed me.' My heart stopped and then kicked back in.

'Were you safe?'

'Yeah,' he said. 'You were right. You *can* hear it coming.'

I went to Jeannie's checkout. 'That's my brother. Can you cover for me while I take him outside for a minute? Tell Daryl I've gone to the toilet?'

She tapped her nose. 'Women's issues,' she said.

We walked across the car park, found a spot under the public toilet roof that was out of the wind.

'What did you need me for?' I said.

He took a couple of deep breaths. Found himself again. 'Some kids at school said some bad stuff about Mum,' he said. 'They said she might go to jail.'

I frowned. 'Why would they say that? She's not going to jail.'

'They said everyone knows she's doing something bad with Jason.'

'Who said?'

'Some grade sixes. One of them said his brother goes to your school and someone told him about a party where some bad stuff was happening and they said it's because of Jason. Why would there be credit card stealing at a party?'

'Skimming,' I said. Yardy's party. 'There wouldn't.'

He wiped his nose on my sleeve. 'They wrecked all my things. They made me feel like I'm a criminal even though I'm only ten and ten-year-olds can't be criminals. Look at this stuff on my bag. I think it's yoghurt.' He put his head down to sniff it. 'Gross.'

'They're wrong. Mum's not going to jail.' I tried to bundle him up in my arms. 'Kids say all kinds of stupid shit.'

'Well, anyway' – he pulled the little notebook and the flamingo pen from the bag's front pocket – 'then I wanted to talk to you about the plan, but urgently, not after school. Not our plan, but a plan to find out what's going on. Like, whether any of this stuff is true. So that's when I called you and then all that other stuff I said, and now I'm here.' He opened the notebook to a new page. I took a deep breath. Kids were supposed to learn this stuff from their parents; about sometimes doing the wrong thing because you wanted to get it right in the long run.

I put my hands on the open pages. 'You know how we've got this plan? To get out of here so we can be safe? It costs money.'

'You think I'm a baby,' he said.

'No I don't. It's just, I know what I'm doing. And I'm going to keep working here, even after work experience is over, and you can't tell *anyone*. Okay?'

'Why?'

'Because this way, we can have the money we need in six weeks instead of six months.'

He frowned, kicked the ground with the heel of his shoe. 'Six *weeks*? That's *forever*. That's six times as long as butterflies live. Their whole *lives*.'

I grabbed his knee to stop the kicking. 'We just have to keep our heads down, okay? Stay out of Jason's way. If we go now, we won't have enough money and then what'll we do? Sleep in boxes? In the park? Do you think Mum wants to sleep in the park?'

'No way,' he said. 'But doesn't your school mind?'

I imagined Miss Fan calling my name from the roll book next week, never really sure exactly who I was. 'I think they'll be okay with it. Now' – I sat next to him with my knees up to my face, like his – 'I have to go back to work, but let's talk about this tonight, okay? I'll bring home some of those chicken wings you like.'

'I guess.'

'You don't have to go back to school today, if you don't want to.'

'Nah, I will. We're doing a science experiment and I'm going to show them this trick Yiannis showed me where you mix two chemicals together and put some soap in and they explode.' His eyes came alive at *explode*.

'Sounds dangerous.'

'Yeah, some kids in America set themselves on fire doing it.' Then he was off, bag bouncing him along the street.

I put the chicken wings in the oven and we sat at the table with our notebook out.

'Where's Mum?'

'Pilates. But Jason went too so I don't know if they're really at Pilates.' He turned to a new page. 'We need to figure out what Jason is doing,' he said. 'Not parrot exporting.' He gasped. 'Unless – maybe that's where Raf's parrot has gone? Exported?'

'It's not parrot exporting.'

'So is it credit card stealing? How many people do you reckon can get robbed like that before the criminals have to move on?'

'Ten?'

'Maybe it's not that then. But we have to keep Mum safe' – he nodded furiously while he talked – 'so we need to find out what he's doing and then we can tell someone.'

The oven beeped. Ben's hands were quickly covered in honey and soy sauce. He talked around the bones: 'The bedroom with his stuff in it is always locked. Jason always locks it. I don't think Mum even has a key.'

'Right.' I tried it every day, gave it a shake. Felt relieved when it didn't budge.

'So maybe if we could get Jason not to lock the door, we could see inside and look for clues? Or we could get a copy cut for ourselves. He must put his keys down sometimes.' He chewed thoughtfully. 'Maybe if Murray distracted him.'

We looked out to the yard, Murray standing in the mud with his nose pointing right at us.

'Did you know that cooked chicken bones can kill dogs?' Ben said. 'They get splinters of bone in their stomachs and die.' The dog did one slow circle of the clothesline. 'I just thought it was interesting.'

I closed the notebook.

'Something exciting for your specials board today.' Daryl had the texta in my hand before I was even in the door. 'Got a celebrity chef coming. One of those guys from the TV, you know the ones. Wear the fancy scarves, get close-ups of them sampling the food? They're doing a special on the food around the Gulf.' He puffed out his chest, like he'd invented food and the Gulf and they were coming just to see him. 'Gotta let all the oldies know he's coming. They're the ones who'll watch some arsehole use a frypan in a supermarket in the middle of the day.'

I wrote a few words about it. Drew a man in a chef's hat and with a big knife in his hand, turned his eyebrows down so he looked like a murderer. Wrote *GEOFF GARLAND* underneath in bubble letters. He was bringing his team of chef bodyguards so none of the old ladies would kidnap him.

'Nice one,' Daryl said, standing close behind me. 'Good use of bubble letters.' He pointed to the board. 'He's coming on Friday. Write that. Eleven am on Friday.' I wrote it. 'Need to make sure they know when to come. Got an order of organic stuff coming from Clare and if I don't sell it to them, it'll just rot on the shelves.' He wandered off, picking his pants from his arse crack.

My phone vibrated. Raf: *Hey SKY what's UP! haha miss you hope no one pissed in any aisles today*. I thought about his warm skin, the way his hand felt when he slipped it into mine.

He seemed far away. Not in the plan. *EARN MORE MONEY.* Not *BRING RAF.* I tried to imagine him leaving Claud behind, walking away from her while she watched from their glowing front door, but couldn't. He would be angry when we left. Probably wouldn't want to visit.

I texted back: *No peeing in the aisles thank god.*

My fingers were slow and stupid on the touch screen. I didn't know what he'd want to know, whether I was just drama to him. I shoved the phone in my pocket.

Jeannie spun around on her stool. 'How're you travelling, darl?' She had her hair pinned away from her face, curled into gift-wrap ribbons at the ends. 'Been almost two weeks. Still loving your new career choice?'

I fiddled with my cash drawer. 'It's not my career choice.'

'Sure, right. You're going to be a vet or something? An astronaut? A tortured writer!' She laughed to herself. 'I was like you. Dropped out when I was fifteen. Thought I was pretty smart. Parents kicked me out right away so I worked in this old folks' home during the day and went back to a crowded dorm at night. Me and eight other girls on bunks. Like an orphanage. I guess you'd call it a women's shelter now. We'd all dropped out of somewhere – school, work, life.' She pulled on the end of a curl and it sprang back.

'And now you're here.'

'Met Les, didn't I? Said he had a farm out here, inherited it from his dad. Didn't tell me it was a garlic farm but it was too late then anyway. Got knocked up, spent the days in the kitchen with my Kylie, waiting for Les to come back from the fields. Stinking up the place.' She smiled and sighed at the same time. 'Drunk, mostly. Banged open the fridge and shouted when there was nothing in it. Then there was Peter and Steven and my career was over anyway.'

'Your old folks' home career?'

She frowned at me. 'Yeah, my old folks' home career. Had to wait 'til my kids were old enough to look after themselves, then I came here. The boss then was this guy Jack. Town bloody hated him but they're like that, aren't they? Close-minded dickheads, the lot of them. He took a chance on me though, didn't he? Still here twenty years later even if he isn't.'

'Did he leave?'

She laughed. 'Yeah, in a manner of speaking. Keeled over in that meat freezer. Treated his liver badly until it fought back. Anyway.' She turned back to her belt, where a customer was waiting. 'Laurence Black, my old friend. What's the bandaid for? Oh yeah, you gotta be careful cutting those onions. Showed Les my trick, maybe I'll show you. How's Doreen? No good once they start breaking their hips, is it? 'Course I hope she gets better. No, 'course. Give her my love.' Laurence Black left, but Jeannie kept her back to me.

Daryl set up an organic display at the end of my lane. Bags of expensive muesli and artisan pasta and oatmeal shampoo in cream-coloured bottles. He stepped back to admire his creation, all puffed out.

'Whaddya think, Skye? I figured you're young, you know how to sell this stuff. Right? You can sneak one across to the oldies, tell them it'll make them live longer or whatever?'

'Will it?' Jeannie said.

'Fuck no.' Daryl laughed. 'But I will live longer, once I get a bonus from this celebrity chef garbage.'

I drew some things on the whiteboard to look organic. Wheat stalks. An apple. A green shopping bag. The oldies started RSVPing right away, coming through my line with their ten-dollar notes already out for tickets. Geoff was a popular guy, apparently. Daryl watched me from the cigarette counter, pointed at the organics stand. I upsold a couple of oatmeal shampoos and boxes of quinoa, and Mrs Forsythe took a whole basket of overpriced vegetables, said she'd make her sons some organic soup to take out on their boats.

'I bought these special new thermoses,' she said. 'They use the power of titanium.' So I sold her an organic tea towel as well, and a sixpack of organic toothpaste. Daryl gave me a thumbs-up.

For three days I convinced pensioners to spend their money on ten-dollar avocados. On my breaks, Daryl said things like, *Better than spending it at the pokies* and *It makes them feel smart and important*. At night I made spaghetti with non-organic pasta and jars of homebrand sauce, read Raf's texts about the mechanic and sent my own about old ladies and vegetables. After we'd eaten I worked on the plan with Ben with our backs against the bedroom door, each of us just waiting for the six weeks to pass. Staring at the walls until we were unconscious and then snapping conscious again like the night hadn't passed at all.

By the time Friday morning rocked around, the organics stand was empty and I was a bit empty, too.

Geoff Garland was a big man, bald head with eyes pushed too far into it. He'd brought a whole team with him – a couple of chaperone–bodyguard types, some people to shuffle ingredients around, a whole camera crew, a prickly woman with a clipboard and a lizard in a glass tank. They got him set up at the front of the store while he waited in Daryl's office. No one ever went into Daryl's office – not even Daryl – but there was no chance he'd see the dodgy marked-down meat in there.

Jeannie appeared at my side. 'Is he serious about that lizard?' she said. She had on a blue dress with lace on the sleeves, cut almost to her bellybutton. Fancied herself a new celebrity chef husband, maybe. The aquarium had been mounted on the cigarette counter, lizard pressed up against the glass with all its toe pads flattened out.

'I think so. Could be weirder, I guess.' I would have to tell Ben about the lizard. Thought about calling him right then, getting the school receptionist to put him on. I got my phone out and took a photo instead. The woman with the clipboard was instantly next to me. She pointed to the aquarium.

'Cedric doesn't like having his photo taken,' she said.

'What?'

'I'm going to need you to delete that.' She stood over me while I flicked to my photo gallery and trashed the picture. Jeannie's shoulders rocked, trying to hold in her laughter.

The supermarket was open while Geoff Garland did his thing, so I watched the show from my lane.

Two twiggy sticks appeared on my belt. A can of cola. I turned back and into the face of Simmo, newly black under his eyes and a few scabs around his mouth. I stared, for a second. It passed slowly while I figured out how to look away without being obvious. Couldn't decide what he'd want me to do so I scanned the twiggy sticks.

'They've gone up,' he said, pointing at the screen.

'Have they?'

'Two sticks for a dollar. Always.'

I scanned them again. A dollar twenty. 'Sorry,' I said. 'They must have changed the price.' I looked over at Daryl, tapping on the aquarium glass, laughing in his beetroot way.

'Fuck that.' He slammed the can on the scanner. 'Look at that arsehole. Gets paid to go round showing other dickheads how to boil an egg and I get an extra twenty cents on my bill. What, the price of cats' anuses went up in China?'

Daryl turned his head towards us.

'I'm really sorry,' I said, trying to keep my voice steady. 'I have twenty cents you can have. Your dog – she'll miss out.'

'Not the point.' He left one of the sticks on the belt. 'Just get one then, right? Cleopatra can eat on Wednesdays and Saturdays.'

'Is that her name, Cleopatra?'

He stared at me, put two dollars in my hand and walked out. Daryl had turned back to the lizard. He'd dropped an insect into the tank and had his nose right up to the glass, waiting for Cedric to jump at it. Like a child, and not a smart child. Jeannie had a family in her lane, two kids fighting over who got to unpack the trolley onto her conveyor belt. I made like I was going to the meat freezer but slipped out the door instead. Followed the man and Cleopatra to the jetty, twiggy stick in my pocket.

He sighed. 'Whaddya want? Come to save my life with yer money, right?' The little dog shook between his feet. He bent down to her and she licked his hand, took a tiny piece of sausage from his fingers.

'Nah. Just wanted to get away from that chef crap.'

'Righto.'

'You're right, too. I bet Daryl put the price up.' Cleopatra got her front paws up on his leg, sniffed the air. 'He's been trying to get as much money out of this celebrity thing as he can. Organic toilet cleaner. Stuff no one even knows how to use, like truffle paste and quince jelly. Making all the oldies think they need it.'

'Dickhead.' Simmo picked at bait dried to the boards, threw it into the water. 'Went to school with him, y'know. Daryl. He was the kid beating up all the other kids. Me included.'

'Oh.' Something got me in the ribs, a bit of a feeling caught there. I took the twiggy stick from my pocket.

'He was a wanker. Still is. He'll get what he deserves one day.'

Ben in the playground, coming into the supermarket covered in yoghurt and whatever other garbage they'd thrown at him. Kids like Daryl. Ben and Simmo hiding under a bench together, Daryl pouring sand on them, jamming sticks into their ribs.

The automatic doors opened and laughter poured out, the amplified boom of Geoff Garland making a tuna salad I couldn't pronounce. Simmo took the meat from my hand and looked me right in the eyes.

'Don't patronise me,' he said, and threw the stick into the water.

I had to stay late, packing up the junk a celebrity chef apparently leaves behind.

'I'll get paid overtime, right?' I said, and Jeannie laughed in her blue dress.

'You won't get fired, if that's what you mean,' Daryl said. I imagined him again with Simmo, bearing down, the other tough kids laughing. I wanted to shake him, for a second, jumbled up in my head with Ben and those kids at his school who didn't care about his balloons and bees. Raf texted me: *Wanna come over after work?* and I wrote back, *So tired. Tomorrow?*

Late in the afternoon, I got a packet of pasta and some mushrooms and went home on the bus, same as always. Past Raf's place with its sunshine windows, past Ben's school dim with the evening.

Ben was hiding by the front door; his little hand stuck out from behind the bushes as I reached for the handle.

'Don't go in there,' he whispered. 'Can't you hear them?'

I put my ear to the door. 'I can't hear anything.'

'They're in there, fighting. I was just building a replica Pyramid of Giza out of matchsticks and they started fighting about me.' His hand shook around my wrist. 'I came out here so I wouldn't have to listen to them but they're so loud. They're so loud. I can hear them even inside this bush, even though it's pretty dark in here.' He pulled on my arm. 'You should come in here too, so it's not as loud.'

'Ben, I can't hear anything. I don't think they're fighting.'

'Mum just said, "We should send Ben away." Didn't you hear her? She said it just now and, hang on' – his head popped out and he pressed his forehead against the window – 'now Jason is telling her he thinks I should live in an orphanage.' His shoulders went around and around.

'Wait a second.' I cracked open the door. The air inside was still and cold. 'Hello?' No answer. I opened it the whole way, stepped into the front entry. Their bedroom door was closed but no light came from underneath. I went back to Ben, closed the door behind me. Jason's car was not in the driveway.

'Mate, there's no one here.'

But he sat, with his hands over his ears, staring right into the window, and he said, 'Please make them stop.'

I went in and made him some spaghetti, fried up the mushrooms and a bit of bacon. Murray's nose went up with the bacon smell. He did a few laps of the Hills hoist, then went back the other way to get his chain untangled. I thought about throwing some out to him but that felt like betraying Ben, so I put it in the pasta instead and spooned it out into two bowls. Took them out to Ben in the bushes.

'Come out, Ben. No one's home except Murray and Bilbo.'

He crawled onto the front step, pushed his body in as close to mine as it would go. 'Maybe I heard Murray shouting,' he said. We ate our spaghetti under the front porch light. Watched the pasta move like a disco under the dancing insects.

12

AT THE END of Dad's street there had been a little antiques shop with a leadlight window. A friend of his ran it, someone he'd met at university. The shop was filled with bizarre knick-knacks: porcelain dolls with heads that came off, single shoes made from exotic animal leather, flick-knives with women's names engraved on them.

Out the back the shop opened into a tiny courtyard garden. That was the best part about it. Three brick walls, each with their own mural, hand-painted by Dad's friend. To the left, Medusa with her snakes. To the right, a minotaur, horns curling right off the wall and into nightmares. And in front, my favourite – a mermaid with a pink and blue tail, her face the size of my entire body and her eyes closed. Thinking.

Each time we visited, Dad bought me something little from the shop. He kept them all on the shelf in his kitchen, all these trinkets in a row.

When Dad disappeared, the trinkets did too.

Raf texted me before seven on Saturday morning: *Come out the front*. He had a plastic bag and he led me over the road to the spinifex block – 'It's so early,' I said – where he pulled out a couple of dry muffins. The ground was hard, rocks sticking into my legs.

'Finally. Okay. I'm going to kiss you,' he said, like the thought had occurred to him right then, leapt right out of him.

'Okay,' I said, or tried to say. My words were stuck in my throat.

He licked his lips, brought his mouth to mine. His soft mouth. It tasted like pie. Maybe that was just the way he tasted, always like pie. I opened my mouth a bit and his tongue shot in and then out again. I leaned into his shoulder.

'When are you leaving?' I said.

'Next weekend. Here to Port Augusta to start.' He sighed. 'Least we get that one week at school before I'm gone again.'

I panicked. 'We do?'

'Isn't your work experience over? I finished yesterday. Got a report saying I was a *very good sport*.'

'I, uh . . . I've got another week. Maybe my boss didn't know?'

'Are you serious?'

'Yeah, he's definitely got me rostered on next week.'

'Shit.' He frowned at his hands. 'What if we go somewhere now then? Somewhere nice.'

'Right now?'

'Yeah, today.'

'Like a restaurant?'

'Uh, no. Here? No. Somewhere good.'

'Like on a date?'

He shrugged, one-dimpled. 'Maybe.'

He had a great-uncle in Wallaroo, a fishing town about a hundred kilometres down the Yorke Peninsula. The uncle was keen to have us for the weekend, and Ben too, if he wanted to come. Raf's brother would take us. He had a rusted-out Commodore but he'd rebuilt the engine himself and it would definitely get there. A kind of road trip.

'Don't you have football stuff?' I said, but they all had the weekend off before their big week of training for the trip ahead.

We asked Mum as a courtesy. She was half-asleep anyway, took five seconds to look up from the couch and grunt. 'Have you eaten?' I said. She just stared ahead. I thought about calling someone, for a minute. Maybe even a doctor. But her phone rang and she cooed into it and waved me away. The deep lines around her eyes moved while she spoke.

'Who'll look after Bilbo?' I said to Ben.

'I gave him a cricket,' he said.

'Just one?'

'He only eats one a day. Or if I can't find any crickets, sometimes I give him a bit of sausage. But he likes to eat stuff he can catch.'

Raf's brother's girlfriend took the passenger's seat, and Ben squeezed between us in the back. Raf reached his arm around the back of my brother, stroked my hair with his fingertips. My body froze, but my skin flushed with goosebumps.

'You ever been to Wallaroo, Benno?'

'Nope. I've been to Adelaide, Noarlunga, Aldinga, Victor Harbor and Port Elliot and I think one time to Normanville to get a vanilla slice.' That had been Nonno, taking us to Normanville. After Dad disappeared. The bakery there was legendary and we had sat on the verandah with milkshakes and talked about everything except Dad.

'But never Wallaroo? I'm offended.'

Ben frowned. 'I'm sorry.'

'He's joking,' I said.

'Mostly joking.' He looked at me across Ben's head.

The morning was warm for winter, and Trey's car didn't have air-conditioning so we drove with all the windows down. My hair whipped at my eyes, but the salted air renewed my skin.

We stopped halfway at a town called Port Broughton, which had a big red pub and a jetty in a huge T shape. While Trey got petrol, Raf took us out to the end of the jetty, where it split into two, and we watched the locals fishing and jumping.

'It must be freezing in there,' I said.

''Course it is. It's bloody winter. Gives you a real rush, though. You should try it.' He pulled off his shirt. His body was hard and dewy with sweat.

'I'll just watch.'

'Suit yourself.' He took a long run-up, hurdled the barrier and leapt into the water, landing with a *slap!* below. Ben looked over the edge, wrapped his arms around his body.

'It's a long way down,' he said. A *woo!* shot up. 'Do you reckon I should try it?'

'Mum would kill me.' Raf called out from the water, something unintelligible, and laughed. 'Go on, do it.'

Ben was tiny, shivering on the jetty in his shorts, but he pulled himself over the barrier and stood there for a while with his back to the sun.

'Come on, Ben!' came the voice from below.

He dropped like a marble, straight and silent. After a second, a tiny splash, and a roar of applause from Raf. They went twice more before Trey found us, shouted about us getting his car wet and stormed ahead. Raf pulled me to him and his breath was all over my face, right up next to my ear. In the car, he wedged his hand between his leg and mine and it was warm and rough.

The whole drive had been flat and dry, but we pulled in to Wallaroo around a new housing estate and at the other end, the water broke through. Trey took us through town and along the coast, past the limestone buildings and the silos and out to a squat weatherboard house one street back from the sea.

'This is it. Unpack your shit.'

I just had a few things in my school bag, but Ben had brought his usual collection of bits and pieces, and they clinked together as we walked. The uncle greeted us at the front door, smiling, arms wide.

'My boys,' he said, and smushed the guys' heads together under his own. They didn't fight him; if anything, the hug lingered. He hugged us, too, me and Ben squashed into one person by a stranger who had shown us more affection in ten seconds than our mother had in three months. 'I'm Reg. But call me Uncle Reg.'

Trey left with his girlfriend and a sleeping bag.

'Where are they going?' I said.

'Where do you reckon?' said Reg, and he winked.

'Camping,' Raf said, pushing Reg through the front door.

He had put on a breakfast spread of fresh fruit and tiny fried fish, and we ate under his pergola and he smoked a metal pipe that he tapped on the table with a click.

It was comfortable. I stretched my legs, extended them all the way under the table until they reached the ends of my toes. Let out a sigh I'd been holding since who knew when. I saw Mum's face for a second, her eyes shrunken back into her skull and her skin pulled over it, tight as cling wrap. Tried to remember her before, when the flat hadn't been sold, but just saw her with her head on the table and the flies buzzing around.

'Uncle Reg,' Ben said, with his mouth full of melon, and the old man turned to look at him, 'have you ever tried turning a frog inside out?'

'No, I never have. It sounds dangerous.'

'It's not. My friend Yiannis showed me once when we went in his parents' caravan while they were out for dinner. We weren't supposed to go in there but he said their other toilet wasn't working so we had to go in there, and there was a frog in the toilet. Do you ever get frogs in your toilet?'

'Sure do. Green ones. Brown ones.' Ben laughed at brown ones. 'You ever seen a snake in a toilet, fella?'

'A snake in the toilet?' Ben's eyes were wide. 'What if it bit, you know. Your, you know.'

'Balls?'

Raf spat his drink across the table.

'Maybe just check before you sit down then, huh?' Uncle Reg smiled and winked again, so easy, like it was the only emotion he had.

Ben and I would share a room, but instead of overlooking a dead lawn we could open the window and hear the ocean, shouts from people walking their dogs in the afternoon sun. There were bunk beds and another single one with clean sheets and a single daisy in a jar.

'He must have lots of visitors,' Ben said.

'I think Raf has a big family.'

'Do you think there are really snakes in the toilet?'

'Hope I don't find out.'

Later on we left Ben peeling prawns with Reg, and Raf took me for a walk down to the foreshore. 'This is where I grew up,' he said. 'My best mate Eddie lived three doors down from Reg and next to us was my dad's friend from the army and on the other side of him was my gran.'

'Is Reg your dad's brother? Your mum's brother?'

He kicked the sand. 'Nah. He's … he's not really my uncle. Not my blood uncle, anyway.'

'Oh.'

He dropped into the sand and bent forward over his knees. 'He's a foster carer. You know, takes kids in when they've got nowhere to go. Just until they're ready to go home again.'

'Why did you need to go to a foster carer?' I sat down next to him. 'Am I allowed to ask?'

'Yeah, 'course you are.' He rubbed my knee. 'Mum was sick. Couldn't look after herself, let alone Trey and me.'

'Sick?'

'She had breast cancer. We were kids, we couldn't help out. Dad was at work all the time and Trey started skipping school so they sent us down here. It was cool though. Gran knew Uncle Reg for years before we arrived. I'd met him heaps of times.'

'You couldn't go with your gran?' I imagined Nonno bent over in his garden, too crooked to take us in.

'Gran? Nah, her house is full of cats.'

'Oh, right. But your mum got better?'

'Yeah, she got better. Remission, anyway. She says you never go round saying cancer is *cured*.' He waved his hand towards the sea. 'So, yeah. Six months here with Reg, cricket on the beach, barbecues at night. Same as now. Nearly didn't want to go home.'

'Do you miss it here? Like, are you homesick?'

'Not really. Even less to do here than in Port Flinders. Same goes pretty much all the way round, 'course, far as Port Lincoln. Anyway.' He leaned back on his elbows, and I did the same. We sat that way for minutes, watching the water come and go.

Finally, I said, 'Well, I am. Homesick, I mean.'

'I know,' he said. The sand was warm between us, our fingers nearly touching.

'I miss getting up in the morning and knowing where I fit in the world.'

He reached his arm around my shoulders and pulled me to him. 'I've got a pretty good idea.'

His body moved against mine and his arm was shaking holding up both of us, but we stayed like that until the tide had come in and the other families had packed up for the night.

'I'm glad your mum's okay now,' I said.

'Yeah.'

I took a deep breath. 'I don't know if mine is.'

The words came out and they hung out with all the other huge things we'd said. Raf shifted his weight. He took a breath, let it out again. His chest rose and fell. Finally, his mouth opened: 'That sucks.'

I let it sit there for a while.

'What can I do?' he said.

'I don't know. I just needed to say it.'

'I'll show you how to fish,' he said. 'This afternoon. In case you ever get stranded on a desert island without me.'

The jetty stretched out white and glossy into the water. On all sides, people dropped their lines over the edge and stared down at them, drew up a stool, laughed with their heads right back. We walked out to the end and I pulled my hat over my eyes, tried to shield them from the glittering water.

'So, this is fishing,' I said.

'I've fished before, obviously,' Ben said. 'I can show you how.'

Raf set each of us up with a reel and a bag of bait that smelled like cat food. 'Just wait here a second,' he said, picking up his phone. 'I'll be right back.' He disappeared down the jetty with his hand to his ear.

Ben pierced the cockle with his hook, pulled it right down. 'Let me do yours,' he said, and slipped another slippery blob on to my line. We cast together into the water, watched our lures disappear into the murky depths.

'I've never been fishing,' I said.

'I reckon I've been about three times,' he said. 'Yiannis showed me how to make a lure out of a real goldfish. You have to embalm it first, but you can do that with PVA. That means it won't rot.'

'Gross.'

'Yiannis said his grandfather showed him how to do it when they went to visit him in Greece.'

The lines moved with the currents.

'Do you miss him?' I said.

'Who?' He gave his line a jiggle.

'Yiannis. Everyone from school. Amir?'

He shrugged. 'I guess. Who do you miss?'

'No one,' I said.

'Nonno?'

'No, I said "no one".'

'Oh,' Ben said, and shook his line. A cold wind had come up and along the water, driving the lines further away from us. Fish curled around each other under the surface, brown ones with rainbow light reflected. They ignored our lures. When we pulled them from the water, the cockles were gone.

'Oh,' Ben said. 'I thought I put that on pretty good.'

Raf came back with cans of lemon squash. 'Hey, Benno, let me help you.' He squatted next to him and showed him how to get the bait right on and around and threaded back in on itself. 'We can go crabbing, if you like. Get a net. Or squid! You catch them with a jig. It's like heaps of hooks all stuck together.'

Ben's eyes widened. 'What do you do with a crab, once you catch it? How do you get it out of the net without getting your fingers cut off?'

'Practice.' He tossed the line into the water. 'The thing about catching crabs is, you gotta get a good little leatherjacket first. Pop them in with the net, or throw them down the bottom and the crabs go nuts for them. Cockles are for babies.'

'*I'm* not a baby,' Ben said, puffing out his chest.

We let our legs dangle over the edge of the jetty. Raf's thong slipped into the water and Ben started laughing. 'Shit!' Raf jumped to his feet.

'Can't you just jump in after it?' I said.

'Oh yeah, it's real smart to jump into the water around a bunch of fish hooks. Everyone will be real happy to hoist their lines out while I dick around trying to get my shoe back.' He laughed, sat one-shoed for a while.

Ben stared at him. Raf pointed to the taut line. 'You got one? Let's reel him in.' A tiny yellow fish swung from the hook, half its face coming away. Ben started to cry.

'I don't know if I like fishing,' he said, and Raf tossed the fish back. It landed with a slap on his floating thong.

'You'll get used to it.'

We sat in silence, staring at the thong. The men around us threw their lines in and out, sometimes with fish glinting in the sun and sometimes with bits of rubbish hanging from them. I reached under Raf's hand, pushed my fingers through his. His hand was coarse and warm, gritty where sand had stuck to sweat.

'Raf,' Ben said.

'Yeah, mate.'

'You know your Uncle Reg.'

'Yep.'

'Is he your mum's brother, or your dad's brother?'

'He's not my mum's brother or my dad's brother.'

'So he's not your uncle?'

'Kinda. A while ago my mum couldn't get out of bed, so he looked after us until she was better. Sometimes we call people like him uncles.'

'Your mum couldn't get out of bed?' I watched Ben's brain tick over. He breathed faster. 'Did they make you leave her?'

'Nah, I mean, sort of. But she was really sick.'

'So they only make you go if your mum is really sick?'

'Yeah.'

'Okay.' He breathed out. 'Our mum isn't sick.'

Raf looked to me. 'That's … good?'

'Shall we go again?' I said.

'I don't even have any shoes,' Raf said.

'You have one shoe.'

He cracked a smile. 'Fine. We can't go back empty-handed.'

'You could dive in and get Ben's fish back,' I said. It flapped around on the thong with its mouth open. 'How long do they last out of the water?'

'Few minutes.' He pulled off his shirt and dropped into the water. The lines moved in his tide.

'Dickhead!' The men got up from their stools and shook their fists. 'What are you doing? Scaring all the damn fish away!'

When he resurfaced, the fish was gone but he held his thong aloft. 'Got it!'

Ben shifted across so his body was touching mine. 'Did you see how I kept the secret then? Like you said. So no one will find out.'

'You did a great job.'

'It's sad how Raf's mum couldn't get out of bed. Do you think he was worried, living with Uncle Reg? It's pretty far from where his mum lives.'

'Maybe.'

'We won't have to do that.'

'No, we won't.'

'Because Mum's coming with us.'

'Right.'

He nodded and redid the bait, hooked it on the way Raf had shown him. Raf disappeared under the water again, appeared a minute later by my side and flicked water from his hair like a dog.

'You're a magician,' I said, and he kissed my hands.

'You wait here with the lines. I'm going to take Ben down to the bait shop.' They ran off down the jetty, Ben shouting, 'We're gonna get crabs!' and Raf laughing with all of his body. I held both lines in one hand, drank my squash with the other. Felt it trickle from my throat into my belly and around in my veins. The sun was hot and high.

'We got a net!' Ben came charging towards me. 'Did you catch any bait for it? We can't catch crabs without any bait. Raf says we can have a crab feast. He says to eat them you just break off their legs and suck out all the insides. From their legs. Is that the grossest thing you've ever heard? He says it tastes good though.'

'Is this true, Raf?' I said. 'From their legs?'

He nodded solemnly. 'From their legs. Although if you get the itty-bitty ones, you can just fry them up and eat the whole thing, shell and all.'

'Gross!' said Ben.

And there we were, on the jetty, three of us packed tightly together, peering into the water for signs of yellow fish stupid enough to bite down on a hook. Port Flinders seemed far away. Wet and dark and in another dimension.

We caught two crabs. Three, if we counted the one that climbed into the net but then plummeted to its death on the sand as we lifted it. Ben was beside himself. Raf showed him how to lift them up by holding their backs and he ran around shouting, 'You hold them by their butts!' and waving them in the air. The first was big, with one huge claw and one tiny claw; the second was smaller, but put up more of a fight.

'That big claw will be magic,' Raf said. 'We'll have to rock paper scissors for it.'

'I'll have you know,' I said, 'that I am the reigning rock paper scissors champion at my old school and I will definitely beat you.'

'You don't even know if you like crab.'

'I'll win it just so you can't have it.'

He punched me lightly in the arm, then hooked his elbow around it. I leaned into him and we walked awkwardly together, a bit out of step, him first and then me, kind of up and down at different times. My head bounced on his shoulder. Ben ran in front of us, waving the crabs around.

Uncle Reg had done his own fishing, and he had a whole

snapper to bake in the barbecue. Ben watched him prepare it, still holding the crabs by their butts.

'Bit of lemon,' Reg said. 'Good whack of pepper. Garlic. Look, you slice the garlic up like this and then you can shove it right in the holes.' He wrapped the fish in foil. The air filled with magic smells – garlic and salt and holidays.

'What about the crabs?' Ben said. 'We caught them with leatherjackets. Have you ever done that? We had to catch the fish first and put the fish in the net – Raf bought us the net from the bait shop but I went with him – and the crabs came to eat the fish and then *whoosh!* we just grabbed them right out of the water.'

'Big day, huh.' He took the crabs from Ben, who flopped on his back in the grass.

'Huge day.'

A couple of Reg's friends arrived: a woman with orange lipstick and a potato salad, and a man wearing boardies with flowers on them, like he was on a Hawaiian holiday. She shifted the salad from one arm to the other, reached her hand out to the surfie guy and he grabbed it. They were part of the ocean, somehow, like they had crawled right out of it.

'Kids,' Reg said, 'these are my friends Gert and Terry. Me and Terry worked on the trawlers together. Years ago, huh.'

'Twenty years,' Terry said, still holding Gert's hand.

'And Gert runs the local rec centre.'

'Doing aquarobics classes for the old folk, mostly,' she said, and she had orange lipstick on her teeth as well.

When the crabs were cooked Raf showed Ben how to break them open and get the meat out. 'Like I told you,' he said. 'You just crack it like this, and there's the good stuff in there. You want the white bits. They're the best.' Ben stuck the leg in his mouth and tried to suck the meat out.

'I think I need a fork.'

'Benno, you think people in old times ate crabs with forks? Crack it and slurp it out.' Ben tried again.

'Ooh! I got a bit!' He spat. 'Ugh, it tastes like garbage that's been floating in the sea.'

'Give it here then.' The white flesh came out in one long tube. 'And you, Skye.' Raf turned to me, balled his hand into a fist. 'We've gotta fight for the big claw, remember?'

'Best of three,' I said. Paper: me. Rock: him. Paper: me. 'My reign continues.'

'The thing about these big claws is, you smash them. Like, with a hammer.' Uncle Reg passed it over. 'So you line it up like this. You don't want to get the shell in it. It'll cut your stomach open.'

'Sounds great.'

The hammer came down and the shell cracked in a couple of places. He peeled it back. The meat inside was white and orange and soft. I pulled it out with my fingertips. It smelled of the sea and sun and the little yellow fish we'd used to lure it in.

'Eat it.'

It tasted like it, too. Like salty chicken, melting on my tongue. Salty, cheesy chicken. 'This is so good,' I said.

Raf stole some from the plate. 'Finder's fee.'

We picked at the snapper straight from the foil. Wrapped our forks around salad and garlic-laden fish and bits of herbs I didn't know. Uncle Reg told stories of the time his dad had spent working in the mines, sixty years ago, heading into the middle of the Earth to find runs of copper in the soil.

'They're still there,' he said. 'Can't go wandering round Kadina in case you fall right in.' He took a big forkful of fish. 'And if you do fall in, you're dead.'

Ben gasped.

Gert said, 'Where're you kids from, then?' Her skin had been prickled with pinkness and she scratched at it while she talked.

'Adelaide,' I said, as Raf said, 'Port Flinders.'

'Oh right, Port Flinders.' Scratch. 'I got a sister in Port Flinders. Nice lady. She's a cleaner at that motel out on the main road. Near the beach. What's it called?'

No one knew.

'Well, whatever it's called. They get her to clear out all the sheets after.'

Terry's fork scraped on his plate. 'Only one reason people stay at a place like that, and it ain't the breakfast bar.'

Gert chewed, pushed her food around. 'Yep,' she said, winked at Terry. Reg snorted, Ben said, 'Huh?' and Raf squeezed my knee under the table and we all shared this joke we didn't understand, for a minute, all of us connected.

Sounds came up from the street. They were different from the trundling trucks and cars along Dyson Road, and they were different from the low drum of the desert. In Wallaroo the sounds were bright. Birds picking stuff out of the sea. People walking their dogs and shouting at other people, but only because they knew them, not because they wanted to fight them. Neighbours in their gardens clinking their dinner plates together.

After the sun had gone down we watched a movie in the front room with the breeze coming through, Raf with his arm around my shoulders and Ben in the recliner by the window, laughing as though he'd just learned how.

13

In the end, I only saw Nonno three more times after Dad left. Mum took me up there in her old bomb, Ben howling in his car seat in the back, and she waited in the driveway for me to go in on my own. Nonno didn't say much, so for a while we just sat in his front room and he offered me tea six times.

Afterwards he took me out to see his chickens, showed me how to collect the warm eggs from the roosts. We picked oranges from the closest trees, and he pointed across the fields to where he'd planted almond trees, because he'd heard a rumour about milk made from almonds and he thought it might be a good investment. Then he opened an old exercise book and found the recipe for Nonna's orange cake so we made that with kookaburras on the breeze.

'Where's Dad?' I said, without meaning to.

He went to pick up the book and the pages fell out like leaves.

We spent the next morning on the beach, hitting a cricket ball around and chasing it into the freezing water. In the early afternoon, we hugged Reg and crammed into Trey's shitty car. Ben pressed his nose to the glass and said, 'Bye,' and kept it there until Wallaroo was out of sight and we were back on the highway. Raf had me under his armpit and I read a book I'd found under the passenger's seat and listened to the way his heart tripped over itself.

Trey dropped us off at the end of our street and Raf climbed out behind me. Ben picked up his backpack. 'Thank you for driving us, Trey.' The car tore away. 'Did you have a fun time?' he said to me. 'I had a fun time. Even though the crab was a bit disgusting. Yiannis says the most delicious food in the world is the Galápagos tortoise. He says they tried to bring them back to England on boats but they kept eating them because they were so delicious.'

'Gross,' I said.

'Do you think Bilbo would be delicious?' He laughed.

'I don't think I want to find out.'

'Ben,' Raf said. 'You go on ahead, yeah? I've gotta talk to Skye about something.'

Off he went, his heart all filled with gladness. I was light as air. I imagined us back there on the jetty with the sun on our skin. Raf with his arm around me, his hand on my hip, smelling like salty chips and deodorant mixed together.

'I had a great time,' I said.

'Me too.' He slid his hand into mine. 'After the footy tour I'll be able to get my licence and we can go out to the Flinders. Camping.'

'Camping? Shit no.'

'Glamping?'

'Worse.'

'Something else then.' He was whispering, pulling my body against his. All the blood drained from me and when he kissed me, hard, for a thousand hours, I felt like nothing at all.

*

Ben was waiting for me by the door, jumping from one foot to the other.

'Skye. Skye! Get inside.' He poked his head out and looked around, like I might have been followed. 'I've found something,' he said.

'Why are you whispering?'

'I don't know. I feel like I'm going to be in trouble because I went into Jason's room when he wasn't here.'

'Where's Mum?'

'I don't know. They weren't here when I came in. I didn't know if they'd gone yet so I tried to turn the door handle to Jason's room and it just opened. He forgot to lock it.' He looked at his skinny arms. 'Or I just have superhuman strength.'

My heart beat a little faster. 'And? What did you find?'

He pulled me into the room, where he'd taken out a few things and laid them on the desk.

'Do you know what this stuff is?' he said, and I did, the burning glass and the stream of smoke, but I didn't say it. 'There're no parrots, so at least I was right that they're not sending animals overseas in plastic tubes. I couldn't find any credit cards either, so you were wrong. But what are these?' He picked up a glass pipe with a bulb on the end.

'I don't know,' I said. Believed myself, for a second. 'Did you find anything else?'

'Weird stuff, like packets of alfoil and little Ziploc bags. Money. Not heaps and heaps of money but some five-dollar notes rolled up with rubber bands around them.'

'I'm going to take a couple of photos and then we should put this back,' I said.

'Why would you take photos?' He frowned. 'Are you going to show them to the police? Don't you remember what the kids said?' He was tugging on my arm, urgent, pulling me down to his eye level.

'Not to show the police.'

'Why then?'

'I thought Raf might know something. He can help us.'

Ben's shoulders dropped loose. 'Oh,' he said. 'Yeah, Raf will help us.'

'Can you remember how you found it? Jason will really lose it if he finds out someone's been getting into his stuff.'

'Yeah.' Ben pulled out the notebook with the plan inside. 'I drew a diagram. See?' Each item on the table had a scribbled version on the paper. We carefully squeezed it all back into its original places and closed the door behind us. I tried to catch my breath but tripped over it.

Ben danced back and forth across the kitchen, grabbing things from every cupboard. 'I feel like a detective.' He put bread in the toaster. 'My teacher said she sometimes has toast for dinner because she can't be bothered cooking anymore, because her baby is taking up all the space inside her body. So then I said, I could cook toast for dinner, so you wouldn't have to.' He peered into the toaster, face lit up with the orange light.

'But I like cooking for you,' I said.

He tucked a tea towel into his shorts, like a waiter. 'We have three spreads available. Peanut butter. Vegemite. And something called *anchovy paste*.' He took the lid off and sniffed it. 'Argh! Ma'am, I don't think I can recommend the anchovy paste.' He put it back in the cupboard.

'Peanut butter sounds great.'

'Please take a seat at the table.' He shuffled around in the kitchen, disappeared out the front door for a minute, came back to spread the toast. It was cold by the time it arrived at the table. Cold, with a little spray of grass in the middle. 'It's like a restaurant,' he said, and got his own plate from the bench.

'You have to think of a name for your restaurant. So people know where to go.'

'Sad Ben's,' he said, and then he smiled.

'Well, Sad Ben's, this toast is not bad at all.'

'It's cold.'

'I like cold toast.'

'I don't mind that you're lying to make me feel better.' He gnawed on the last of his crusts, got a faraway look in his eyes like he was thinking deeply. After a bit he said, 'Does the stuff I found mean the police really will take Mum to jail?'

'Are you going to tell them?'

He crossed his arms. 'Definitely not.'

'And neither will I. So, no.'

'You just looked pretty scared when you saw it, and then you said Raf would need to help us so I thought it must be bad.' He took my empty plate, slotted it on top of his. 'What do you think it's like in jail? Would Mum go to a jail with murderers in it? I think they put murderers in their own special jails, with very high walls and guard dogs, and if you try to escape they just shoot you.'

'Who told you that?'

'Amir, I think. He liked to talk about jails.'

'Why does an eight-year-old like talking about jails?'

'Dunno. He's weird.' And then he laughed.

We watched TV for a while, some old movie with aliens in it. I got him into the shower, sat outside the door on Mum's plastic stool so he could talk to me. He told me stories about places he would go when he was all grown up, hunting for dinosaur bones on African plains and buried Aztec treasure in the rainforest. His voice ran frantic and urgent, the way it always did. I watched through the window for Jason's car, its one dim headlight. Ben had disappeared into the bathroom fog. 'Did you know' – he shouted over the water – 'a baby blue whale weighs *three tons* when it comes out? And they're mammals, so after it's born it just eats its mother's milk and gains like, a hundred kilos every day for the first year of its life?' He made a whistling sound. 'One time I found a baby bird in the playground, but it only weighed about fifty grams and when I picked it up I realised it was dead.'

'That's sad,' I said.

'Yeah, but then I gave it a funeral and Amir sang a song about how the bird's suffering was over and now it could fly free, so that made me feel a bit better.'

Headlights lit up the hallway, for a moment, and moved on. I let out a slow breath.

'Let's get you out of there,' I said. 'It's getting late. Don't want to let Mum see you up past eight.'

Water had streamed out through the crack in the glass, and Ben stood in it and shivered in his blue towel. 'Jason should use all those five dollars to get a towel heater,' he said. 'I feel like my bones are going to rattle right out of me.' Then he laughed.

'Put your PJs on.'

'But they're covered in sand and fish guts.'

'Trackies, then. Or a t-shirt at least. Look at you, you're turning into an ice princess.'

He smiled, lips thin and blue. 'Maybe a snow queen. She was evil, you know, originally.'

I rubbed his arms through the towel. 'Get dressed. Your toes are going to fall off.'

As he went to the bedroom, the hallway lit up again. A car whirred to a stop and doors slammed shut. Someone was in the driveway. I slipped on the chain lock, peered through the peephole. Jason's old Ford was parked in the street, and in the driveway was a red car I'd never seen before. Jason stood next to it with one hand on his hip and the other wrapped around Mum. Kurt was there, too. He had Jason's same bald head. They might have been laughing. It was hard to tell; laughing and yelling were so alike from behind.

I kept the chain on and went to the kitchen. Everything was

dirty, piled high in the sink with food crusted to it, some of it growing green edges.

'Skye!' The door banged, chain lock pulled on its screws. 'Open the damn door.'

'I'm on the toilet!' I waited a few seconds longer. Washed a glass and poured myself a drink. Jason pounded on the door again. Ben came out in shorts, knees visible where he'd grown taller than them.

'What's all the banging?' he said.

'Mum and Jason are home. I'm trying to decide whether or not to let them in.' I tipped the rest of my drink into the sink and went to the door, pushed it shut so I could get the lock open. Jason burst through it, still shouting.

'Where do you get off, locking us out like that?' He slammed the door open. It made a cracking sound as it hit the wall behind.

Kurt stood behind him, then Mum with her face all lit up. 'Don't worry about it, Jase. It doesn't even matter. Tell them! I'll tell them.' She was flushed red from her neck up, eyes shiny. 'We bought a new car! I mean, it's not a *new* new car, but it's pretty new. It's ex-demo. You explain it, Jase.'

'Yeah.' He shook his head, like he was trying to get his thoughts in order. He pressed the remote in his hand and the headlights went on and off. 'Big twin-turbo. Goes like the clappers.'

'The seats have bum warmers in them.'

Kurt said, 'Goes zero to a hundred in seven seconds,' right as Mum said, 'Goes zero to a hundred in seven seconds.' Kurt laughed and punched Jason's arm.

'You got a good one here, brother,' he said. Mum beamed like she was in a pageant.

'And the headlights turn on by themselves when it gets dark!' She giggled into her hands. 'I've never had an ex-demo car before. Remember my shitty old car, Ben? Remember the time you got your fingers stuck in the boot?'

He frowned. 'Yeah, of course I remember. One of them got broken.'

She rubbed his head. 'Well, that'll never happen in this car. You can't even close the boot, you have to press a button on the remote thingy.'

'That's heaps better!' He pushed past Mum and ran around the back of it, tried to pry the boot open with his bare hands. Mum pressed the button; it floated up like it had a balloon attached to it. 'Cooooool,' he said.

'Ben, it's cold.' I followed him out, grabbed the waist of his shorts. 'You should get back inside, or put some shoes on at least.'

'Yeah,' he said. 'You're right. My toes are like tiny little ice cubes. You could chop them off and put them in lemonade and that would be a pretty good drink, wouldn't it?' He gave a shrill laugh. 'Don't, though. I need my toes to walk. Do you know your toes are how you balance when you walk? I guess if we were kangaroos we would use a tail, but humans haven't had tails since … well, *ever*, unless you count when you're still in the womb. I don't think I count that, though.'

Jason looked up from where he was polishing the bonnet with his jacket. 'God, you talk a lot of shit,' he said, and nothing more.

Mum made us look at the car for a few more minutes. Showed us the dials inside, the way they lit up blue when you had the headlights on. It told us how far it could drive until empty (four hundred and nine k's), and the name of the song that was playing on the radio ('Wrecking Ball'), and how cold it was outside (8.4 degrees). At the last part, she agreed it was too cold for Ben to be outside without shoes on, and Jason pressed the button to lock everything up. The whole car bleeped in the darkness, flashed the driveway into a false daylight.

'Gonna head off,' Kurt said. 'Cheers for the car, Jase. It'll come in real handy when the baby gets here.'

Inside, Ben turned on the crap heater in the lounge room, shoved his feet right up to it.

'Have to warm up my feet before I get frostbite. But not too fast. You can get hyp*er*thermia from heating up too fast. But did you know, people who get hyp*o*thermia, the last thing they do is take off all their clothes? They get so confused they think they're hot so they take everything off, even though they're so cold their limbs are probably going to fall off.'

'That's weird,' Mum said. She was smiling at him, standing in the doorway with her arms folded across her chest but with a look on her face like she couldn't believe he was hers. He smiled back up at her. Wriggled his toes in front of the glow of the heater.

'It's too late by then,' he said. 'Once you've taken off all your clothes, you're dead, even if they find you. That's what happens on Mount Everest. All the people who die on Mount Everest get left up there because it's too hard to bring them back down again. But it's so cold they're just preserved there. When other people climb it, they use the dead bodies to navigate. Isn't that gross?' He pushed a moth into the heater and it hissed and popped.

'Grosser than setting moths on fire?' I said.

'Yeah.' He screwed up his face. 'Heaps grosser.'

Jason grabbed Mum's shoulder. 'Gonna hop in the shower,' he said.

'Okay, darl. Did you see how I knew the same thing Kurt knew? Did you hear him? "You got a good one here", he said.'

'Yeah, I heard,' Jason said, went to the bathroom and closed the door. His big voice boomed underwater, singing something out of tune. Mum touched the keys on the front table, looked at Ben again with her big eyes.

'Hey, Benny.'

'Yeah?'

'Let's take the new car for a spin. I'll show you how the windscreen wipers shoot soap all over the window.'

'Really?'

'Yeah, we can drive down to Port Pirie and get a soft serve from McDonald's.'

He was already up, trying to find his shoes under the table. 'Can we get chocolate fudge sauce?'

'Yeah, 'course,' she said. Twirled the keys around on her finger. Jason's booming still coming from the bathroom, steam streaming out from under the door. He would be twenty minutes, at least. Never thought about saving water. Always had it going so hot, like a sauna.

'What about me?' I said.

Mum turned to me, dropped the smile a little but not completely. 'You want a sundae, Skye? Didn't know sixteen-year-olds still ate sundaes with their mums.' She punched my arm, just a soft tap near my shoulder. 'Go on, get a jumper on.'

'Will Jason mind?'

'Mind? Why would he? I chose it.' But she looked to the bathroom door as we left, told us to be quiet when we shut the flyscreen door.

The road was practically empty. A few trucks shot past with their big lights in our eyes. One overflowed with sheep, still alive but with the saddest faces, all drooping down like they were trying to drip right out of the truck and onto the road. For a while we followed behind one filled with pebbles, and they shot out and nicked the windscreen, bounced off into the night. Ben squealed every time, and Mum laughed. She laughed and Ben squealed and I thought about how long it had been since I'd heard both sounds. Watched the way Mum's face got tight at her ears, where her mouth curled around at the ends, and Ben's skinny face with his teeth bursting right out of it. I wanted to hug both of them. Sat in the back seat by myself instead, leaned against the door and tried to remember the way they sounded in case I needed it later.

Later. When we were gone. After we'd stowed away in Ben's bushranger room and got the train to Adelaide.

I thought about what we'd do when we arrived. It would be

colder in Adelaide. Raining, maybe. We could get off at the station right in the city and find a motel to stay in for the night. Catch a taxi out to Nonno's farm the next day, or maybe after two days so we had a chance to see the city a bit. I could take Ben to the museum, or the zoo, or both. We could go to the reptile enclosure and see some proper lizards, a few snakes, a crocodile. I still wasn't sure whether Mum would be there with us.

'You been to the zoo, Ben?'

He twisted around to look at me. 'What zoo?'

'The Adelaide Zoo. You know, near the river.'

He frowned. 'Oh yeah, I went with school. Do you know they have *pandas* there? Do you know how much it costs to buy a panda for your zoo? When we were at the zoo, Yiannis asked the panda keeper how much, and she said it might be five hundred thousand dollars. Do you even know how much that is? You can buy an Aston Martin DB9 with that much money. Or two if you get second-hand ones. That's the car James Bond has.'

Mum squeezed his knee. 'Not as good as this car though, right?' She grabbed the steering wheel with both hands and we surged forward, close to the truck full of pebbles. Our headlights reflected back from its metal belly. 'Watch,' she said. Took off around the outside of it, floored it down the wrong side of the road. It was so dark we could only see the metres in front of us. No streetlights. Not even any moon, only a sliver of it hanging lonely in the sky. My guts pushed back against the seat as the truck disappeared behind us. Mum slipped over to the left-hand side, let the car slot in, find its rhythm again.

'That was awesome!' Ben fiddled with the dashboard. 'Not very fuel efficient though, see? We went from 397 kilometres left to only 382 kilometres.'

'Helpful passenger, you are.' Mum took her eyes off the road to admire him. The car filled up with the sound of her phone ringing. 'Ooh!' she said. 'It comes through the stereo.

Hands-free, you know, so we don't crash.' She pressed a button on the wheel. 'Jase?'

His voice was low and steady: 'Where the fuck are you?'

She looked at Ben, forced her face into a smile. 'You're on speaker, doll.'

'And?'

'And the kids can hear you.'

'So you *did* take the car. Who said you could do that?'

She was nervous, gripping the wheel so tightly her knuckles were white. 'I said.' Her voice came out narrow, like it was squeezing through the hole in her face without permission.

'What's that?'

'I did.' Even quieter. 'I said I could take it.' Jason's breathing was heavy on the other end. Ben fiddled with the dials, turned Jason's breath up and down. Mum slapped his hand away. 'We're going to Port Pirie to get sundaes. I thought I'd bring you back one. Strawberry, right? On the top and bottom?' She was talking fast, trying to get it all out before the breathing stopped. Ben tapped all the buttons again. 'Ben, stop it.' *Tap tap tap*.

'What's he doing? Better not be mucking around with anything.' The lights on the dashboard were blue and green and red and Ben touched them all, and Jason's breathing went up and down and Mum turned around and shouted, 'Just stop it!' and Ben pressed the big one on the steering wheel and Jason's breathing stopped. The radio came back on. Mum took a deep breath, put the indicator on and pulled over to the side of the road. The truck full of pebbles went past, roaring along until its light disappeared around the bend.

Mum was quiet. She put her head on the steering wheel, wrapped her arms around it. Her back rose and fell but no sound came out. Ben looked at her. He looked at me. The car's engine whirred and then shuddered into idleness. A man on the radio crackled something about a wind warning for coastal areas.

Two more trucks went by. Right up close to the car, so we shook in their currents. Mum turned the key and the car sighed into silence.

Ben squeaked, a funny noise from the back of his throat. I reached over to him and squeezed his hand; it was damp and shaking. 'Mum?' he said. She grunted. 'Sorry I pressed the wrong button.' She shook her head, shoulders moving up and down. Somewhere under her hair, she was crying.

A whisper: 'I told you to stop.'

My heart caught a bit, skipped like it was stuck on repeat. I squeezed Ben's hand again and smiled at him in a way I hoped was comforting but he probably couldn't see me anyway, in the dark. I cleared my throat. 'He didn't mean to.'

Mum sighed. 'Shut up, Skye.'

'And anyway, Jason was being a dick.'

'I said, shut up.'

Ben was grabbing my hand right back, turning his head from me to Mum and back again. 'Are we still going to get sundaes?' he said. 'We should get sundaes. I think McDonald's is open until ten o'clock.' Voice rolling along, faster and faster. 'Look, if you press this button the clock lights up even though the car is off. It's only nine fifteen. We've got heaps of time. Maybe we can even do dine-in, if you want. You can come on the playground with me, Mum. Go down the slide? You love doing that.' His whole body jittered. Floppy hair bounced with him, so he looked like he was dancing.

Mum turned the key. The dashboard lit up again, one dial after another like a private jet. She pushed her hair back from her face and pulled down the sun visor. A light went on above it. She peered into the tiny mirror, patted her eyes where they were puffy from crying. Then she pulled out of the emergency lane and did a sweeping u-turn across the highway.

'Aren't-we-getting-a-sundae?' Ben said, in one urgent breath.

'No,' she said. Stared straight ahead with her hands on the wheel. Ahead of us, a truck's tail-lights disappeared into the blackness. Across the fields, the train let out its long moan.

Jason was waiting at the door when we pulled in. We couldn't see his face, with the light shining from behind him, but his arms were crossed and he had his legs wide apart. Blocking our way. Mum turned off the ignition and the three of us sat there for a bit, until the headlights turned off on their own.

'Okay,' Mum said. 'Okay.' Ben went to open his door. 'Wait. Ben. Jason's going to be pretty mad, okay? We shouldn't have taken his car without asking.'

'*But it's your car,*' I said. '*You chose it.*'

She didn't look at me. 'Just wait here for a minute. Both of you.' Her door clicked open. Jason shifted his weight, started pointing his finger right in Mum's face. She bent around it, crooked and twisted to avoid being jabbed in the eye. Head down. Arms by her side. It was hard to tell if she was talking, but Jason's voice came through. Not the words, but the sound of the words. Sharp. Like they were coming in at Mum from way up high, like he was throwing lightning at her. She kept standing there with her shoulders rolled forward.

She came back to the car and clicked the door open. Ben was already climbing out. 'Come inside.' Voice straight and even.

'No thanks,' I said.

'It's not a suggestion.'

I went in, closed the door behind me.

Jason said, 'Ben, go to your room.' He protested, my brother, said he wasn't going to his room and if Jason had something to say he could say it to all of us, but it didn't matter. 'I can stand here all night,' he said, with his face scowling half onto the floor, and eventually Ben left. Pulled the door closed tight behind him, then pulled it again so it latched.

The three of us stood in the hallway. Mum, shoulders down. Jason, face lit up with anger. Me, small and quiet inside my body, a much tinier version of myself right down by my knees, but upright on the outside. Ready for a fight, if that's what he was offering. I wasn't Mum. I wasn't going to roll my shoulders forward.

Jason looked to the spare room, maybe to check the door was really closed. He coughed. Mum rubbed his arm and he pulled it away like she was on fire.

'You got something to tell us?' he said to me. He talked fast, trying to make sense of the words as he spat them out.

'Me? About what?'

'Nothing you fucked around with while we were picking up the car?'

We'd been so careful, putting everything back exactly where Ben found it. He had the diagram and everything.

'No,' I said.

His feet fell heavy on the lino. 'You're a liar. Linda, she's lying.'

I looked at them, from one to the other. Mum couldn't even lift her head, she was that scared of him. She slunk around in the dark part of the hallway.

'Lemme ask you again.' He turned to face me. 'What were you doing in my room?'

Mum's thin voice: 'Our room.' He ignored her.

'I wasn't,' I said.

Mum made some involuntary sound with her throat. Jason hopped from foot to foot, ran his hand across his head a couple of times. 'That's my private shit. It's mine. Jesus.' He started pacing along the hallway. Stopped at the bathroom door, leaned against it with his head down. 'What gives you the right? You think this is your house? Like I didn't work my fucking arse off to –' Mum grabbed at him. 'You!' He turned to her. 'Might've mentioned your kids that first day. No? Like it might have been important? In hindsight?'

She was nothing. A bit of paper crumpled on the floor. Squeaked out at him: 'You're right.' And I stood there with my heart pounding, waiting for Jason to do something, to come over, to lift his hand to me, to do something, anything.

'Why's it such a big deal?' I said.

He came closer. 'You're so smart. Why don't you tell me? Smart girl. So smart.' He laughed, coughed. Mum said nothing. Twisted herself around so she wasn't facing either of us but still looked like she was. He came at me with his arms like cages. Pushed me against the wall, put his hands flat above me so I was inside the cave of him. His breath reeked, rings of sweat stained on his t-shirt.

'I don't know what you're on about,' I said, and swallowed a couple of times, tried to get the spit to go back down.

'Last chance.' He drew up so close I felt the heat from his skin, the sweaty, slobbering anger.

I took a deep breath. Watched the hallway slide away from me, pulled myself up as tall as I could. Sucked in all the courage I had, all the bravery I'd ever collected from watching Ben going around in the world exactly the way he wanted.

'I already told you, I don't know.'

He raised his hand, curled it into a fist. Mum squeaked again, invisible in the corner behind the pot plant. He pounded against the wall, first, like he was having a practice run.

'They'll see that at school,' I said. 'Don't want to hit me where they can see. People'll ask questions.'

He brought his face right up to mine, putrid breath pouring from his mouth. 'Fine.' My heart raced, watched him bring his balled-up hand like it was in slow motion. Pain shot from my ribs to my guts as he punched me, at the *ugh!* shooting out of him. I stopped myself from doubling over. Went rigid with the cannonball pain. Scooped up the vocal chords I'd dropped into my belly and said, 'Piss-weak.'

Jason turned, went to his bedroom and slammed the door. The floor danced beneath me.

'Thanks for your help,' I said, but she was silent.

'Skye?'

Ben's voice came soft and worried from his side of the room.

'Just going to lie down for a sec,' I said, and eased my body down. 'Just for a sec. Then we'll go to sleep, okay?'

We spoke quietly, in the darkness. Like we were hideaways. Mum and Jason moved around in the kitchen, clanging plates together and arguing. I could never grab the words of their arguments. That was probably a good thing.

Ben shifted under his sheets. 'What happened?' he said. 'Was Jason angry about me going into his room?'

'No. Don't worry about it.' A dull ache stretched from my bellybutton around to my spine. It was hot, too. Radiating like a star. I let my hand rest flat on my belly, pushed my fingers into the worst of the pain. It helped a bit. Made it seem like I was the one doing the injury.

'We're gonna leave soon, right?' He didn't even speak, just exhaled the words. 'I've already started packing.'

The plan wasn't finished. It was still just *EARN MORE MONEY.* I hadn't been able to find out where Nonno lived, either. Somewhere in the hills, somewhere in Happy Valley, where Dad had sometimes stopped off at the tiny petrol station on the corner and got us a Frosty Fruit. That wasn't much to go on. Couldn't rock up to the train station in Adelaide and ask them for directions to a petrol station. But what would we do instead? Stay here, wait for Jason to corner one of us again? The pain in my guts flared.

'Yeah,' I said. 'Really soon. I've just gotta do a bit more work at the supermarket, then we're out. Okay? All you have to do is go with the others in the walking bus and keep quiet.'

'I'm not very good at keeping quiet,' he said. 'My new teacher says I talk too much. He says no one cares about my stupid stories. I told him, they're not stories, they're facts and information and it's good to learn things.' He sighed. 'He sent me into the corridor.'

'I like your facts and information.'

He said nothing for a minute. Then: 'Can I get in with you?'

I pulled up my blanket. 'Duh.' He climbed in, nudged his small body against mine. His knees and elbows were cold but sweaty, fear creeping out of them. When he breathed, his ribs popped and cracked. I wrapped my arms around him and it was like hugging a Rubik's cube, the sharpness of his bones.

'Mum is coming with us, right? Back to Adelaide?' I lost my nerve for a second, thinking about her hiding behind the pot plant. 'Skye?'

'Yeah,' I said. 'Of course.'

'Why hasn't she talked about it?'

I thought of her standing quiet in the corner. 'She's just keeping it secret so Jason doesn't find out.'

'Oh. That's smart.'

'Yep.'

He fell asleep quickly. The arm I had underneath his head had gone numb but I used it to move the curtains aside. Looked at the moon, its thin crescent above the fence. Thought about the plan again, about getting to Nonno's and finishing school. Wondered what it might be like, five years from now, to look at the moon again. And then I was asleep, too.

14

A FEW MONTHS after Dad left, I went on an excursion down at the docks. There was a Greenpeace ship there and we went with school to tour around it. We were allowed to go right into the belly of it, down where you could only see water through the portholes. Everyone said it was a big deal, Greenpeace being there. It was the last place they were docking before they went to save whales in Antarctica, so there were journos all over the place.

In the morning Mum had the newspaper and there was a photo of the ship on the third page. I looked and looked for myself, looked through all those people climbing on every part of it for the hat I'd been wearing.

And there at the edge, next to the painted rainbow, was my dad. He had his back to the camera, staring up at the sails, but he had that band t-shirt on and I could tell it was him by the way he was slouching.

In the morning the sky was orange, opaque, and Ben was gone. I was on the phone to Raf in seconds, barking at him around the panic in my throat.

'We'll find him,' he said. 'He can't have gone far.'

'Who knows how long he's been gone? He's *smart*. He could be anywhere. What if he hitchhiked? What if he's stowed away on the train? He could be in Alice Springs. He could be in Adelaide. He could be anywhere but here.'

'I'll be there in five minutes. I'll run. Stay where you are.'

'And do nothing? Are you joking? I have to look for him.' Pulling on my runners. 'I don't know where to start.' Dragging my hair into a ponytail. 'At the beach? Would he be at the beach? What was the name of that pizza place I took him to? Should we call the police? Do you think Mum knows he's missing?'

'Skye!'

'What day is it? Monday? Will you get in trouble if you're not at school?'

'Probably. Will *you* get in trouble if you're not at work?'

A small panic grabbed me. 'What? Why would I be at work?'

'Work experience? They'll wonder where you are.'

'Oh! Yeah. No? Who cares?'

'Okay, just let me get my shoes on, yeah? We'll start at the start.'

I tried to think of every single place he had been, made a list that started with him pissing on the foreshore and ended with him curled up in my bed. He might be at the spinifex block, or at the jetty, or in the chicken shop. He might be in Wallaroo. He might be at the train station. The tip, the post office, the supermarket. The hospital.

'Do we call the police?' I said. 'Is he a missing person?'

Raf peered into his phone. 'Nah, let's not call the police yet. We'll probably still find him on our own and then we would have wasted their time. You know what the police do when you waste their time?'

'No? The only time I've ever met the police was when they visited my school.'

'Well.' He tapped the screen a few times. 'You don't want to waste their time.'

We went south, first, along Raf's street and across the creek. I didn't know what we were looking for. Clues? Ben's red jumper hanging from a tree? Was he the kind of kid who would leave clues? Notes, maybe. I looked for them, for his jangled handwriting to lead us to him. Raf tapped his phone a few more times. The creek was full of water and he frowned at it, didn't make eye contact with me.

'He's not in the water,' I said.

'No, yeah, he definitely isn't.'

'He wouldn't even come this way. We always go down the main road.'

'Yeah, yeah, you would, from your place. This is nowhere near you.'

I grabbed his hand, pulled him along with the current, which slammed along the withered beds on its way to the ocean. We reached the main road and climbed up onto the bridge. People had started their days, flipping their signs over to OPEN, standing out on the street with mugs in their hands.

'Okay, let's ask them. Someone must have seen him.'

We went everywhere. Into the pub, which wasn't open yet but still had a sad old man with his head down on the bar. He grunted, and the publican polished the space around him while he spoke to his glass. She hadn't seen a kid. Not a kid in a red jumper, or a kid in a hat, or a kid with pelican shoes. We went to the supermarket, where Daryl's eyes went all over Raf, and Jeannie said, *Everything all right, love?* but the automatic doors were already closing and I thought of Raf asking me, just for a second, if I should call work, but there was no time for that. We went to the chicken shop, and the other chicken shop, and the doctor's surgery, in case he'd had an accident and someone had taken him in, and the train station, where a woman waited to be taken somewhere else, and down to the jetty. But he wasn't building anyone into a sandcastle. He wasn't getting stung by a jellyfish. He wasn't anywhere.

A shadow was suddenly on us. It had a thick smell, a corpse smell. The drunk from the pub. He lurched towards us with his arms out, missed Raf's shoulder and went stumbling into the sand, fell to his knees.

'You right, mate?' Raf shoved him with his shoe. 'Bludgers.'

The backs of my knees were suddenly warm. I turned around, came face to face with him, dick out, pissing on my shoes.

'Are you *serious*?' Raf kicked the sand into his face, into the hole where his mouth had opened into laughter. The morning collapsed on me. And then the week on top of that, took me by the shoulders and forced me to the sand, too, into the wet sand.

Raf went down the list, putting furious lines through the places we'd been.

'School,' he said. 'We haven't tried his school. We should have gone there first. Why didn't we go there first? It makes so much sense that he'd be at school. He wouldn't want to get in trouble. He'd definitely go there. Quick! Skye, come on.'

My heart pounded, out and around the corners and across the creek and past the caravan park and to the final stop of the walking bus. The school gate croaked behind us, slipped into its compulsory latch. The woman at reception blinked, pushed her glasses up her nose. 'Ben Teller?' She clicked around on her computer. 'Wasn't here at the bell.'

My heart dropped. 'Did anyone call to see where he was?'

She clicked a few more times. 'Says we left a message with his father.'

'Right.' I thought of Jason, turning over his five-dollar notes on the glass table, letting his phone ring out in the next room.

I burned from head to toe. Couldn't catch my breath all the way, like it had stuck to the top of my throat. 'We're going to have a look around.'

'Is something wrong?' she said. Saliva caught on the hairs above her lip. Droplets on a leaf.

'Yeah, something's wrong. My brother is missing.' Raf slammed the door behind us. The receptionist blinked out, put the phone receiver to her ear.

'Those clouds look bad,' I said.

Raf squeezed my hand. 'He's a resourceful kid. I bet he's found a dry spot somewhere.'

We hunted past the kids bottled into their classrooms, their fishy mouths opening and closing with lessons.

In the corner of the playground, near the boundary, under the fence with the wattle falling over it, I saw his little shoulders. Their right angles, the way they hunched over his whole body, as though he hadn't grown into them yet. He was facing away from us but he'd brushed his hair so it shone.

'Raf! Raf, he's over there.' I pointed. We ran and tripped and collided with our relief. Ben looked up at us.

'I was looking for your parrot,' he said. 'Parrots can live to be a hundred years old. Yiannis says people who live to be a hundred years old can't even go to the toilet on their own. He says they have to carry a bag around in their pyjamas.'

'Oh yeah?' I said, breath in torrents.

'His papou is a hundred and one years old. Yiannis helped him go to the toilet once. He said he smelled like if an underwear drawer had bird crap in it.'

'Ben!'

He gave a crooked little smile. 'Anyway, I wanted to show Bilbo where I come at lunch.' He pulled the tortoise from behind his back. 'We're not supposed to bring pets to school but he's so quiet I just keep him in my bag under my desk and if my teacher asks what the scratching noise is I just tell her I have nits.'

'We were worried about you,' I said. 'I went to get you out of bed and you weren't there.'

'But I was at school.'

'But it wasn't even seven thirty.'

'I got up early so I could find some frogs. I heard them during the night. Did you hear them? When it rains all these frogs just appear from nowhere but it takes a few weeks for the tadpoles to hatch and it rained the whole time when we first got here so I've been waiting for them.'

'Did you find any?'

'Nah. I found a big centipede, though. Most centipedes don't have a hundred legs. I don't know why they call them centipedes.'

'I nearly called the police.'

'They might have brought their dogs with them. They're called K-9, did you know that? There's a whole squad of dogs and they're called K-9 because it sounds like "canine". Don't you think that's clever?'

'Super clever.'

'They could've taught Murray some manners. Right and wrong.' His shoulders shook. In a quiet voice, he said, 'I did run away, today. I went to school but I was still running away. It was just the only place I could think of running away to.'

Raf took out his phone and I heard Claud's panicked voice answer.

'He's at school,' Raf said. 'We're here with him.' Ben pushed his nose under my arm, stuck his little head out at me.

'I'm a tortoise,' he said. 'You smell weird.'

On the other end of the phone, Claud let out all her breath and I heard her echoing voice: 'Where was he? At school? What a bloody legend.'

*

Daryl was waiting for me by the automatic doors. Shirt pulling near his bellybutton, hands on his hips.

'You're late,' he said. 'What the hell was that stunt earlier?'

'It's only nine thirty. I had an emergency.'

He raised his eyebrows. 'An emergency, huh? What kind of emergency?'

'Probably none of your business.' The words fell out, waiting for him to grab them and shake them, but he didn't.

'It is when you're on my payroll.' He handed me the texta. He was amped up, all this positivity leaking out of him. He moved quickly, easily, like something was lifting him off the ground.

'Why're you so happy?'

'You should know,' he said, and jabbed his finger into my ribs. I winced; Jason's fist, the bruise that stretched from bellybutton to breastbone. 'I've got a promotion. They're moving me to head office. Pay rise, too. Thirty-two dollars an hour.' He puffed himself out, his accordion sides, until he was shaped like a gold trophy. 'How about that?'

'Great.' I crossed out the old prices, wrote in the new ones. Put a sticker over the part of the meat that had turned grey in the freezer, so no one would notice it until they got home.

'It's in Port Pirie. They've got me starting the week after next.'

'Good for you.'

He dragged a crate along the floor, sat on it with his eyes pointing up to me. 'That deal we made, though.' His fingers made their way to my left hand. I kept scribbling with the right one, crossing out the numbers and writing new numbers. His sweat on my skin. The ragged breaths popped out of him as clouds in the cold room. I said nothing. 'Skye. I put myself on the line getting you these hours. We had a deal.'

Five dollars. Three dollars. A pack of steaks that expired yesterday, cross it out, put a sticker over the date. Six dollars. Four shiny chicken breasts, half price. His hand on my hand.

The cold air, pulling my throat open to get past the rising bile. Eleven dollars for a lamb leg. Two schnitzels at seventy per cent off. I put them aside to buy myself later. The clock in the freezer room said it was nearly ten.

I thought of the money growing in my account. Tried to remember what I'd said to Daryl that day, exactly what I'd promised him. I looked down at him, his hair slicked back in a greasy wave, bags under his eyes, trousers pulled tight across his thighs.

'No we didn't.'

He smiled, squeezed my hand harder. 'I scratched your back.' He had his other hand on the back of my head and he pushed hard against it. 'You gotta scratch mine. It's only fair.' He gave my hair a sharp tug, pulled my mouth right into his lap. The smell. Shit. He let go of my hand, unzipped his fly. Blackness. The whir of the freezers. The texta still in my hand like a knife. Both his hands on the back of my head. I couldn't breathe, didn't want to, couldn't get the air into my chest but felt every bit of his wet skin on my cheek, on my neck. Tried to pull my head back against his hands. Tried to turn my face away but couldn't. Tried to get my brain together. He let one hand go from my head, just enough, and I bit the chafed flesh inside his thigh.

He jumped, pushed the crate away. 'You little bitch,' he spat. Someone was shouting in the store. 'This isn't over. I should fire you.' He limped out, heavy on the side where a little bitch had got her teeth into his skin.

After he was gone I pulled up my shirt, touched my skin where purple and blue had bloomed across my abdomen. *EARN MORE MONEY.*

I wrote the numbers, faster and faster, eight dollars, six dollars, a dollar fifty. Grabbed the bin and coughed my empty guts into it, the hot rash of reflux in my throat. Crossed out the numbers, put the stickers on, shook the texta to get the ink moving. In the freezer room, the outline of him still hung where he'd been, bits of his sweat stuck to the frozen air.

Ben and I sat at the kitchen table with the notebook open. It was dark already. Mum and Jason had taken the new car somewhere, told me again to keep out of his stuff and balled up his hand while he said it.

'It doesn't have to be perfect,' I said. 'The plan. We can figure some of it out when we get there.'

'I still think it's weird Mum never mentions it.'

'But it's a secret. Would you go around talking about a secret all the time?'

He gasped. '*Me?* Never!'

'So you understand.'

He chewed on his pen. 'I think we should leave at four o'clock. Nighttime is darkest before the sun comes up so if we leave at four it should be very dark and then the neighbours won't see us. If the neighbours see us, they'll probably tell Jason and then he'll come after us.' He wrote *FOUR OCLOCK (A.M.)* in big letters on an empty page.

'I looked it up and the train is at seven. We can hide in your bushranger bunker if you want, but I don't think it really matters. No one from school will be there yet. I mean, who catches the train at seven o'clock in the morning?'

'Maybe adults going to work in Port Pirie?' Ben wrote *ADULTS –> PORT PIRIE* with a few question marks. 'It will be cold. It might be warmer if we stay in the bunker.'

'We can figure that out when we get there, I guess.' I took out my own pen. 'So we catch the train at seven, and it gets us to Adelaide right before lunchtime. About four hours. Then we can transfer from that train to the other one, which will take us into the city.'

'Then what?'

We sat in silence. I flipped to *EARN MORE MONEY.* Ben added *GO TO NONNO'S FARM* and was quiet again.

'How will we find him?' he said finally. 'Did you find his address?'

'No,' I admitted.

'Didn't you call him?'

'Not yet. I wanted to wait until we were definitely coming.'

'Are we *not* definitely coming?'

'We are, definitely.'

'So shouldn't we tell him?'

When I was about five, Dad turned up at the apartment we were living in, down near the marina. Ben wasn't born yet, but Mum threw her huge belly around every corner and in the afternoons I rubbed her feet in front of the TV. That night Dad knocked on my window. His face took up the whole thing, smiling and trying to pull the blinds apart. Get your bag, *he said. And I said maybe we should ask Mum first, tell her where we were going so she didn't worry.* Nah, *he said, with his eyes all lit up,* she'll just say no. Easier to ask someone to forgive you.

'He'll be excited to see us,' I said. 'I don't want to spoil the surprise.'

Ben turned a couple of pages. Underneath *ADULTS –> PORT PIRIE*, he wrote *SURPRISE SKYES NONNO.*

'When we get to the main train station, we can go to one of the motels and stay there for a night. You'll be tired. It's a long way to go on the train and we should have a rest before we go up to the farm. Nonno will probably make us work right away, picking oranges.'

'It's not orange season,' Ben said.

'Well, something. He's probably still got some goats or chickens or something that needs looking after. He must be old by now. Sixty at least.'

There was a noise in the street and we both turned to look at it. Ben closed the notebook. Waited a few seconds with our breath clamped in our chests. Nothing.

'We might even spend two days in the city. I thought I could take you to the zoo and the museum. Stuff we haven't been able to do since we moved here.'

'That sounds good,' he said, and wrote *GO TO MUESEUM* on the paper.

'Once we're with Nonno, he'll help us with the next bits. Mum will get you booked in to school, and me. I can get a part-time job somewhere and we can make new friends and live on his farm until Mum finds us our own place. You'll like it there.'

'Tell me about the farm.'

I told him what I remembered of the last times I'd been there. The way the breeze came down the hill and into the valley and shook the fruit around. The neighbours, far down the road, calling to each other and singing. The smell; wet eucalyptus and pine needles and dirt being turned over. A pub down the road that served roast lunches on Sundays and the local shops with sky-high vanilla slices and waiting for Dad to come out of the petrol station.

'Mostly it's just quiet,' I said. 'Not quiet like it is here, like the rest of the world doesn't exist. Just peaceful.'

He closed his eyes. 'Peaceful sounds nice.'

I took the notebook from him, turned to a new page. 'The main thing is that we're all there. Okay? We don't need to think of all this stuff right now, but we do need to stick together.' I drew a really bad pair of stick figures and made them hold hands. 'People might come looking for us.'

'Who? Jason?' he said.

'Maybe. Maybe other people from here. If they do, I'm not going to let them separate us. Okay?'

'Okay.' He grabbed the pen and drew a third stick figure – straw for hair, like Mum – then yawned. 'I hope Mum comes home before I go to sleep,' he said. 'So I can hug her.'

'Why?'

'Because I miss her.'

I put my arm around him. 'I know this is a bit scary. We'll be fine. Mum will love being at the farm with us.'

'Yeah, I know.'

Moonlight slid between the curtains and fell in shards across his *Thomas the Tank Engine* sheets. His small body, the tiny curve hidden there. I took out the notebook again. Turned to the page with the plan.

At the bottom of the page I wrote a few more words. A secret plan of my own.

15

For ages I carried a photo of Dad in my pocket. Me and him on a merry-go-round. One weekend Mum did the washing for the first time in her life and the photo was in there, in my jeans, and then the water came through and it wasn't anymore.

Raf's footy tour was due to leave on Sunday. They were going all around the Gulf, up to Port Augusta and down to Whyalla and all the way to Port Lincoln, where the final was. The guys and girls had separate buses but everyone knew what happened when they got there – the post-game parties and the midnight streaking down the main streets.

He arrived early in the morning. Ben answered the door, whispered '*Raf*!' as loudly as he dared and attached himself to Raf's leg. Raf was smiling. He put his hand out and I took it, found my memory in the rough edges of his fingers and his warm palm.

Mum and Jason were sitting out on the back verandah, talking to Murray and maybe to each other, so we lingered in the doorway for a minute. Ben stared at us. I wanted him to leave, give me a second to think about what I could say to Raf. I wanted to tell him about Daryl and the supermarket, but the words didn't come and the TV was too loud.

'When do you get back again?' I said instead.

'End of the term,' he said. 'Goes into the school holidays if we win the whole thing. They take us down to Adelaide to go to the Royal Show.'

'Oh, cool.' My chest got tight. I tried to say I would miss him. A bit of spit just came out instead, landed on my t-shirt.

'We probably won't win, though.' He squeezed me closer. 'I mean, I might, but the rest of the guys aren't taking it very seriously this year. Dicks.'

'Hey, Raf.' Ben sat on the floor in front of him. 'When you get back, maybe we can catch the train somewhere all together.' He looked at me and tried to wink. 'Have you been to Alice Springs? Did you know in summer it can be fifty degrees in Alice Springs? I think that's hot enough to cook an egg on the road. Maybe you wouldn't want to eat it though, if it's been on the road. Dirt and stuff.'

Raf smiled. 'Sounds good. It'll be the holidays so we'll have heaps of time to do whatever you like.'

There was a knock on the sliding door to the verandah, and Mum called out: 'You kids here?'

'Let's go,' I said. 'Over the road. Find another hopping mouse.'

'Ooh yeah!'

We walked across to the spinifex block and I lay with Raf on the dead grass and the sky was so big, sheets and sheets of cloudless eternity.

'So,' I said. 'Two weeks.'

'Two weeks.'

'What are we going to *do*?'

'Sext?'

'You do that?'

'First time for everything.'

Ben kicked dirt into the air, squealed like he was being chased. 'Raf! There are so many *ants*! Do you think they're termites?'

'Could be,' Raf called back. He rolled his head to the side and kissed my cheek. 'Got something special planned for when I get back.'

'Sounds scary,' I said.

'Could be.'

Ben dropped to the ground on Raf's other side. Raf pulled his phone from his pocket. 'Shit,' he said. 'I'm gonna miss the bus.' He went to kiss me, looked at Ben, changed his mind. 'Cheer for us. Loud, so we can hear you on the other side of the Gulf.' He scrambled to his feet.

'Bye, Raf!' Ben said. We watched him run, footy bag bouncing. When he was out of sight, Ben said to me, 'He's nice.'

'I know,' I said.

'Have you ever been to the tip? It's over the other side of the block and I went there once after school and found a TV.'

'A TV? What'd you do with it?'

'It was too heavy to carry so I left it behind. But there might be other cool stuff there.'

'Okay, you lead the way.'

The morning was warm and humid. He skipped through it, swatting flies and pulling tiny black ants from his arms. Sure enough, behind the empty block was a rotten old tip, piled high with people's junk and the junk's junk. Ben had found – or cut – a hole in the fence and he slipped through it.

'The TV was this way,' he said, and I followed behind.

We found all kinds of stuff. Nothing good, but everything with its own story. A food processor with worms living in it. A suitcase with *MACPHERSON* stamped on the front. Mugs and plates smashed into pieces. Piles and piles of tyres. Ben opened the door of an old fridge and something scuttled out.

'A *scorpion*!' he shrieked, ran behind me like I could protect him from it.

'Want me to step on it?'

'No! Don't kill it!' He stared at it until it disappeared under the rubble. 'Their bodies glow, you know. Yiannis had a pet one and his dad bought him one of those black lights and it looked like it was glowing in the dark.' He reached for my hand and we walked together. 'I think they have live ones at the museum. Maybe they can show us how they glow, when we go there.'

'Sounds good,' I said.

'They probably have other things too, like centipedes and spiders.'

'Gross.'

'Maybe bird-eating spiders. They don't eat birds but sometimes they eat lizards.' He let go of my hand and ducked through the hole in the fence again. 'Pretty much all omnivorous animals eat lizards.'

I slid through behind him. 'That was fun,' I said. 'Disgusting, but fun.'

'Yeah,' he said. 'Fun things usually are.'

We were halfway home when we heard Murray barking. He was really going for it, loud and throaty barks and deep growling. People in the other houses had come out to look, standing on their porches and peering down the street, as though the dog were a spectacle, something exciting to watch.

Ben looked at me with his eyes wide. 'That's Murray,' he said.

'I know,' I said.

He raced ahead of me, pockets jangling with all its trinkets as he went. The people on their porches watched him go, looked back to me, looked in the direction of the barking.

'Everything okay?' said one of them.

'I don't know,' I shouted.

I went after him, running harder than I could ever remember running, just throwing everything I had into getting back to the house. The front door was wide open. Mum stood in the hallway with her face red and blotchy and her fingers in her ears and I shook her – 'What's going on?' – and she blinked a couple of times and pointed towards the yard.

And then Ben's screaming.

Howling. Like the sound was being forced from his body. I ran to the back room, Mum trailing behind me.

Ben: on his knees, his face on the floor and the screaming echoing against the lino. Body shaking. I ran to him. 'What is it? What's going on?' and he pointed without looking to the garden.

Mum: standing in the doorway with her face half-painted and her robe coming open, sighing.

And Jason: beer in hand, laughing, kicking the homeless tortoise back to the dog, and the dog sniffing for it, blind, barking at the air, barking at the ground. Picking up the tortoise and its broken shell and crunching it in his jaws and all of us hearing it, the crunch amplified as though he'd hooked up surround sound just to make sure we all knew what was happening. *Crunch.*

I rocked Ben back and forth and he pulled out his toy cars and started throwing them at the glass door. Jason spun around and yelled at him: 'You want to fucking pay for it?' and Ben just threw them and then picked them up and threw them again, until he finally made a tiny crack in the glass and Jason came storming in.

And grabbed him.

Grabbed him by his throat, just picked him clean off the floor.

Mum gasped.

Jason shoved Ben against the wall and he kicked his legs and his knee had a graze where he'd fallen on the nature strip and he kicked and kicked and Jason held him there, put his face very close to him: 'You don't keep animals in this house.' Ben's little legs went like mad, like he was riding a bike up a very steep hill, and with his hands he pulled at Jason's hands, grabbing and scratching. Murray screamed and yanked on his chain and the Hills hoist groaned and moved in its concrete footing. I felt paralysed. Couldn't make my legs go over there, couldn't make my hands slap the shit out of him. I just stood there like a useless prick, doing nothing and saying nothing.

Mum moved in my peripheral vision, a step forward and then a step back. Jason's eyes flicked over to her.

'You understand?' Jason said, to both of them at once.

Ben nodded, a bit, as much as he could nod with the hands around his throat, and Jason dropped him. He gasped for air, tried grabbing it with his fists and shovelling it into his throat. Then I could move again. I ran to him and did all the things I knew to get him restarted. Rubbed his back, rubbed his head, held him and rocked him and picked up his toy cars so he could smash them into each other.

Mum kept standing there with her robe open and her face red and her eyes wet, but she didn't say anything. Jason looked back at Ben.

'Be a man,' he said. He took Mum's hand and they went to his bedroom and closed the door, the soft pads of her slippers down the hallway and his steel-capped boots on the lino.

I grabbed Ben's shoulders and looked right at him. 'You wait here for two seconds, okay?' His neck had come up in red welts, finger-sized beginnings of bruises. 'Okay?' He moved his head minutely, up once and down once.

I got a towel and opened the back door a centimetre at a time. Murray snapped at thin air, dancing on his three good feet and his one bad foot. His chain whipped against the metal of the clothesline, clunked and rang with each step he took.

'Murray!' Nothing. 'Murray, stop!' He kept on pulling. His clouded eyes showed no signs of anything. Anger. Sadness. Regret. It was just his body, his determination to get off that chain. And then what? Jason would run him down with his own car.

Inside I found a bit of meat in the fridge, brown at the edges, four dollars a kilo marked on it in my own handwriting. Murray sniffed at the air, lifted his nose towards the bit of carcass. 'You want it?' I said. 'Go get it.' I chucked it across the yard and he went after it, right to the end of his chain.

I couldn't look at Bilbo. Tossed the towel in the general direction and scooped him up in it. For a second, his legs moved under my fingers. But the shape of him was all wrong, with the towel wrapped around him, like tectonic plates shifting.

Ben grabbed the towel right out of my hands and held it close to his chest.

'We have to go to the vet,' he said, his voice coming out in ribbons.

'Jason said the vet's not in.' The tortoise bound in the towel. He couldn't breathe in there, even if he wanted to.

'Maybe Raf knows.'

'Raf'll be on the bus already. Are you okay to walk?'

'Yeah.'

'Listen,' I said, very close to his face. 'I'm going to grab some things. I want you to stay exactly right here. Don't move a muscle.'

'I have to move my chest muscles to breathe,' he said.

'Just those then.'

I grabbed our school bags and shoved in everything in reach. A change of clothes for him. A change of clothes for me. Shoes, socks, undies. The picture he'd drawn of us and Mum and Bilbo on a leash. The blacksmith book. The cars he'd thrown at the window. A rock with *You rock!* written on it. My phone and wallet were in my pocket. I went to the kitchen and took muesli bars, a block of cheese, half a loaf of bread.

Things we could eat on the train. Things we'd need in Adelaide.

Jason's door stayed closed. We went out the side door, through the laundry, and clicked open the gate to the street. The people who'd been out before had mostly gone inside; the same woman who'd called out earlier was still there on her porch, drink in hand. She watched us go but said nothing.

We walked across the empty block to the other bus stop, where we could wait without anyone seeing us. He sat on the kerb. I sat next to him. The warm concrete pinched the backs of my thighs. Ben put his hand inside the towel, snapped it back like he'd been bitten. Quick breaths, in and out.

'Tortoises aren't supposed to feel like that,' he said. 'Do you think he's dead?' He began to open the towel. It flapped in the afternoon breeze and bits of shell came away with it, green and brown. Ben's body shrank away from mine but he said nothing until the tortoise was exposed to the air, when he let out a whimper, then folded it all up again. 'He *is* dead,' he said. 'He's dead.'

'He might not be.'

His voice was wet with sadness. 'Yiannis says chickens can live without their heads. And cockroaches. He says cockroaches can live for a month without their heads because they breathe through holes in their body.'

I put my arm around him, squeezed him close to me.

'He says they can just keep on surviving without their heads until they starve to death or a bird gets them. *And*,' he said, and I heard the breath rushing in and out of him all at once, 'their heads can survive on their own, too. If you feed it, it might even live for a whole day.'

'Gross,' I said.

He nodded, patted the towel again. 'Not tortoises. Tortoises just die.' He stood. 'We have to bury him.'

At the end of the empty block we found a bit of earth soft enough to shovel with our hands. Ben got down on his knees, dug into the ground until his fingernails were black and red. I picked through the dirt pile, found spiders and centipedes and threw them as far from Ben as I could. The towel didn't move. It was crisp along the edges where blood had dried.

'You okay?' I said to the back of Ben's head.

'Do you think this is my fault? Because I said the thing about Galápagos tortoises being delicious?'

'Oh Ben, no. No. Of course it isn't.'

'It's just I said Murray might think he was delicious and it turned out Murray did think he was delicious. I didn't have to say that. I could have just said, *Galápagos tortoises are delicious*, and not said the thing about Murray.'

'It's not like he could hear you,' I said.

'I guess.' He took the towel and folded it around itself a few more times to make a package. He was gentle, placing it in the hole he'd dug with as much delicacy as he could muster.

'Do you want to say anything?' I said.

'No.' He pushed the dirt pile back into the ground until the towel had vanished. We stood there a while longer, Ben staring at the ground and me watching him, the way his body had curved forward and his brow shoved down.

'Do you want to get an ice-block?' I said.

'Okay.'

We walked into the afternoon. Ben's throat had turned vicious shades of pink and violet. I pulled out my phone. Claud's number stared back at me.

'Skye?' she said. 'Rafferty's already left.' I waited for a second, tried to make my own voice solid and even. Coughed. My chest was so tight behind my ribs.

'I know,' I said finally. 'Can you come and get us?'

*

We waited on the gutter. Ben touched his hand to his throat, touched it again, again. Rings of purple, red veins where the skin had torn. We played noughts and crosses with a stick in the dirt. It was getting close to dinner time. The sun sat low across the spinifex block and I strained to see into the shadows it threw. A couple of kids kicked a ball around; their shouts carried loud across the flat road.

'It's not okay, what Jason did to you. You know that, right? You didn't do anything wrong.'

Ben said nothing.

It was less than ten minutes before Claud pulled up. She jumped from her car, gathered Ben and his trinkets into her arms. He let his head drop forward and she gasped, buried her head in his soft hair. He crouched into her like she was a nest.

'Get in, Skye,' she said. Her face was so dark, eyes furious and bloodshot. I climbed into the back seat and she bundled Ben in after me.

She set each of us up with a bowl of ice-cream and we sat in front of their huge TV and watched Trey play on his Xbox. I ate Ben's. After the ice-cream was finished, she made us ham and cheese sandwiches cut into little triangles, brought them in on a tray with flowers on it. Ben didn't eat any of it. She sat next to him and put her hand on his knee.

'Bad day, huh?'

'My tortoise got eaten by a dog.' He was so quiet, like someone had put him inside a box.

She whistled through her teeth. 'That doesn't sound too good.'

'I watched him. He picked him up and he crunched him like a lolly.'

'That's awful, sweet pea.' She pulled him into her lap and he curled up in there, a baby possum in its pouch. He closed his eyes. After a few minutes, his breathing had eased into a steady rhythm and he was asleep. Trey went outside and his car started up.

Claud turned to me, spoke in a low voice. 'So?'

'Mum's boyfriend.' I didn't know where to start. At the apartment? Snapping my bra strap in the hallway? Telling Ben he talks a lot of shit?

'What did he do?' she said. 'Are these marks his?' She pointed to Ben's neck, where the bruises were flowering.

'Yeah.'

'I'll kill him.' Ben stirred. 'What happened?'

'I don't … I can't remember.' The tortoise and the dog and Jason laughing, Mum watching from the door, Ben with his feet in the air. 'I don't know.'

'Did he touch you?'

'Not this time.'

'Skye. Oh, darling.' She picked up her phone. 'I have to call the police.'

'No! You can't.'

She pulled me close. 'They'll make sure you guys are safe.'

'They'll take him away.'

'Who, Skye?'

'Ben. They'll take him away from me.'

'I *promise* they won't. Just let me call them, okay? We'll see what they say.' She held the phone to her ear. I heard the muffled grunting of a person at the other end. Claud nodded a couple of times. I tried to breathe, could only think of Ben without me. Me without Ben. 'Okay then,' she said. 'Thanks for your help.' She put the phone down.

'What did they say? Are they coming to get him?'

'The guy'd left for the day.'

I let out my breath. 'Oh.'

She grabbed my hands. 'Stay here tonight. I can't bear you kids going back to that monster.'

'Thanks.'

'The guy we need to speak to will be back in the morning and I'll call again then. Okay?'

'Please don't.'

'Everything will be all right.'

Ben hiccuped in his sleep, breath shuddering out like he'd been crying.

After dinner I used Raf's computer, brought up the train website and booked two tickets – thirty-five dollars each, the cheapest ones they had. When they'd printed, I checked my internet banking. Twelve hundred dollars. Half of what I'd hoped to leave with, barely enough to cover us for a week. It wasn't enough, wasn't nearly enough.

I closed the laptop. It would have to be enough.

16

*S*OMETIMES *D*AD WOULD *pick me up from the flat and take me into the central train station. We went on Sundays and stood under the flickering timetables with our tickets in our hands. We always caught whichever train was leaving next. Sometimes we ended up in Belair and sometimes at Gawler.*

Once, there had been a fair on – the signs were everywhere – so we walked and walked to find it but it wasn't anywhere, and then the last train was leaving.

My alarm went off at three fifteen. I listened to Ben sleep for a full minute, standing over him like I thought I was his guardian angel. He was smaller than yesterday, tucked up in Raf's sheets, a soft snore choking out of him. My need to keep him safe wrapped tight around my lungs.

'Time to go,' I said.

He rolled to face me, eyes closed. 'Go where?'

'Home.'

He blinked a couple of times, looked at me with his eyes puffed up. 'To Jason's? No thank you.'

'Not to Jason's. On the train.'

He frowned, took a second just swirling the idea around in his head. Then he jerked upright. 'But Mum's not here yet. She's not here yet. We have to wait for her.' He scrambled out of bed. 'I'll go and get her. You can stay here and I'll go and get her.' His bruises stood out black and angry in the light from the street.

'I had to change the plan a bit. It's okay though, Mum will understand.' Standing in the hall with her dressing-gown flapping open. 'She'll catch up with us. Okay? I'll call her from the train and she'll get the next one and we'll all meet up in Adelaide.'

'Why can't we wait until she's ready?' He stared at me, so bleary-eyed, trying to connect whatever he'd woken from with the strange room.

'Oh, I already bought our tickets. If we don't get this train we can't get a refund and I worked so hard to save up for them. You know? Mum doesn't want us to waste all that money.'

He chewed on a fingernail. 'Well, okay.'

'Grab your shoes.'

'Is Claud driving us?'

'It's so early. I said we'd walk down.'

'Okay.' He rubbed his face. 'We can't forget anything,' he said. 'If we forget anything and we have to come back they'll put us in *jail* and Mum won't even visit because we left her behind when we promised to take her with us.'

'Stop it. That's not happening,' I said. 'But we do have to go. Now.'

He grabbed my hands, looked me dead in the eye, as serious as he'd ever been about anything. 'There's something I have to do first though. At Jason's house.'

'I don't want to go back there.'

'It's just one thing.'

'I don't want *you* to go back there.'

'It'll take five seconds.'

'What is it?'

'I can't tell you. It's just a thing and I have to do it and I don't want to say it.' His frantic face, eyes flicking everywhere.

I sighed. 'Okay. But you have to be *so quiet*, Ben.'

We closed Claud's door – Raf's door – and stood in the moonlight, Ben's eyes big and his neck stamped with fingerprint bruises. The streets were empty. All the houses locked up tight, people inside in their beds with the radio on or someone snoring next to them. We walked to Jason's house, out across the train line and over the canal and the bridge with its missing railings.

'What are we doing here?' I said.

Around the side, the gate was latched but not locked. Ben clicked it open. A bat flew over. We were like burglars, breaking into the worst house in the street in the dark shadows before daylight.

'You keep watch here,' he said.

'If Jason sees you, it's over. Do you understand?'

'*Yes*. Let me go.'

'I don't want to.'

He snatched his hands away and hissed at me: 'It's just *one thing*.'

'Okay. Sorry. Be so, so quiet.'

'I *will*.'

I saw faces in the trees and under the parked cars and in windows, heard human voices in the cry of the bats and the owls. Tried to turn off the movie in my head. Kept an eye out for the guys making early starts to get into their utes. Stared at the stars, the way they came over the spinifex block and exploded, distant fireworks.

I imagined Mum hearing Ben in the house, crawling out of bed and seeing him there in the hallway.

Then he was back, dragging Murray's chain, the dog yanking and pulling and whining. Ben said nothing. He closed the gate, dropped the chain, and let Murray limp-run blindly down the street. The air was so cold at night, without clouds to blanket it, but we stood there until the dog had disappeared around the next corner.

'I want to say goodbye to Bilbo.' He grabbed my hand, dragged me towards the spinifex block. I looked at my phone. 'Do we have time?'

'If we're *super* quick.'

The pile of stones marking the spot had been scattered, but Ben knew where to find him anyway. He knelt in the dirt, put his hands flat on the mound.

'Sorry Murray ate you,' he said.

I stopped to look at the house, at its Hills hoist without its dog, at the tree in the backyard stretching into the sky. At the room in the front with the curtains closed, imagining the people inside, wondering what would happen when the sun came up.

The train line stretched out dark before us, moonlight striking the tracks. We walked along them with our bags thumping against our backs, the sound amplified a million times in the absolute quiet of the sleeping town. The station was still and silent.

'The bushranger hiding place should be just by the entrance,' Ben whispered. 'The map in the book said it was near the gates but over to the left a bit.' He blew out his breath in front of him. I rubbed my hands together, shoved them into the pockets of my jacket. 'Here!' It was roped off; a sign shouted DO NOT TOUCH. He slipped under the barrier and pulled on the trap-door's handle. 'I can't get it open. Help me.'

'Maybe we shouldn't.'

'People will see us if we don't.'

'There's no one here. We can wait in the waiting room, it's warm there.'

He pulled again on the handle. The door didn't budge, just groaned a bit in its metal skeleton. Ben's shoulders dropped. 'Fine.'

We sat in the back corner, tried to push ourselves right into the wall.

Sometimes a noise came from town, someone shouting or a glass breaking. A car engine started, then another, people driving out to the mines or the boats, pointing their headlights into the blackness. Animal sounds, too – a few bats talking and a pair of possums boxing on the train station roof, barking and hissing.

'What's that sound?' Ben gripped his bag tight, white-knuckled.

'It's just possums.'

'They sound angry. Possums have sharp claws. And teeth.'

'They're only angry at each other. Put your bag down.'

He shook his head, pulled his hood over it. Sank deeper into the metal bench with his knees up to his face. He seemed tiny and afraid. I wrapped parts of myself around him, the bits of me that weren't shivering. The night seemed never-ending. My phone told us it was a quarter to five. More than two hours until the train.

'We've got a while to wait yet, mate,' I said. 'Tell me something interesting. One of your facts.'

'I can't remember any,' he said. 'I was thinking of facts all day yesterday and then today I woke up and you told me we were leaving and I couldn't remember them. It was like my head pushed them all out so I could concentrate properly on getting to the secret room at the train station.'

'How about I tell you a fact, then?'

'Okay,' he said. 'I probably already know it but my brain has just forgotten it.'

I squeezed him. 'I went to kindy with this girl called Mackenzie. She was mean to everyone, but especially to me. Said all kinds of bad things about my dad. Heaps of lies. She lied about everything. Anyway, she told me if you drank a juice box too fast, your brain would get air bubbles in it and you'd die.'

His eyes widened.

'So this other kid decided to test it out. He had an apple juice and at recess we went down behind the swings and all crowded around him, and Mackenzie was standing in the middle going *You're gonna die, James!* but he was trying to be really tough. As tough as you can be when you're four, I guess.' I thought of his face, all pinched into the middle, frowning like he was going to conquer the world. 'You've never seen anyone drink one so fast. Fifteen seconds. Sucked so hard on the straw his lips kind of went back into his mouth.'

'Did he *die*?'

I let the pause draw out. Ben stared right at me. ''Course he didn't. He did a huge burp and we went back to the sandpit. Turns out you can drink a juice box as fast as you want and not die.'

'I think I knew that fact already,' he said, and turned back to the open doorway. That wind was so cold, like it had fingers made of ice and they were grabbing my legs. The freezer room popped into my head, Daryl swaying side to side, first his head and then his body catching up. I thought of him getting to work that morning, having to write the specials on the board himself. I thought of Jeannie, too, and the grandchild she'd been knitting for in Darwin.

Ben let his head drop onto my shoulder. The sun came bending around the station, dropping into the pit of the tracks. A few more cars got going, one playing loud music all the way down the main street, out onto the highway heading north to Port Augusta. From the raised platform I saw the ocean gleam, throw its white skulls into the sand. The town glowed orange and red in the sunrise. I took a muesli bar from my backpack and chewed on it and Ben's head bounced up and down on my shoulder as I ate and he shivered the whole time.

'How you feeling?' I said.

His teeth clicked together. 'Nervous.'

'What're you nervous about?'

'Everything. Being far away from Mum. Not being able to find your nonno. What if we can't find him?

'We'll find him.'

'What if Mum comes after us and she can't find us and then we try to get back to her but she's looking for us so we never find each other again?'

'She'll know how to find us. I've got my phone.'

He nodded, satisfied. It was six o'clock. People would start to arrive at the station, soon, to head into the city for work. We'd practised our speech: our grandfather was sick in Adelaide so we were going to see him. Our mum was already there. She was meeting us at the station. I had to finish an assignment first otherwise we'd have gone with her.

A woman arrived, pink umbrella in hand. She talked into the palm of her hand, bounced on purple sneakers. She had black hair and the platform light reflected off it. Hair so shiny it was like a mirror. I touched my own hair, the ratty ends. Ben's had grown past his ears. Things I hadn't thought to notice before. She didn't look at us, just talked into her hand and pressed a finger against the receiver in her ear.

'I don't think she's from here,' Ben whispered. I was relieved to go unnoticed.

It was just the three of us on the platform for another fifteen minutes. She smoked a couple of cigarettes, paced along the platform into her own nicotine clouds. Trucks came to life on the highway. Belted down towards the ports, or took their herd of cattle out to be made into dinners. Blew their horns closer to town than they were supposed to.

'What time is it?' Ben said. Eyes flicking around, bags carrying them. The day looked so long ahead of us.

'It's six thirty.'

'Why did we leave so early?'

Mum and Jason were usually still in bed when we left for school. Door closed. We would be well and truly on the train by the time they thought to take a morning piss. 'Because it was in the plan,' I said. He nodded, and his legs went up and down like he was riding a bike.

Two men came to the waiting room door. Big guys, one with tattoos across his neck and under his collar and the other nearly bursting out of his shirt. They nodded to the woman in the purple shoes. The tattooed guy took a cigarette from his pocket and handed it to her.

They looked surprised to see us there, in our corner of the room. Looked at me, at Ben, and then at each other. Sat in the opposite corner, on separate benches but with their knees together, and drank from the same plastic coffee cup, one of those reusable ones with a coloured cap on top. Ben pushed our bags further under the seat and sat on the floor in front of them.

'People think we're running away,' he whispered.

'No one cares what we're doing,' I said, but the men looked at us and the woman paced inside her volcanic eruption, and Ben leaned hard against the bags so they were invisible. Six forty. I imagined Mum climbing out of bed, bleary. Jason snoring with his mouth hanging open. Mum in the kitchen, getting a glass of water. Looking out the back to the naked Hills hoist, no Murray chained to it.

My heart beat faster. Maybe she would notice the dog missing, come looking for us, to make us look for him.

I took a deep breath. She wouldn't be awake yet. She'd get

a drink straight from the tap in the bathroom, the way she always did. No one would notice Murray missing until Jason was up. Burning toast in the kitchen, shouting at Mum, seeing the empty yard. He might not even look for him right away. Might be relieved, first. One less thing to worry about. Our door would still be closed but he'd think we were at school by then, me taking Ben to the walking bus and then to my own bus, finding Raf behind the gate.

Air caught around the edges of my mouth. Tried to creep back in while I breathed it out. Raf streaking down the main road in Whyalla, making out with El in Port Lincoln. I didn't even know what the places looked like but it was easy to imagine them there, together in the moonlight, ocean in the distance. I thought about texting him but it was so early. He'd be drooling into his pillow at whichever motel they were staying.

The men in the corner had their cheeks together. The tattooed one pushed his fingers between the other one's fingers. They'd stopped looking at us. An older lady and a small child had appeared on the platform. The child held her nose near the smoking woman and said, loudly, 'Smoking is bad for you.' The woman ignored her. Grandma picked her up under her armpits and held the girl tight to her body.

Six fifty.

Mum had an alarm clock by her bed and sometimes it went off early in the morning. I could hear it from our room where I lay awake under the slimy curtains, wondering why she needed to be up at seven. Front door opened and closed, car started. I would lie awake and watch the ceiling move and twenty minutes later she'd be back, door banging shut, Jason grunting. It could be this morning. She could have set her alarm this morning.

Ben shook next to me. His body was limp with lack of sleep. 'There are muesli bars in the bag,' I said. 'You should have one before you pass out.'

'Three o'clock is really early.' He pulled up his eyelids, let them stick to their heavy hoods.

'It was your idea. To hide in the darkest part of the night, remember?'

He yawned. 'Oh yeah.'

The train pulled in at sixty fifty-eight. It was two minutes early and that made Ben nervous. 'Why is it early? Is it so they have extra time to get the police on board to find us? Is it because Jason called the train company and asked them to wait for him?' He got up and jumped around a bit with his bag bouncing. 'Trains are never early. Trains are *late*.'

The tattooed man said, 'Settle down, lad. She comes when she wants,' and his accent was round and wild.

Our seats were in the economy section, which included all of the train except the sleeper carriage. We found one we both liked in the middle car, which was nearly empty. I looked for Mum on the platform, in case she had come to find us, and couldn't quite figure out if that would be good or bad.

At seven o'clock, the train picked up its legs and began to move. 'Oh,' said Ben, 'they meant it *leaves* at seven,' and he relaxed back into his chair, though his eyes kept moving around the empty seats.

Somewhere down the back, a baby cried and a low voice soothed it.

I touched Ben's shoulder. 'I'm going to call Mum now, okay? She'll be awake and wondering where we are.'

'Okay.' He swung his legs, gave me a big smile. I walked down the aisle to the back of the carriage. Hid my voice in the rattle of the walkway between the cars. Watched Ben's little head going up and down, safe in his knowledge we would all be together again soon.

Then I took out my phone, and I called the police.

*

Ben made a friend in the restaurant carriage. Her name was Evie and they sat in a vinyl booth and shared packets of chips. I bought one, then her dad bought one, then I bought another. Ben pointed out the window and explained the countryside to her. The silos tall with grain and the tumbling fishing boats and the wide fields of green wheat.

After three hours, the scenery began to change. I pressed my face against the window, watched the suburbs unravel around us. The train slowed as it wound through the outskirts of the city. Ben went to the toilet and changed out of his pyjamas.

We pulled into Adelaide's central train station at lunchtime and its big clock chimed twelve while we climbed down the stairs. Ben took his school bag and became lost under it, a bouncing bit of blue canvas along the platform. We stood under the timetables for a minute, watched the numbers change. The familiar place names. The same smell – something like the dust from the street mixed in with the algae from the river. It felt strange to be back, like I'd left my body there all that time and only just re-entered it.

I'd been there heaps, caught the train up and walked into the mall with Kirrily, gone back the other way to the park and eaten fish and chips in the rotunda. And with Dad, of course. This time I took Ben out onto the closest main road and we went down the hill to find something to eat. We couldn't keep carrying our bags forever. We'd get lunch, check in to a motel, have a good night's sleep on real beds. That was the plan.

The police hadn't been in the plan. Not the one we'd written together, anyway.

I checked my phone. Nothing but a notification from some game Ben had installed.

The street was jammed tight with people on their lunchbreaks, and we slipped into their moving bodies. They walked fast, had places to be. They swung shopping bags by their sides and their bones grunted in the cold air. A couple in front of us argued until she threatened to leave and they kissed. A guy behind us shouted into his phone, loud enough that people around us were staring at him. An old lady tapped him on the shoulder. Through her tight mouth, she said, 'No one needs to know the shape of your bowel movements.' Ben laughed.

We broke away from the crowd, slipped through the arcade to the McDonald's behind the old cinema. I watched Ben eat, cramming a thousand fries into his weird little mouth. I had a salad and a frozen Coke, paid for it all on my card. I felt like a millionaire with all that money in there. Maybe we could even watch a movie on the rental things they had in the motel rooms.

'Gotta go to the toilet,' Ben said.

'Thanks for sharing.'

I picked at my salad. The seats were hard and my back hurt from all the sitting we'd been doing so I pushed it up against the chair, straightened up. I closed my eyes for a second so I could think about something else. Nonno's farm. The year we'd climbed the fence to steal peaches from his neighbours a kilometre down the road.

I heard a tray scrape right next to me. Opened my eyes and two guys looked back at me. They had their food spread all over the table and when they smiled I got a whiff of stale smoke. It made me think of Jeannie, just for a second.

'Nice tits,' one of them said. The big one, beanie pulled down half over his eyes and a ring through his lip. He took a bite of his burger. 'What's your name?' Bits of bun and lettuce sprayed out at me and I said nothing.

The other one was smaller, and he disappeared a bit into his chair, like he was trying to hide from himself. He had a grey hoodie with a symbol on it I'd seen before but couldn't remember where. He asked me, too: 'What's your name?' but with his mouth only open on one side. Maybe he didn't want to ask at all.

I thought of Raf pointing to the clouds.

'Leave me alone,' I said. They both laughed, whacked the other's shoulder. The smaller one fell forward under the force of his mate's hand and banged his elbow.

'Piss off, Kieran,' he said.

Ben appeared next to me, school bag in hand. 'Come on, mate,' I said. 'Time to go.'

The big one slapped my jeans as we left, sucked his tongue between his teeth. No one said anything, though the place was packed.

We decided to go back up the road towards the hills. The Botanic Gardens were there, and we could have a rest for a bit before we had to get serious about finding a place to sleep. The internet said there was a motel down on West Terrace, and we could even get an orange juice delivered to our room. We just had to get back there by five to check in.

So many people. It had been months since we'd seen so many in one place. They crammed onto buses, smoked in packs outside the university gates, crossed the road on the green light buzzing like rows of soldiers. We weaved our way through them, trying to find the habit again.

The Botanic Gardens welcomed us with big iron gates. We'd been there heaps of times when Ben was little, probably because it was free. Mum had taken a picnic down to the pond with the lily pads and we'd pretended to get lost in the rose garden. Once, Dad had brought me to an *Alice in Wonderland* play. Not a normal play, but a performance that went through the whole garden. We had to follow it around, like we had gone down the rabbit hole as well. Kids from my school were there and we all laughed and chased after the white rabbit until afternoon tea was served.

Ben and I walked right through the gardens, around the kiosk and the duck pond, where families picked at loaves of bread and threw croutons into the water.

'They shouldn't do that,' Ben said. 'Ducks aren't supposed to eat bread. They're supposed to eat snails and mealworms, but if you feed them bread they fill up on it and they don't have any room for snails and mealworms so they die of malnutrition.' He scowled at the families. A couple of dads looked up at us, just a split second to register the way our family was different from their family. Pushed their prams back to the kiosk, probably got a latte to take out to the deck.

We made our way through the back gates, over the road and onto the grass. A couple more families in groups, folding tables set up with potato salad and bowls of bright jelly. Kicking a footy around. I put my hand in my pocket, took out my phone to send a message to Raf. It was one thirty. I put the phone back in my pocket, thought of Raf and Yardy and El all laughing about me. Stupid Skye. Too scared to stay home so she ran away.

'Don't they have jobs to go to?' I said.

Ben shrugged. 'Maybe they like being with their families more.' I tried to read his face, but it was plaster. All his feelings crammed up inside him.

'We could watch a movie in the motel tonight. They have pay TV, I think. We can pick up some of that gross coloured popcorn from the supermarket on the walk back.'

'Okay,' he said. A bus came around the crescent, dropped a load of schoolkids off at the zoo entrance. They dropped into line in their yellow uniforms like dandelions, marched in through the learning gate while a teacher barked at them. All laughing at once, a chorus of childhoods.

The police would have been to the house by now. They must have. Mobilised their units or whatever it was they did on TV, rammed the locked door of the spare room to find Jason's gear.

I tried not to imagine Mum but I did anyway, shouting at them to at least let her put some clothes on, being led away from the dirty house with her dressing-gown flapping open. Handcuffed? The skin around her wrists would be dry where she got eczema in winter. Bags under her eyes. Watching from the back seat of the cop car while they searched Jason's house, unless they took her back to the station first. Would they take both of them together, or separately?

Was she afraid?

The fig trees curled out around us and the wind was fresh and dry. At three o'clock, the roar of lions came across from the zoo. Feeding time. Ben mimicked their low rumble. One of the groups kicked a ball towards us and a girl came running after it. She chatted with Ben for a minute and he told her about footballs and how they were made from pig's bladders. She told him they were about to go to the beach to see the whales. I watched the families in the park, trying to see what it was that glued them together.

'Can we go see the whales?' Ben said.

'What whales?'

'That girl who was *just here* said there were whales at the beach. Can we go see them? I've never seen whales. I saw their skeletons at the museum once but never actual whales. Did you know that you can suffocate a whale if you sit on its blowhole? Imagine if they got a penguin stuck in it.' He took a deep breath.

'Ben! Okay. We can go and see the whales.'

We walked down along the river, watched a rower shoot along with his wooden arms. We waited, same as anyone else, trying to blend.

'I haven't caught this tram since I was a little kid,' I said. 'Dad took me on it to go to the Show. Twice, I think. It was a different one then, though. An old one. It rattled a lot.'

'I've never been on it.' Ben looked down the street, copying the four other people at the stop who were also looking, like they could make it come faster if it knew they were waiting. It came into view around the main square, pulled up a couple of minutes later with a squeal. We took a seat near the back so we could see everything. Ben pulled my head right down to his. 'Are people looking at us?' he said.

Maybe they were. Flicking their eyes over the top of us.

'No,' I said, but I thought I saw them do it anyway, sometimes frowning and looking at their phones but never talking. Most of them got off at South Terrace and disappeared into office buildings. 'They're gone now anyway.' We were both quiet, then. I felt the day before squeeze me, all the energy I'd had to *EARN MORE MONEY* and to leave Port Flinders leaking from the parts of me that were still upright, which wasn't all of them. Leaned against the window with my nose pressed into it. Felt a bit sick, all the scenery flicking past. The tram stopped a couple of times to let someone on or off but I slipped low into my seat, trying to be invisible, to be inconspicuous. Ben watched me and did the same, but then we were two kids trying to be invisible on a tram on a school day, which was worse, so he told me about whales while I tried not to fall asleep on the window.

The tram glided to a stop at the beach and its familiar smell – salt, sand, ice-cream – overwhelmed me.

It smelled like breathing.

People had gathered at the end of the jetty. Some of them had binoculars, like tourists on a boat, but the whale was close enough to see without them. Its dark shadow under the water, the rocky mountain of its wet back in the sun. Ben squealed when he saw it. Charged right at the barrier and hoisted himself up, half-fell over the side in his excitement.

'Careful!' A man pulled on the back of Ben's jumper. 'You fall in and that whale might eat you.'

'Oh, no,' Ben said, spilling over with glee. 'That's a southern right whale. They don't have any teeth, they just suck in krill like this.' He clenched his teeth and noisily drew saliva between them. 'Also, they have the largest balls of any animal in the world.'

We laughed – me, and the man who'd saved Ben from the whale, and the woman standing next to him. All of us laughing there in the late-winter sunlight, not thinking about how the police had come and taken Mum away with her dressing-gown open.

The man looked at us again. Looked at Ben's jumper and at his own hand. Poked the woman next to him and said something right into her ear.

'Mum would like this, don't you reckon?' Ben said.

'Yeah,' I said, not looking at the whale. 'Let's bring her, when she gets here.'

'She'll be here soon.'

'Really soon.'

The people eyed us like they knew us, up and down, whispering to each other. After five minutes no one was looking at the whale except Ben, hand up to his face to keep the sun out. A woman in a yellow dress had her phone to her ear, facing away from us but with her eyes pointing right at us. The man next to her squeezed her hand. Her face lit up red and nervous, like she was trying to chew her lip right off. A murmur went around – not words, just a hum from one person to the next.

'Ben,' I said. 'Maybe we should move on. Try calling those numbers, see if we can find Nonno.'

He looked right out to sea. The whale blew a spout of water high into the air, and Ben clapped and whooped but the rest of the crowd mumbled, grunted, murmured some more. The woman in the yellow dress slipped away from her husband and down along the jetty, stood on the kerbside as though waiting for someone.

'Ben. I really think we should go.'

He clapped his hands. 'There *is* a baby one! Look, Skye! See, when the big one moves out to sea a bit you can see the other shadow next to her?'

'It's great, mate.' I grabbed his hand. 'Let's go.'

A car pulled up. Dark windows, extra antennas, the whole bit. Two men got out, straight and tall, pulled on their hats and adjusted their belts.

Cops.

The woman in the yellow dress pointed to the jetty. To us. Ben yanked his hand away from mine, shouted: 'I'm not ready to go yet!' and people turned to look at him, then to the police, murmured and hummed and buzzed in their one collective lump of people not minding their own business, and I tried to pull Ben away but he'd wrapped his legs around the jetty railing and he would not budge.

The numbers from the page I'd torn out. I hadn't meant to memorise them but that was the thing about looking at them over and over, trying to find the courage to dial them, thinking of my dad, G Esposito, Seaford Downs. They flew round and round and I grabbed them as they shot through, ten numbers I'd read until my eyes fell out and had forgotten to forget, and I pulled my phone from my pocket, watched the cops come bumping through the crowd with their shoulders forward, shoving people into the barriers, coming right for us. Dialled the numbers, one after the other in the order I'd remembered, let my finger hover over the green button for a second or maybe two seconds, reached for the words I would say to him when he answered.

They moved right past us, the cops. Went to the ice-cream van by the barrier and bought a couple of soft-serve cones dipped in chocolate. The whale breached and landed heavily on the waves. No one was watching us at all.

17

DAD HADN'T KNOWN where Nonna was buried. He must have, once, but we didn't visit her until I was eight and she had been dead then for twenty years and he had forgotten. When we went to the cemetery he stopped the car at the booth by the gate and asked for directions.

'We don't do directions anymore,' the man said. 'We give out GPS coordinates. You can program them into your phone.'

We followed the GPS coordinates to a wide lawn with rose gardens around the outside. She had a plaque on the ground with her name on it and DEARLY MISSED *underneath. He stood in front of it for ages. I had a posy of white carnations from the supermarket so I put them on the plaque and I stood, too, not knowing when we were supposed to stop.*

We got to the motel by four thirty, waited in line behind some people with backpacks who talked quickly in another language. It would be sixty-two dollars a night and there was no minimum stay. The guy at the check-in counter looked from me to Ben and back a couple of times, then at my bank card, then back to me.

'Just the two of you, then?' he said.

'We're going to a conference,' I said.

'Oh yeah?'

'It's a dinosaur conference,' Ben said. 'We're going to see a presentation about how they know dinosaurs had feathers.'

The guy behind the counter's name tag said STUART. He frowned.

'We'll only be here for a couple of days,' I said. 'Our dad's coming too, he's just paying the taxi driver.'

'Yeah,' Ben said. 'He's paying the taxi driver.'

'He told us to check in. You know, save some time.'

'How old are you?' Stuart said to me. 'Fifteen?'

'Me? Oh, no. Eighteen.'

'You got some ID?'

'It's in the taxi. With our other stuff.'

'Not in those bags you're carrying?'

Panic. 'These are just clothes.'

'Lot of clothes for a couple of days.'

Ben said, 'We need different clothes depending on which dinosaur we're talking about.' The guy behind the counter stared at him.

'Where are your parents?'

'We told you, paying the taxi driver.'

'And your mum?' He leaned closer. A short line of people had gathered behind us. 'Come on, guys. Cut the bullshit.'

No story came to me. I looked for one, frantic. Our mum was having a baby. We were foreign exchange students. We were Jehovah's Witnesses. The line behind us murmured and shifted. Ben tugged at my t-shirt. All the words I knew were stuck in my throat.

The police hadn't taken us to their station. It was weird – the first thought I had about that was that Ben might have liked it.

Uniforms, flashing lights, criminals. He probably had a few facts about police stations. Serial killers, maybe. But they'd taken us to an ugly brown building instead, down behind the Town Hall, pushed us past people in suits eating salad from containers. They'd asked me a few questions while Ben stared at a toy box in a windowless room, and taken us out to a waiting car with a woman inside.

I watched the social worker from the back seat, the way she frowned into the road, the back of her neck flushed pink. She took us out through tree-lined streets and past unfamiliar parks and schools with ovals that could host the Olympics. We came to a stop outside a white plaster house, pine trees and gums all around it, parrots shouting from them. I got out. Took my bag from the boot, and Ben's, too. He still hadn't said a word. Not on the drive, or any time before that. I kept thinking I'd lost him, without the sound of his stories to orient me.

We lined up, like we were waiting to go into a classroom. Two women appeared at the door, flung it right open with big smiles on their faces. I reached behind me to squeeze Ben's hand but couldn't find it. The social worker pushed my shoulder a little, gave me a shove towards the door.

'Hello,' the women said, in unison. One had dark, cropped hair and a mouth that curled up at the sides. The other was a ginger, red hair bursting out of her head like an abandoned doll. A dog came running up behind them, poked its head between the redhead's legs, and the house loomed warm and golden. A proper house, with a hallway and lights along the walls that lit yellow instead of blue. A rug running from the door to the back room.

I took a deep breath and looked these strangers up and down, not sure what they could offer us, or what they planned to. Ben took my hand and it shook, so limp, a flag on a stick.

'Come in,' said the buzz-cut woman, shouted 'Perry!' at the dog, and to us said, 'I'm Lavinia. Please, for the love of God, call me Vin. This is Therese.' In the front room a fire crackled. The house smelled of it, of the charcoal and the logs. And it smelled of something else, too. Biscuits or cakes, like it was trying too hard to be a proper house. Vin led us down the hallway, into a glossy back room with leather couches and windows all the way around, a white kitchen with silver appliances, a tartan dog bed tucked away in the corner. Through the windows I saw crouching trees with their bare branches, and a swimming pool with the cover on.

'Fancy,' I said, not meaning to. Ben's eyes were wide, red at the edges.

'If you come back this way,' said Therese, 'I'll show you to your rooms.' She slid across a door at the edge of the kitchen, which opened into another hallway. 'We built the extension last year. You get your own door out to the garden so you can head out there anytime. Maybe not in the middle of the night, though, this time of year.' She smiled at us, turned the handle of the first door.

'This is yours, Skye.' Vin put her hand on my shoulder. All the comforting was going to make me lopsided.

But the room. The room was perfect. It took me a minute to get it all inside my brain. A white bed with white sheets, bedside table with a yellow lamp shaped like a monkey. Chair in the corner, bookcase next to it overflowing with spines and covers and pages. A purple throw rug over the chair and a speaker dock for a phone. On the ceiling, a glass chandelier. Not a posh one, but star-shaped and glittering. I dropped my bag by the bed and lay down on it with my hands folded across my stomach. My heart raced under them. Raced and shouted but I watched the chandelier move with the breeze through the door, hypnotic.

'You don't have to do anything right now.' Vin had her hand on the knob. 'Take as much time as you need.' She closed the door behind her. Near-silence. I pulled out my phone, tapped out a few words to Raf. *Stuff's gone pear-shaped. Miss you.* Deleted them. Pressed the call button, hung up straight away. Flicked through to a photo of the two of us at the spinifex block with the universe above our heads.

I shut my eyes and the train came rushing through, its horn sounding across the wheat fields. The ground bucked beneath me, the steady rumble of the carriages over the tracks. Waiting for the train to pass. Watching it head into the distance with all its people on board, over the bridge, by Jason's house, past the tip. A dog walked the streets, scrounging for food in total darkness, limping into three good feet. The train was gone.

My eyes flicked open. A tree rapping against the window. A bird, a small one, crooning on the fence. No train.

I breathed out. Slept right through dinner, and when I woke, the first strokes of sunrise had lit up the fairytale window.

A different woman came to see us the next day. We sat in the front room with the fire going, and she rested her hands on a folder open on her lap. Ben wouldn't sit next to me. He stared at this woman from the other couch. I wanted to reach my hand out to him but his body was all closed up inside itself. Wanted to ask him about his room, whether he'd slept like I had, dragging heavy and safe into the floor.

'Skye?' The woman pointed to me and nodded. She had a striped shirt on and the collar went right up around her ears, like she was trying to hide in it. Like a tortoise. A jab of sadness in my ribs. 'And Benjamin?' Ben nodded, weird mouth all bunched up.

'I'm Yasmin.' Yasmin. She was soft and pretty. And young. Younger than Mum, no wrinkles around her eyes. She spoke with a bit of an accent; American but not. 'I guess you know why you're here.' She said it like a joke, her voice going up at the end, then coughed into her fist. 'The thing is, Skye' – she looked down at her notes – 'you're sixteen. The law says sixteen-year-olds are allowed to look after themselves, but not other minors. Do you understand what that means?'

'Yeah, my mum's deadshit boyfriend is legally better at caring for Ben than I am.' Ben kept sitting, so upright it was like he had a wall behind him. Politely. Still and quiet, mouth zipped shut.

'If that were true, you would be with him, and not here.' She pushed her hair behind her ears. 'I'm just here to meet you both. I'm what they call a case worker, which is a fancy name for someone who helps to look after you for a while.'

'We met a bunch of you yesterday,' I said.

She shifted in the chair. 'The department sends me to make sure you're safe and that we can get you back into the best possible situation.'

'Are you sending us back?'

'No. There are … complications at their end, at the moment. You'll probably be here a bit longer yet.'

Ben's chest moved in and out, faster and faster. He stared straight ahead and his breaths were puffs of anger trying to smash their way out. His hands had gone white from clenching. Mouth forced down, eyes pinched together to keep the feelings in.

Yasmin's folder was much thicker than the one the social worker had yesterday, and she flicked back and forth, searching for the information she wanted to give us. She told us about Vin and Therese, the other kids they'd looked after, how experienced they were, how nice the neighbourhood was. She told us she would come to see us every day for the first week, then twice a week after that until we were settled.

That was a lot longer than the 'couple of days' they'd told us about at the department building. Ben stared. I knew he heard them, too, the words she was choosing to leave out. Words like 'six months' and 'foster care'. We'd seen the kids in the system, when we were living in the flats. They'd disappear for a couple of months because someone put a cigarette out on them, and then they'd come back. Sit on the porch steps the same as before, but different as well.

Yasmin didn't tell us where Mum was. Didn't tell us whether they'd taken her away with her dressing-gown flapping open, whether Claud had been there too, whether Jason had gone in a separate car. I tried to ask her but the questions came out in different words; I tried to say 'Is my mum in prison?' and it came out as 'Do you have a business card?' and I tried to say 'Why didn't she protect Ben?' and it came out as 'Where's the nearest corner shop?'

She had all the answers to those questions. The corner shop was down this road and left at the end, near the park. Her business cards were still being printed but she would give me one as soon as they arrived.

Folder closed. We had enough information for one day.

I walked Yasmin and her folder to the door. She stepped out of it, then turned back to face me.

'Bye,' I said.

'You can call me Yas.' She reached to put her hand on my shoulder but ran it through her hair instead. 'Let me know if you've got any other questions, in the meantime. Vin's got my number.'

I thought of fruit-picking at Nonno's farm, of the numbers I'd memorised from the phone book. 'Yeah, I have another question.'

'Go for it.'

'Why aren't we staying with my nonno?'

'Nonno?'

'My dad's dad. He lives not that far from here.'

She frowned, reached for her folder. 'They didn't mention a dad's dad.'

'I don't get why we wouldn't just go to him. We used to stay there heaps. He lives on a farm.'

'The department is pretty thorough about these things. If there was someone else you could go to, they would've found them. Is he old? Maybe he's too old.'

'I don't know. I don't think so. Last time I saw him he was still picking fruit. Old people couldn't do that, could they?'

'I'll find out for you, okay? Vin and Therese are really great women with lots of experience. They'll take good care of you both, for now.'

'Then what?'

'Part of my job is to help figure that out. I'll be back tomorrow and I should have more information then, okay?' The day was bright and it clipped the edges of her face. 'Try to relax. Get your things unpacked.' She closed the door. Ben hadn't moved.

Therese made a casserole for dinner and we all sat around the table, including their dog, which lay across Vin's feet, and their cat, which perched on the dresser behind Vin's head. She looked like an evil villain. I tried to catch Ben's eye, to show him, but he stared into his bowl of meat.

'So.' Therese gave us both a big smile. 'You've probably guessed I have a super boring job. An accountant. But did you know Vin's a *zookeeper*?' She was talking to us like we were babies, but Ben's eyes went up. 'Yep. She works with all the native Australian animals. Don't you, Vinnie?'

'Koalas. Echidnas. Platypuses.'

I looked over at Ben. 'Platypi?' I said.

She shrugged. 'They're very shy. You're lucky to see one, let alone two.'

Ben's body vibrated, like it was full of platypus facts he wanted to share.

'I haven't been to the zoo for ages,' I said. 'We were near it the other day, when we first got back. Heard the lions roaring. But we didn't go in.'

'I can take you,' Vin said. 'If you like. We get in for free.' She was looking at Ben, just with her eyes. 'I'm bringing home some babies in a couple of days. Echidnas. Round-the-clock hand feeding.'

Ben's chair scraped along the floor, his knees going up and down.

'What are baby echidnas called?' I said, to her, and waited for him to take the bait.

'*Puggles*!' he shouted, threw himself across the table at Vin. The cat leapt off the dresser. 'Baby echidnas are called *puggles*. Did you know Australia is the only continent in the world that has monotremes? All their babies hatch out of eggs and then they feed them with milk. The other one is platypuses. Did you know when scientists first discovered a platypus they thought it was a hoax? They thought someone had killed a duck and sewed its beak to a beaver and just invented the whole animal because they're like otters but they live in burrows and lay eggs but they're also mammals?' He took a deep breath and turned to me. 'And it *is* platypuses. Not platypi.'

'I think both are correct,' Vin said gently, and she was smiling. Ben ate a big forkful of casserole.

'And,' he said, mouth full, 'it's octopuses too, or sometimes *octopodes* but never octopi.' He looked at Vin. 'Do you have any octopuses at the zoo?'

'No octopuses.'

'Pythons?'

'Lots.'

He took a deep breath. 'Tortoises?'

'Yep. We have Aldabra tortoises. Giant tortoises.'

'They can live to be two hundred.'

'Is that right? They're hibernating at the moment but I could take you to see them when the weather's a bit warmer.'

Ben nodded. 'Maybe.'

After dinner we sat for a bit in the front room, fire still going. Therese had the big armchair by the door and Vin was on the couch. Ben sat next to her. He leaned towards her, just a little. Enough for his ear to connect with her shoulder. She didn't do anything, just let him leave it there, both their faces lit by the stupidly textbook glow from the fire.

'Lavinia,' he said.

'Call me Vin,' she said.

'Do you mind if I call you Lavinia though?'

'Not a bit. Benjamin.'

'Lavinia, if you take us to the zoo, will the other kids know we're just staying with you for now?'

'What other kids?'

'The other kids visiting the zoo. Because our mum is coming really soon and if we go to the zoo with you and then go again with her, people might get confused and think she kidnapped us.'

'Not a chance. All kids at the zoo care about is seeing the lions and going to the kiosk.'

'Not even those tiny monkeys with huge eyes?'

'Mandarins?' I said.

'Tamarins?'

'Oh yeah, tamarins.'

'Some of them care about tamarins,' Vin said. 'They might just think I'm your cool auntie, if they think anything.'

'Okay.'

He relaxed the way he did with me, with the logic and science of the world explained. He moved his head from her shoulder to the space under her arm, and she let her hand rest on the small of his back.

On my couch, there was just me.

My phone beeped. *We're in the semi-final!! Can't wait to see you.* Raf's bright face wide open, Yardy next to him with a cigarette hanging from his lips.

*

Yas came back the next day. The three women sat at the kitchen table, left the door half-open like they wanted me to hear what they were saying. I pulled myself up on a stool by the door. Rocked back and forth while I listened.

'Benjamin will be going back to school on Monday,' Yas said. 'We have a place for him at St Eleanor's Primary.'

'And Skye?'

'Glenside High. But she won't go Monday. I have to take a statement from her first and I don't want to do it while Benjamin's here.'

'Then when?'

'Tuesday.' Yas's folder opened, paper rustling. 'I'll take her out to do it, if you can get Benjamin settled in. He's in Judy Russell's class.' The sound of something sliding across the table.

'Oh, she's so nice. We had Richie with her, remember, Vin? And Ava, I think.'

'I remember. She *is* nice!'

'Why do they need a statement?' Plates collided, one of them whispered *Shit!*

'They think the call might have come from her. The mother says Skye didn't have a phone, though.'

'She does have one. I saw her tapping away on it last night.' Silence, then: 'Why does it matter?'

'She says the kids didn't know what was going on. She's contesting the protective order, saying she was keeping them safe the whole time.'

'Can she do that?'

Yas was quiet for a moment. 'I mean, I guess she can try whatever she wants. The boyfriend's locked up, the house was full of paraphernalia. It's going to be an uphill battle for her one way or another.'

'Especially if she was high the whole time.'

My heart skipped a beat.

'The police say she wasn't.'

'That's something, at least.'

'Tea?' said Therese, and there was the clinking of china and things shuffling around. Ben's door cracked open.

'Are you okay?' he said.

'Shh.'

'I found this book in my room about the universe. It's old, though. It doesn't even have anything about the "Curiosity".'

'The what?'

'The robot they sent to Mars.' He closed the book. 'What're you doing?'

'Listening.'

'Are they talking about us?'

'Kinda. Why don't you go back to your room?'

'I want to sit with you.'

'No.'

'But I want to hear.'

'Tough on those kids,' Vin said.

'No, you don't.'

'Just let me sit with you for a second.' He tried to shove his head under my arm.

'Could you just *go away*?'

He stepped back, mouth turned down. 'Sorry,' he said, like I'd pulled out his whole heart. I reached into the space he'd made between us.

'*I'm* sorry. Ben. I'm sorry. Come here.'

He walked to his room and closed the door. I stared at it for a bit, the polished white wood. His perfect room behind: safe, quiet, his.

'Yeah,' Yas was saying. 'You know how Skye was skipping school to work full-time? The guy, her boss' – paper rustling – 'Daryl O'Mara. He's in hospital. Assault. Kicked a guy's dog and the guy punched him back, apparently.'

'Jesus.'

'Quite a place, this Port Flinders.'

We had our first weekend in foster care. I couldn't stop thinking of it like that, *foster care*. The way the house always smelled of baked goods, the way you could always hear laughter from the park down the street. It was like being in one of those TV shows, a perfectly manufactured life that was actually an experiment.

Ben had forgotten our argument. Not forgotten, probably, but filed away in his encyclopaedia of things. I saw him there in my head all the time, the hurt in his face. Sometimes I came out of my room and sat with him at the kitchen table and we looked into the backyard together, and he told me the things he knew. I recognised some of the stories – things about bees tied to balloons and making tear gas from pumpkins. Sometimes I came out of my room and sat at the kitchen table and watched Vin show him pictures of the animals she worked with.

'These are the babies,' she said to a photo of echidnas, their spiny jellybean bodies.

'Puggles,' Ben said.

'They're orphans. That's why I'm hand-rearing them.' The link was blatant and I thought of Mum and Dad and Nonno and all the people who hadn't hand-reared us. My body burned under this layer of fatigue but I sat next to Ben and he took the pictures one by one and looked at them all. He picked one out to show me.

'This one is a sugar glider,' he said. 'It uses flaps of skin to glide from one tree to the next.'

'Membranes, actually,' Vin said. 'It's called a *patagium*.' Ben frowned. Committed the word to his brain, stored it away.

Sometimes I came out of my room and watched him with Therese at the kitchen table, pulling out his skinny hands and painting his fingernails blue and red. It was the only whimsy she had, she said, painting fingernails. Accountants didn't have much whimsy. Ben let her do it, fingers splayed and flat on the table, watching her neat, organised strokes and breathing in the chemical smell.

'Ethyl acetate,' she said. 'That's the smell. Most people hate it but I secretly love it.' She winked at Ben, painted his smallest fingernail red as guts. I watched him store that away, too, in his Dewey Decimal mind.

I thought about what I could teach him – how to mark down meat in a supermarket freezer, how to listen out for the train coming, how to leave behind the only guy who's ever liked you. Nothing useful.

Sometimes I came out of my room and sat by the front window and stored my own stuff away instead. I watched the people go past with their different families and their animals and kids on shoulders and babies in strollers and bubbles and laughter and all the things people took around with them and filed it.

Ben's room had floor-to-ceiling bookcases, box after box of toys. At night I took something from the shelves and climbed in next to him and he read aloud from books with inscriptions in them. He asked me if I was angry, and I said I didn't know what I was so he hugged me and told me it was okay to not know all the time.

'Mum will be here soon,' he said.

'Right.'

'She just needs to figure out her complications.'

'Yep.'

'How long, do you think?'

'I don't know.'

'A week?'

'Maybe.'

And at night I waited, in my own perfect bedroom, for a knock on the window. Jason's bald head, Mum's claw hands on my monkey lamp.

Ben was small inside his blue uniform, track pants loose around his waist and jumper with cuffs past his wrists. Therese asked what we would normally have in our lunchboxes and I told lies for him: chocolate, chips, raspberry lollies. Lunch orders, usually. Pies with sauce, or pasties if we needed to get our daily vegetable intake up.

Vin took him in her work ute. Bound him up in the back seat of the cab and he waved to me with a big smile on his face.

I waited by the window for Yas's car to pull up, alone in the house. I thought of leaving, slipping out that shiny white door and catching the train down to Kirrily's house. Finding the man with his legs cut off. I thought about it for ages, his head exploded all over the tracks, not sure why I was thinking it but doing it all the same. I opened Raf's text again. Tried to type something back to him, something that said *Congrats!* but also *COME GET ME* and *WE RAN AWAY AND THEY FOUND US*. I went with *Congrats!* He sent back a thumbs-up.

It was after ten when Yas arrived. Hair pulled back, serious business suit on. 'Let's go down to the shops. There's a café there that does a great milkshake.'

The ache was catching up with me, Ben and my plan on the table outside Joe's with our paper straws. Mum crept into my brain again with her dressing-gown flapping.

We walked to the café. The sun had come out, bright and delighted. Everything had a gumleaf smell. I stepped on the lilly pilly fruit and felt it burst beneath my shoes.

Yas pulled me into a seat by the window. She spread her papers all over the table: Mum's police photo, Ben's class list, a report from my old school. 'Have a seat.'

'Sure,' I said.

Yas pulled a bit of paper from her folder. 'So, I'm sorry to do this to you.'

'Uh-huh.'

'But we're going to need to take a statement. Nothing scary. A few things about life at home and why you left. You don't have to tell me anything you don't want to, though. No one can force you to say anything.' She reached for my hand. 'You're not in trouble.'

'Yeah,' I said. 'Yeah, I know. Why would I be?'

'You're not.'

'Yeah, you said that.'

She smiled, flagged down the waiter to ask for a latte and a vanilla shake. We sat uncomfortably.

'We'll just have a chat,' she said finally.

'Okay.'

She laughed awkwardly, a little hiccup of a thing. We sat in the window together, like we were mates. That was part of her whole deal, getting chummy with us so we trusted her. I didn't. Not yet. Another drone from the government. It was impossible to know either way.

'So, here's what's happening. This is stuff I'm comfortable telling you, you understand, because you're older. But I don't think Ben needs to know any of it yet, okay? Can we just keep it between the two of us for now?' She smiled, so I nodded. 'What's happened is, after you left, the police had reason to go to your house.'

'What kind of reason?'

'They had a, uh … suspicion. They had a look around, and they found some things that shouldn't have been there. Especially with you and Benjamin living there.'

I asked the questions I thought she wanted me to: What kind of things? Why did they take her in? What does it mean to get out on bail? But I knew it already. Daughter's instinct.

'The police will have their own ideas, but I need to know what you know about what was happening in the house. Like I said, you don't have to tell me anything you don't want to, but it might help us figure out what to do next.' Pause. 'And then the other part is – and you really need to keep this from Benjamin for now – your mum is going to ask us if you can live with her again.'

'Up there?'

'Probably not. It's still early days, but she has a case worker too, like you. It seems she's hoping she can move back to Adelaide, find a place here for you all to live together.'

The apartment, Amir and Ben running in the canal. The water against the rocks. The far-off cry of the train. The train. The way it had dislodged Ben when he didn't hear it the day we started our plan, the haunted sigh of it across the fields. And then the commission flats, the kids with their eyes hanging open in the stairwells and Ben flying down the drive on his trike and –

'What kind of place?'

Yas shrugged. 'It could be any kind of place. A unit, a house. The important thing is that she has a stable place for you guys to go. But even then, we have to make sure it's safe for both of *you*.' She put her hands on top of mine, carefully, as though I might attack her. People kept doing that. Touching my shoulders, my hands, my elbows. Bodyguards. 'It's important that everyone is fully aware of the potential risks. Do you understand? I want to hear your version of the story so I know whether you're likely to be in danger again.'

It was Ben I thought of. All the time. Tucked away in his room in the extension, shoving square pieces into square holes. I was exhausted by the burden of taking him away from Mum but also of not protecting him from Jason. He didn't get it. He knew so many things, but not these things.

'We only left because of Jason.' Anger welled in me, in its red rapids. 'I don't know anything about this other stuff you're talking about.' The stuff in the spare room, the afternoon I'd watched Mum through the door. Jason's fingers on Ben's skin. I couldn't stop seeing it.

She frowned. 'The most important thing, Skye, is to be really clear about what happened while you were living there. Nothing you say will jeopardise you or Ben.'

'What about me *and* Ben?'

'What do you mean?'

'What if I do say to you, yeah, Jason tried to crush my brother's windpipe because he threw a toy car at a window?'

'Did he do that?'

I paused. 'That's not the point. Will you take him away?'

'Jason?'

'Ben. Will you take Ben away? If I tell you what really happened, is someone going to put him in some kind of hospital for kids with really fucked-up childhoods?'

'Oh, Skye, no. Look' – she scratched her head; flakes of skin dropped onto her neat dress – 'you're sixteen. Our system says sixteen-year-olds can live as adults, if they want to. But you don't have to. As long as you want to be with Ben, you can be with him. None of us are going to separate you. Okay? You're not in trouble.'

'Why do people keep saying that?'

'We're just trying to figure out what was going on there. How far this – what was going on.' She put her phone on the table. 'I have to record our conversation, okay? Why don't you start from the start? How did you know Jason?'

I told her some of the things. The auction and the move and the rain. Murray and Bilbo. Not Raf's text messages, or how much I needed to see him, but the new car and the trip to Wallaroo. Jason counting out his five-dollar notes, throwing the table into the TV cabinet. The almost-faded bruise across my ribs. I told her about the train, the cold morning waiting for the train in the dark. Waiting and waiting for the train to come and take us to our new life that was actually just our old life.

We went through the park, stopped at the edge of a duck pond to watch a mother duck with her tail of ducklings. The spring air was everywhere. Pollen, suffocation. The trees along the creek had exploded in veils of pink flowers and I couldn't escape the smell of it; that newborn, hopeful, renewed smell. Yas sat on a rubber swing and gave a little shove back and forth. I took the one next to her and did the same.

'Swings, huh?' Yas said.

'Yep.'

'Haven't been on one since I was a kid.' She kicked up the bark with her sandals. 'So, hey,' she said, still swinging. 'I did some searching. For your dad's dad.'

I stopped my own swing. 'And?'

She threw her head back, let out a big sigh.

'Your nonno died, Skye. A couple of years ago. I'm sorry.'

My plan: *EARN MORE MONEY, GO TO NONNO'S HOUSE*. All that time I'd imagined him at the end of this long and shitty journey, the way he would welcome us into his house and make us feed his animals and prune his plants and stay out of his way, but only because he was old. For a minute my eyes ran hot with tears but then they were gone, pushed down with all the other unfair bullshit that had happened.

'And what about my *actual* dad?' I was yelling but I didn't care, didn't care that kids were staring at me from their safe little playgrounds. 'He left us, you know. I was like, seven, and he left us and that's why all this bad shit happened, isn't it? If he hadn't left us I could have stayed with him on weekends and no one could have forced us to go with Jason and that dog would never have eaten Ben's tortoise.'

Yas let her feet drag in the bark. 'He was the first person we looked for. I promise. But he's just dropped off the map.'

'*Fuck*, Yas.' She didn't say anything, just got off her swing and came and put her arms around my shoulders and swatted the air and the blossoms almost bloomed in real time while my chest burned. Eventually she said, 'I have to take you home,' and I didn't even bother asking which home she meant.

Vin had picked up the baby echidnas. She had them in a cat box with thick blankets, and she invited me to look inside before she even spoke to Yas. 'They're only a couple of weeks old,' she said. I said nothing. She looked over my shoulder, frowned, turned back to me. 'Biscuit? I got those ones you said you guys always had, with the three kinds of chocolate.'

'No thanks.' The front door closed. I sat next to Vin and poked my fingers into the cage. Would they bite me? Would I even feel it?

'We can talk about it, if you want to. Or not. Totally up to you.'

'Nope.'

She put her hand on my shoulder and it hissed on my skin, my need for somebody to parent me, to care for me, shot right through my arm and into my chest and lodged in there, so I let her even though it burned.

She went to pick up Ben later in the afternoon. He went to the cat box first, opened the door and put his hand in there. He'd pushed his sleeves right up.

'What happened to their parents?' he said.

She stuck her finger through the grate door. 'Same as all the others. Humans. Someone probably found these in a pouch after they hit the mother with their car.' She smiled. 'They always say it was someone else, though. Just found them on the side of the road! Can you imagine! Hitting an animal and driving away!'

Ben's eyes were wide. 'No, I *can't* imagine!'

Dinner gurgled on the stove. I went to my perfect bedroom, lay on the perfect bed and watched the stars on the ceiling spin around and around.

They'd told me I'd start school the next day. Not the one from the plan near Nonno's farm – Nonno's *old* farm, Nonno's *once* farm – but a big one down the road with more than a thousand students. I couldn't imagine that many people at once, and me dropped in the middle of them.

My phone: *we won! will be in Rads on Thurs.* I thought of the night at Yardy's, sitting on the end of the jetty listening to his dreams. Claud in her warm house with the front light on.

I wrote, *I'm here already,* and he wrote, *I know.*

18

TWO YEARS AFTER Dad left, we had a concert at school. I was in the orchestra, banging a triangle with a stick. We'd been practising for months, every lunchtime on a Wednesday in the assembly hall.

Mrs Sadananda, had asked us for suggestions for songs. Said it might encourage parents to come along if we were playing their favourites. I didn't ask Mum for her favourite but I knew Dad loved Elvis. Mrs Sadananda printed a big list of his songs and asked me to show her which one he liked the best.

'"Hound Dog",' I said.

On the night of the concert, Mum ironed my uniform and did my hair properly with a ribbon. There was a big crowd of parents. Rows and rows of them, encouraged to come along because we were playing their favourites. 'Hound Dog' was right there in the program, after 'Enter Sandman'. I played the triangle better than I'd ever played it before. When we were finished, I looked and looked for my dad in the audience. Mum told me later his favourite was 'Blue Suede Shoes'.

*

School had the same tall gum trees as Vin and Therese's house, brick buildings and clusters of people everywhere. Circles on the lawn like séances, kids with their closed-in friendship groups. I thought of Kirrily first, always finding me in the yard at lunch. Then Raf, Raf, Raf, the burnt oval and the guys on the railway tracks. A different planet.

Parts of it were the same. Go to homeroom, sit through the roll. They must have had the 'foster kid' memo because I didn't have to introduce myself even though I had a little speech planned. *Hi, I'm Skye* – Raf again, pointing up – *and I ran away from my mum's druggie boyfriend to protect my brother.* I was even disappointed not to be able to say it, not to see the looks on their faces.

There were classes as well, must have been, but by the time the morning was over I couldn't remember them. I sat at lunchtime in a garden bed with the trees shading it, pulled out the bag of junk food I'd tricked Therese into packing. Thought about Nonno dying on his farm with his stupid goat. Thought about that housekeeper finding him bowed over his kitchen table. Thought about the fruit trees growing wild without him, or cut down to build new things, or being picked at by strangers. I thought about what I'd said to Yas but mostly what she'd said to me, about Ben not being taken away. Of course he could be. Probably even more likely since I'd tried to kidnap him.

I went to some more classes. Opened my box of homemade food under a different tree, and another different tree. Talked to a girl waiting behind me in the bathroom – she had a brother, too, but he was older and no one had lifted him off the carpet by his throat.

Each night I lay in the white bed and imagined myself climbing through the window and never coming back.

*

On Thursday morning I listened to a man in a cardigan talk about revolutionary wars until I couldn't listen anymore and picked up my bag and left. No one said anything, not him or any of the kids taking notes or the ones on their phones. There was a bus stop further down the road and I waited with my whole body crunched into the bench. I'd never just blown off school to catch a bus, not like this without a reason. I took a seat near the back and it rolled along to a shopping centre, where I became anonymous. Nothing weird about a sixteen-year-old wagging school. I was just like every other kid with free periods or notes to get out of PE. Classical music played from invisible speakers, not too loud; everything soft and vanilla and easy.

I still had nine hundred dollars in the bank. I tried to find the urgency I'd felt to earn it, the life-or-death feeling of getting out. But it wasn't there, not surrounded by women with blow-dried hair and children wearing tiny versions of adult clothes. None of it seemed to matter. Jason locked up, Mum trying to pull her dressing-gown closed. Murray limping his way between Sad Tom's and the butcher in search of a feed.

It was like a hallucination I'd had.

In the shopping centre there were heaps of stores I'd never had enough money to shop in. Clothes actual teenagers wore, not hand-me-downs or stuff from the op shop. Brand names and real jeans. I reached for my bank card.

I bought a maxi skirt with a blue floral print, cross-over tops with gold and silver embellishments, a shirt with lemons all over it that showed my stomach. I bought distressed skinny jeans and boyfriend jeans and shorts up in my arse crack, and something called a shift dress and another thing called a skater dress, and black ballet flats and silver ballet flats and a lace-up bodysuit.

I stared at my reflection in every single thing and tried to see it the way others might. Wondered what Raf would think of me in half-see-through stripes. In an embroidered bomber jacket

I just saw Mum in the driveway in her dressing-gown, trying to pull herself together. I took it off. Bought a pair of rainbow thongs and a wide-brimmed hat and a beach towel shaped like a watermelon. Tried to breathe in between.

At the store by the supermarket I chose a tiny pair of pink flamingo studs, tapped my card on the machine and waited. Stretched my fingers out of their tight grip around the bags.

The chick looked at me and looked at my card. She had one hand on the store phone. 'Sorry, it's been declined.'

I took in the spread of bags around me, breathed in whatever perfume they were pumping through the air-con and said, 'Finally.'

Yas's car was parked out the front. I dropped my bags by the front door, clicked it open slowly. She was alone, standing at the hall table with something in her hands.

The plan. That notebook Ben had chosen. She peered into it like she'd never read anything so interesting in her life.

EARN MORE MONEY.

She paused on a couple of the pages, frowned, made a note in her diary.

GO TO NONNO'S HOUSE.

And on the last page of the plan, towards the back with a few pages between so Ben wouldn't be suspicious. She stopped there, looked and looked at it, sighed deeply.

CALL THE POLICE.

'Can you take me to the Show?' She dropped the book, tried to pretend she hadn't by crossing her arms and talking fast.

'Skye. Didn't see you there. You're quiet. Wow. How was school? Good?'

I ignored her. 'I mean, I could catch the tram but maybe I'm a flight risk. That's what they call it, right? A flight risk?'

She slipped some papers into her folder. 'The *Show* Show? With animals and stuff?'

'Right. Showbags. Laughing clowns.'

'I don't know.'

'I'll pretend I didn't see you reading my private notebook just now.'

'Oh, the *Show*. On my way home, as it happens.'

'Great. I'll get changed.' I gestured towards the pile of shopping. 'Must be something to wear in all of this.'

We got in her little red car and drove through the city. All the people. I still hadn't got used to it, the way they buzzed around with all their different reasons.

As we pulled into the showgrounds, she looked across at me. 'I have to put a recommendation to DECD, about your mum having visitation rights. Are you sure there's nothing else you want me to say?'

I thought of Ben in his bedroom with puzzles meant for babies and about the constellation on my ceiling. 'No.'

'I know you called the police,' she said. 'You won't be in trouble.' And the car squeaked to a stop, its tiny engine resisting the bitumen.

'Here's good,' I said. The ferris wheel loomed ahead of us, smaller than I remembered. Yas slipped me twenty dollars from her purse.

'Call Vin when you're finished, yeah? She'll come and get you.'

'Thanks.'

'Don't mention it.'

The sounds hit me right away – combined shrieks of happiness and fear and too much sugar. The grinding of the big wheel making its way around, the megaphone announcements at the arena, the *thock* of the woodchopping. It smelled of sausages on sticks and fairy floss. Parents came out with kids dragging behind them, whining about not wanting to leave or not getting enough showbags or not having some other thing they were lucky to even know about.

I was early by a couple of hours so I took Yas's twenty and bought myself entry. Took myself to see the baby animals, sat with fluffy chickens and a staggering lamb and watched a cow give birth to another cow. I found the produce hall and grabbed a bit of every sample I could find, stuff I'd never tried before like pâté and possum meat and organic apple cider. The people behind the stalls were glossy, city people. It was nothing like I remembered. I took as many sausages on toothpicks as I could manage, tried to make myself invisible in the crowds.

Quarter to five. Young families had started to make way for groups in school uniforms and they were so easy and loud that I wanted to hide. All those sounds banging together, automated voices shouting prices and prizes.

I didn't see Raf until he grabbed me, face full of goodness. 'Skye.' He pointed up.

'Still going with the whole *sky* thing, huh,' I said, but my heart pounded, all the anxieties in my shoulders and my ribs and my knees.

'I missed you.' He kissed me near my ear. Soft, warm. 'I'm starving.'

'I ate every single sample.'

'Well, I'm gonna get a baked potato. Claud's favourite. She forced me to make them my favourite.'

He ate from a foam box, standing up beside the food cart. A kid puked into her glittery top hat. Raf led me by the hand through Sideshow Alley, down to the one where you threw ping pong balls into dishes, and he fed the guy dollar after dollar. Eventually, a ball dropped into a blue dish. Raf picked the biggest toy from the top shelf and I hugged it. It smelled like plastic and factories. We took it on the pirate ship ride, then to buy showbags. Raf got an Adelaide Crows one and he bought me three different kinds of chocolate ones. When we came out, it was dark. Rows of white lights gave everything a ghostly glow.

We sat on the side of a hill and watched the cars go round the arena. One was lining up to jump through a flaming hoop. None of it seemed real, stuck inside a circus with this guy I knew from somewhere else. The spinning, flashing lights of the rides with bodies screaming inside them.

If Ben had been there he would have told us about the kids who died on the rides. Fell out of the cage and into the crowd below. Caught their jeans on the crossbar and had their head cut off.

I pulled on the oversized glasses from 'The World's Least Crap Showbag!', looked over at Raf. The light from the flaming hoop was reflected in his eyes.

'This has been really nice.'

'Yeah.' He reached across to me. Always touching, always some physical contact. 'Are you okay?'

'Don't.'

'Mum wanted me to ask.'

'I wish she hadn't said anything.'

He sighed, put his drink on the ground. 'I mean, I was gonna call her about the win anyway.'

'What did she tell you?'

'Everything.'

'Everything?'

'Yeah, everything. I'm really sorry, Skye. That stuff he did to Ben, it's not right.'

'No shit.'

'I could've stopped him. Pissed him off out of town. Told the cops.' It was dark in the arena. Four cars jumped one after the other through the flaming hoops.

'You didn't know.'

'I wish you'd told me.'

'Sorry.'

He hugged his knees to his chest.

'You know what I did before we moved to Port Flinders?' I said. '*Nothing.* Went to school, did my homework, hung out with the one friend I had, took Ben to school, cooked dinner for Mum. How did I even get here, Raf? My mum's been in *jail.*'

'Just the holding cell,' he said.

'You know that, too?'

He scratched his head. Bought himself some time. 'The whole town knows, Skye. Half the deadbeats in the place were tied up in Jason's bullshit.'

'Like who?'

'Joe?'

'Milkshakes Joe?'

'Yeah.'

'And?'

'Sad Tom. Dini who runs the pub.' He pulled the plastic packet off a Redskin. 'Yardy.'

'Yardy?'

'All of them, I guess. Our squad, Yardy and fat Hamish and El. Not Seb. Bunch of the seniors, even a kid in Year 8.' *Bang!* The sky lit up like daytime. A kid squealed. 'Yardy tried to get me into it a couple of times. Said he wanted me to make enough to go to that training program.'

'But you didn't?'

'You think you can still play footy if you get caught dealing *ice*?'

A boy down the front cheered, flapped his hands around his face.

'I was the one who called the cops,' I said. 'Like, to arrest my own mother.'

'That was the right thing to do, I reckon. Anyway' – he took a deep breath – 'Claud had already called them.'

'What?'

'Or child protection. Someone.'

'But I asked her not to.' He stuck his hand in a showbag, pulled out a tiny Snickers bar and held it out to me. 'No thanks,' I said.

He unwrapped the chocolate and bit into it. 'She was freaking out. They'd probably been to Jason's already by the time you called.'

'So I didn't even *do* anything?'

'Nah, screw that. You got Ben out of there. No one else was going to.'

The crying pulled my ribs tight, grabbed and twisted and burned them.

'Hey.' He dropped his arm around my shoulder. 'You've got huge fucking balls, Skye Teller.'

'Ovaries.'

We sat and I relived all that time again, playing like a movie in my head. Every minute I'd spent watching Mum transform further into Jason, his balled fists. Our escape train booming beside the wheat fields, the way the stalks had turned from green to yellow while I'd been watching and waiting.

'When do you go back?' I said.

'Tomorrow.'

The air had got cold without me noticing. 'And after that? When will you come back?'

'Christmas holidays?'

I saw it, just for a second. Me and Raf in a yellow brick house with a Hills hoist spinning in the wind and a gum tree stretching into the sky. I put my hand into his hand. Fireworks exploded, rained their sooty bodies onto the grass, and when their thunderclaps chased after them I said, 'I'm scared,' so only I could hear it.

*

Vin's echidnas got bigger. She showed Ben how to feed them from a syringe and he made a chart to track their weight gain. One afternoon, after school, she took us both to the zoo and told us everything she knew about wombats. Ben watched her so closely while she talked. Afterwards we went to the restaurant and I ate chips while he kicked bark around the playground and shouted wombat facts to the other kids.

One night, after Therese's chicken stroganoff, my phone lit up: *Hey Skye. Heard you're back. Feels like ages. Got so much to tell you! Kxxx* and I imagined crawling back into my old body. Catching the train to see Kirrily at Noarlunga, our old apartment being close enough to smell. *Defs,* I wrote, and stopped. I hadn't talked to a real friend for months, didn't know if I could even remember how or where to start. I put my phone back in my pocket.

Raf texted every day. All kinds of things – a photo of the baby eagle that did eventually turn up by the oval, maths questions, a bit of a poem he'd found on the internet, a photo of his half-eaten pie. Nothing from the rest of the town. Not Joe's, closed until further notice, or Sad Tom's, chickens dried out in the bain-marie. I opened them at school, on my own under the gum trees, read them all from start to finish. Sometimes the crying started way down in my guts and made my face explode on its own. Other times I felt nothing. I read *Much Ado About Nothing* aloud in class and people watched me do it without making me feel stupid. Sometimes Claud texted as well, always just to say she was thinking of us. I was thinking of her too, but I didn't know how to tell her.

One afternoon I was waiting for the bus with some kids I recognised from my Maths class. The Maths class I was nearly failing, but they'd said I would get special consideration. The guy in the group turned to me and said, 'Where're you headed?'

'Just home,' I said, and I said it again. 'Yeah, home.' My yellow lamp and my ceiling of stars. I took Perry for walks along the fruit-stained footpaths and through the park, stopped at the café down the road for a milkshake. At school, a couple of girls asked me to sit with them. They didn't ask me why I was new and I didn't tell them. The nights were getting light and warm.

Yas knocked on the door one morning before eight. Vin opened the door with an echidna in one hand, milk bottle under her arm.

'Yasmin,' she said, and looked up at the clock. 'We weren't expecting you for another hour.'

'I know. Got an early start, had to ... it doesn't matter.' Yesterday's hair, fluffed out at the sides where she'd slept on it. She did a double-take on the echidna. 'That's a real echidna, right? I'm not imagining it?'

Vin frowned. 'Is everything okay?'

'Yeah, yeah, of course.'

'Come through.' Vin popped the animal back in its crate, slipped the lock closed. Yas dropped her pile of folders on the table. 'Can I get you a coffee, Yasmin?'

Yas shook her head. 'I'm good. Let's sit.' I took the chair at the end of the table. I could see Ben from there, through the sliding door, doing his baby's puzzle on his bed. 'Can Ben hear us?' she said. 'He probably doesn't need to be part of this conversation right away.'

'I don't think so,' I said.

'Okay.' She opened a file. 'We had a development late yesterday. Your mum's interim protection order was finalised and the courts have allowed' – she looked down at her paperwork – 'three hours a week, supervised.'

'What does that mean?'

'It means she can see you, but one of us has to be there.'

Vin got up and put the kettle on. 'When does this start?' she said.

'As soon as you like.'

I thought of the last time I'd seen her, disappearing with Jason while Ben's throat bloomed into blackness. I tried to place her in Vin and Therese's house. Mum in front of the fire. Mum by the pool. Mum in my bedroom, with its ceiling of stars. 'I don't want her to come here,' I said.

'She won't, not here.' Vin poured herself a cup of tea. 'It's good for it to happen in a neutral place – the park or a café. This is your space, Skye. You and Ben need to feel safe here.'

Yas took us through the options, the likely scenario. We could meet her at the park. There would be lots of other kids around with their families, so we wouldn't stick out. If we felt like we needed to leave, we could. Yas would be there, and Vin and Therese. If Mum put a foot out of line, they would bring us back here again.

'I need to ask Ben,' I said.

He had his head bent over his puzzle, slotting pieces into rectangular and triangular holes. He'd been able to do puzzles like it practically since he was born but he seemed deeply focused. Eyebrows down. Tongue poking out in concentration.

'Ben.' I knelt beside him. Didn't know how to choose the right words, thought of him with his head in Vin's lap, watching the wombats at the zoo, going to school with his face always clean. 'Mum wants to come and see us.'

'Finally,' he said, jammed a circle piece into a hexagonal hole. Jammed it again, turned it on its side and rammed it as hard as he could.

I grabbed his hand. Held it in mine for a second. 'Yas said she could come and visit us at the park. You know, the one around the corner with the pool? You don't have to, if you don't want to. Vin and Therese can tell her we can't go.'

He tipped all the pieces out again. 'Will Jason come?'

'Jason? No way. No. We never have to see him again.' He nodded. 'Anyway, we don't have to decide right now. We can go next week. Whenever we're ready.'

'Okay.' He left the room. The door to the bathroom slammed shut. I picked up the puzzle, put all the pieces back in.

Vin's voice came from the next room: 'He wet the bed again.'

'Did he tell you?' That was Yas.

'No. He wrote a note to his teacher.' The sound of paper rustling. Yas's sharp breath in, a tiny *Oh!*

'That poor kid.'

'He misses her.'

'The mother?'

'Yeah. He has a picture of her in his school bag. Perry found it next to the old apples right at the bottom.'

'Oh, the little love.'

They were quiet for a while.

'What about Saturday?' Yas said. 'Is that too soon? He must be desperate to see her.'

I couldn't quite remember what she looked like. All the versions of her mashed up together in there: fucked up on the floor with Jason; big hair and tall boots with that guy who'd worked at the pharmacy; ironed and responsible in her bank uniform.

I walked out to the kitchen. 'Ben says okay.'

Vin spoke even more kindly than usual: 'How about Saturday?'

'Fine.'

The numbers all came back to me at once. G Esposito, Seaford Downs. And then G Esposito, Reynella. I closed the door to my room and dialled Nonno's number, put the phone right up to my face so I could feel the sound coming through.

The number you have called has been disconnected.

Saturday.

For three days, I thought about her. I helped Therese make lunches for Ben in the white kitchen, sandwiches cut into shapes and sliced-up apples and every flavour of chip in one Ziploc bag, and I thought of her. I took Perry for a walk around the block, talked to the man on the corner with his lines of white roses, picked the cherry blossoms, and I thought of her. I read *Much Ado About Nothing* again, sitting in the front window with the fireplace empty and the sun through the window, and I thought of her.

Yas came once more that week, on Thursday. The police were finished with the house, she said, and Mum was going to be allowed to go back to collect her remaining belongings. It wasn't a lot. The new red car had been impounded, and when they'd really looked, *properly* looked, there wasn't much worth keeping at all. A few boxes of clothes we'd never unpacked.

We could go too, if we wanted. Pick up our own things. Or the case worker could pick them up for us.

'No thanks,' I said. Then: 'There's nothing there I need,' and then I felt stupid, like I'd blurted out a tacky line from a book. But the relief was overwhelming, the feeling of never going back. I didn't need to ask Ben; I'd crammed everything he had into that one bag, the day Claud had come to take us away.

On Saturday morning Therese packed a picnic lunch. The proper way, into one of those baskets with two lids. A checked tablecloth, knives and forks with rubber handles and plastic cups with removable stems. She made all kinds of things: vegetarian sausage rolls, quiches the size of fifty-cent pieces, layered sandwiches with different-coloured fillings.

'You've done this before,' I said, and she said, 'Once or twice,' but it still felt like this time was especially for us.

We took Perry and the basket and photos of the echidnas on Vin's phone. The park was close, a couple of blocks, but we walked through sludge to get there, pushing hard through the sweet air and laughter. Ben gripped my hand. Breathed short bursts in and out, took a few steps forward and a couple back.

Vin bent down level with him and said, 'We can always go home,' and he didn't say anything but moved forward again, and back, and forward.

It was packed. Kids running everywhere, shouting like they were being chased by wild animals, and parents looking on from their barbecue boundaries with boredom. Mum was supposed to meet us near the pool. In the warmer weather we smelled it, the chemical combination of chlorine and the gum leaves floating in it.

There she was. On the edge, sitting on a low wall, looking at us. She'd seen us first. Watched for us to come, waited.

Ben stopped, but his whole body was warm and soft. Breathing out. He twitched at my side. Hopped from one foot to the other. I let go of his hand but he grabbed it back, harder than before. Mum lifted hers to wave. We walked towards her in one mass, me and Ben in the middle like we had a group of bodyguards.

'Linda? I'm Yasmin. I'm your children's case worker.'

Mum put out her hand to shake Yas's. 'Hi,' she said. 'Hello.'

Vin stepped forward. 'Hi, Linda. I'm Lavinia, this is my partner Therese.' Vin spoke without emotion, measured, no judgement. Mum had painted her eyelids green.

Ben pointed to a cat on her scarf. 'Vin, this looks like your cat.'

'So it does.'

'Lavinia's cat is called Tickles.' He was relaying the information to Mum but not looking at her, talking from the side of his mouth. 'She's a Maine Coon.'

'Right,' Vin said. 'The biggest breed of cat in the world, right, Ben?'

Mum's eyes went between the two of them, searching for her place in the conversation. 'Maybe,' she said, coughed a bit, started again. 'Maybe we could get one, in our new place.'

Ben looked at me, looked at Vin. 'Maybe,' he said, still not looking.

Mum looked up at me. 'Skye?'

I had nothing to say.

'Shall we sit?' Yas said. The picnic basket came out. We sat on the grass like a regular family, assembling the plastic cups and taking out the sandwiches. Mum and Ben sat really close, like they were hatching an egg together. She gave him a box. He was hesitant to begin with, like he might find a bomb inside, but eventually a stuffed toy dropped out.

'An echidna,' he said, his voice flat.

'It's … you know, all its parts are like they are in real life.'

'Anatomically correct.'

'Yeah! They told me you'd been learning about them.'

He turned it over in his hands. 'Lavinia's a zookeeper. She's got real baby ones at home and she's showing me how to feed them with a bottle.'

Vin pulled out her phone. 'We have some photos, if you'd like to see them,' she said, but Mum's eyes stayed on Ben.

'I bought it from that shop with all the science stuff you like,' she said. He ran his finger over the glass eyes, the stitched feet. 'Do you like it?'

'The ones at home are so small they don't have proper spines yet,' he said. 'Just short ones. Like how babies don't have proper teeth.'

'I knew you'd like it,' Mum said, and smiled with her lips tight.

The afternoon sun beat brightly on the park and Perry ran laps of us, barking at things she imagined in the trees. Mum put her arm around his shoulder, pulled him into her. Yas watched them and wrote notes in her folder.

'There's one kind named after David Attenborough. He's Yiannis's favourite adult.'

Mum's face lit up with recognition of our old life. 'Have you seen Yiannis?' she said.

'No.' He took a deep breath. 'When I get home I'll show this toy to the babies and see if they think it's their mum. They probably won't.'

Yas wrote faster. Therese went and sat on the other side of Ben, not too close, maybe just far enough to reach out if she needed to.

'Why not?' Mum said.

Ben put the echidna on the grass. 'Mums all smell different. You smell different, and Claud smells different, and Vin and Therese smell different.'

'Oh yeah?'

'Yeah. But today you smell like someone else's mum even though I can see you and I know you're the same one.'

She adjusted her scarf. 'That's because I'm wearing this new perfume.'

'Oh,' he said.

Therese coughed loudly. 'Shall we eat?' she said.

The sandwiches were spread into fans on their paper plates and she'd squeezed tomato sauce into smiley-faces on the sausage rolls. The others all took one. The air between us was dense with conflict and I felt sick enough without eating.

Mum leaned into Ben. 'I'm sorry about your turtle,' she said.

'Tortoise.'

'Aren't they the same thing?'

'No.' He took another sandwich and ate the filling first, balled the bread into white marbles in his fist. 'I think I'd like to go in the pool,' he said to Yas. 'My feet are very hot.'

'Sure, mate,' she said. 'You can leave your shoes here.'

He ran off down the hill, hopping and shrieking across the hot pavement. Vin mentioned a TV show she and Therese had been watching. Yas talked about the trip she was taking over Christmas, down the coast to where the sea was turquoise. I played the lines I'd learned from *Much Ado* on repeat in my head. Mum rubbed her hands together, took a sausage roll but didn't eat it, slipped her feet in and out of her sandals. Finally, she said, 'Could you give us a minute?' I went to stand up, but she said, 'I meant them.'

'Skye?' Yas said.

She wasn't the mother we'd left flapping open in the driveway. Her hair was clean and pulled up into a ponytail, eyes lined with black pencil and mouth with pink lipstick. She wore jeans and a long-sleeved t-shirt and a scarf with cats on it, and she looked like every single other mother in the park. Like the mother who'd worked at the bank and made me bring receipts from the supermarket.

'It's okay,' I said. All three women left, set themselves up on a nearby bench and made out like they were talking to each other but all looked right at me. Mum swivelled on the grass until we were sitting side by side. She stuck her legs out straight in front of her and moved her yellow shoes from side to side.

'I would have left on my own, you know.' Her voice wavered. 'After Christmas I was going to. I had a bit of money put away.'

'Okay.'

'I did. You always think you know better than me, but you're just a kid.'

I couldn't help it, I started laughing. It jumped out of me, a frog from a toilet or a scorpion running from a fridge, some tired and furious part of me just escaped and it was laughter and tears all at one.

'*I'm* just a kid? How do you think we left, huh? How?'

'I . . .'

'We would've have needed money, right? Someone would've had to save up, to get us away.'

'You?'

'Of *course* me! You know that job I got? The one you and Jason told me I had to get?' People were looking at me, not all at once but a few sideways glances and shifting uneasily.

'You're making a scene,' Mum said.

'I don't care. Do you know how I got that job? How I was making enough money to get me and Ben on the train and right the fuck out of Port Flinders? My boss there, big guy, maybe you saw him around. He touched me.' She gasped. 'He touched me and I *let him* because I was so afraid' – tears banked up in my throat, in my nose, all pushing at once to get out – 'I was so afraid I would lose my job and Ben would be stuck there forever.'

At his name, Ben looked up from the pool. 'Stop, Skye.' Mum stuck out her hand like she was going to cover my mouth and I shoved it away.

'I'm not going to stop yelling because *you* feel bad.' I pushed my fingers into my eyes. 'I'm going to stop because Ben might hear me.'

Mum sat rigid, breathing fast. 'You could have …' She frowned. 'You could have told me.'

'No,' I said. 'I couldn't.'

Yas had moved from the bench and I fell into her shadow. 'That might be enough for today.' She gave Mum a gentle smile.

'You want me to leave?' Mum grabbed for her handbag.

'Just for now, Linda. Maybe next weekend we can try the other park, that one with the adventure playground.' Vin and Therese were there too, kind but forceful in that way they were. Mum stood, brushed herself down. Vin went with her to the pool and Mum stroked Ben's shiny hair, squeezed him into her arms until his face popped out the other side. I remembered him the day he ran away, pretending he was a tortoise.

'Sorry, Yas,' I said. She'd dropped down next to me, file closed in her lap. 'That was shit of me, saying that stuff where Ben might hear.'

'Don't say that, Skye. No one expects you to be okay with all of this right away.'

'Ever?'

'Or ever. If that's how you feel, that's okay too.' She held out a smiley-faced sausage roll and I took it, looked at it, copied the expression with my own mouth but it felt ugly and weird.

'Am I broken?' I said.

'You? God, no.' She squeezed my hand. 'You're an absolute champion.'

Ben came back up the hill and grabbed his echidna from the grass. 'Mum looked different,' he said.

'I think she was pretty tired,' Yas said.

He pushed the spines of the toy echidna into his fingertips. 'Maybe next time she'll look like the old version of her. When she's less tired.'

But I had seen her. Not the old her, not the same. Some of her other self with the stuffing punched out. Maybe she wouldn't go back like she had before. Maybe the real Mum was different now. A woman who'd absorbed a terrible man but kept herself inside there too, not perfect, not exactly right.

Vin took Perry's leash and wrapped it around her hand. 'Shall we go?' Yas and Therese packed the lunch back into its basket. The other families had started to leave, too, dripping out of the park with tired children whining behind them. In the street, the sun reflected bright off the pavement. The adults walked ahead and talked quietly so they could still hear us. Ben threw his echidna in the air and caught it again.

'I think I still like tortoises best,' he said to me. 'Echidnas are cool, but tortoises carry their homes around with them everywhere they go and I think that's better.'

'You reckon?'

'They can go anywhere and all their stuff is still right there. If I was a tortoise I'd take my toys and a book about space and pyjamas and a snack and paper for writing down notes about the things I saw.' He looked up at me. 'You'd take your phone and probably some pictures of Raf and sunglasses.'

'Sounds right,' I said. The fruit of the lilly pilly trees hung heavy on their branches and we ducked under them, cool in the shade. A man waved and shouted, 'Hi, Perry!' and the dog pulled towards him. Ben bent down to let a ladybird crawl onto his finger.

'I don't know why they call them ladybirds when they're not all ladies,' he said. 'And *none* of them are birds. It would be more accurate to call them "red spotty beetles". Some people think the yellow ones are poisonous but they're not.'

The day wrapped warm and easy around me like a cloth.

'Yiannis told me ladybirds *bleed* from their *knees* when they're stressed out.'

'That's crazy.'

'Yiannis never lies. You can ask him yourself. Lavinia said he could come over for a visit next week or the week after and Erin is going to come too.'

'Erin?'

'Yeah. From school.' The ladybird cracked open its shell and flew off. I grabbed his hand and he squeezed mine back. 'She's my friend. Yesterday I showed her how to tie a balloon to a bee.'

Acknowledgements

Thank you:

Mum and Dad, for supporting me in so many ways beyond what's reasonable to expect of two people and for always doing so with sincere and warm hearts.

The amazing team that brought this book to life: Geordie Williamson, Mathilda Imlah, Bri Collins, Libby Turner, Alex Craig, Jo Butler.

Allison Tait, for all the reasons previously stated but especially for getting me through the 'I never wanted to be a writer in the first place!' moments.

Erin Van Krimpen, who has a very big brain and has been like my own personal Google but with a much handsomer dog, and is also the most tremendous pursuer of fairness and equity and compassion.

Peter Ireland, Katelin Farnsworth, Gerry Mellor and Helen Perris, for generous and ferocious assistance in the development of this story.

My family, Gaz and Georgia and Lily, who make me laugh every day.

Everyone who read my first book and sent beautiful messages and emails and told their friends about it, and who support Australian writing and the continuation of a sustainable arts industry across all mediums.

And my own little brother, Jonathan Spargo-Ryan, who taught me how to find lizards under rocks.